NEVER
BROKEN

NEVER BROKEN

A Lisa Jamison Mystery

Lori Duffy Foster

LEVEL
BEST BOOKS

First published by Level Best Books 2022

Copyright © 2022 by Lori Duffy Foster

This novel is entirely a work of fiction. The names, characters and incidents portrayed in it are the work of the author's imagination. Any resemblance to actual persons, living or dead, events or localities is entirely coincidental.

Lori Duffy Foster asserts the moral right to be identified as the author of this work.

Author Photo Credit: TSF Photography

First edition

ISBN: 978-1-68512-068-9

Cover art by Level Best Designs

This book was professionally typeset on Reedsy.
Find out more at reedsy.com

To the more than forty million people who remain enslaved throughout the world. May we open our eyes and set you free.

Praise for NEVER BROKEN

"A dark, gripping plot and a daring main character you can't help but fall in love with. It's my first Lisa Jamison mystery but it won't be my last!"—Steve Hamilton, Edgar-Winning Author of *The Lock Artist* and the Alex McKnight series

"Kindhearted, tenacious, and fearless newspaper reporter Lisa Jamison wants answers no matter the cost. Lori Duffy Foster's *Never Broken* is a compelling mystery that explores the resiliency of the human spirit. A page-turner with a protagonist we can all root for."—Bruce Robert Coffin, award-winning author of the Detective Byron Mysteries

"Smart, brave, and filled with compassion, journalist Lisa Jamison is the perfect sleuth for these challenging times. Add in a plot that keeps readers guessing, and you get *Never Broken*, the 'stay up late can't wait to read the next chapter' latest release by Lori Duffy Foster."—Elena Taylor, author of *All We Buried* and the Eddie Shoes Mysteries

Chapter One

Lisa Jamison knew she should be taking in her surroundings: the worn brick buildings with shard-lined windows; graffiti so old the slang was almost retro; the stench from the nearby creek, which many of the deserted factories had used as their own waste dump for decades; the cigarette butts; the crushed beer cans; the McDonald's cups; the occasional used condom or syringe.

But she was having trouble keeping her balance on the broken sidewalk in her leather boots and, besides, she was already familiar enough with these streets. To David Glass, the head of the Seneca Springs Industrial Development Agency, this neighborhood was a treasure, an antique that would become invaluable with restoration. That was the analogy he had used during the press conference just an hour before.

To Lisa, this had been a free hotel room during her teenage years. She'd spent more than enough nights in these abandoned buildings, nights when she'd worn out her welcome on a friend's sofa and had yet to convince someone else's mom to feel sorry for her. She shuddered despite the midsummer heat. It would take a lot more than a couple of wealthy investors to change her vision of Iron City Heights.

Lisa could see her car from two blocks away, the only car left where earlier television news vans with satellite trucks had parked her in. The TV crews got what they had come for—some good video and a soundbite—and left. That was always the best time to do real investigative reporting, when the television influence was gone. No more *Quotable Quotes*, no more practiced smiles, no more carefully intoned voices. Guards came down as the cameras

1

shut down, allowing Lisa to get real answers to real questions.

She groaned as she reached in her jeans pocket for her keys. Projects reporters weren't supposed to have daily deadlines, one of the perks of the job that she relished. But she would have to write something about this press conference for today's online edition and tomorrow's *Sun Times*. She needed deeper information for a newsroom-wide project on the new development, and that meant covering it as if every aspect of the development itself were her assigned beat. Lisa's job was to look at the bigger picture while examining the tiniest of details for any signs of illegal or unethical activity. Hopefully there was nothing to find, but if there was any evidence of wrongdoing, she wanted to be the one to uncover it.

Her interview with the project's developer, Bert Trammel, had gone well, even though it was unplanned. She had followed him to his BMW, which he'd parked several blocks away where the neighborhoods were a little safer and better patrolled. They had walked with two junior partners from his firm. Lisa wasn't surprised to find they had left an intern with their cars to keep potential thieves away. Nor was she surprised they had each driven their own cars. She was certain these guys wouldn't be back until the area was fully sanitized and wrapped up neatly with a bright red ribbon that needed cutting.

But the walk was worth it. Trammel loosened up after Lisa feigned excitement over his work with question after flattering question about his past projects and praise for his performance at the press conference. It wasn't hard to see he was vulnerable to such tactics with his slightly loosened silk tie, his rolled-up Armani shirtsleeves, his dark hair with just a touch of silver in precisely the right places, his perfectly timed pauses and pronouncements and his constant smile no matter the question or the source. He was smart and he could be intimidating, but he was also an egotist, and egotists were easy to break.

What she needed from him were details of the tax deal and the lease agreement his company had negotiated with the city, details that were included in a contract David Glass had promised her days ago but had yet to produce. She knew the basics—that the city had agreed to keep ownership of the property and lease the land to Trammel's company in exchange for monthly payments. The monthly payments were likely lower than the potential property taxes that Trammel would have to pay if he actually bought the property. Such deals were not illegal or unheard of. They were a common way of attracting businesses and creating jobs. Developers could save millions in taxes, especially once improvements were completed and property values soared.

But Trammel Enterprises had turned down offers from the county IDA for locations in the suburbs that would be more appropriately suited for its high-end mall, condos, and spa. Iron City Heights had once been labeled toxic, a federal Superfund site. Though the EPA had declared the buildings and the river free of contaminants years ago, the neighborhood still carried that stigma, along with the possibility that more chemical hazards would be discovered when construction and demolition got underway. It was a big risk for any company, especially when there were other options.

"But here's the thing," Trammel said, stopping just a few feet short of his BMW and turning to Lisa. His face had brightened in a way that it had not during the press conference. Lisa would even call his smile a grin. "The city has agreed to take on any further clean-up costs related to toxic waste and to rid the area of contaminants in a timely manner. People love this stuff—toxic-waste dump turned into a place of beauty. They'll be drawn to it, not repulsed by it. And the county couldn't even come close to competing with the city's tax deal. Our payments are ridiculously low, and they'll never change throughout the course of the ten-year lease. When the lease expires, we get to buy the property at the current value. Couldn't pass that up, now could we?"

Trammel signaled to one of his junior partners, a tall thin man who had unlocked his car and was about to step in, urging him to join them. He was young, like most junior partners in Trammel's firm, and probably single. They had to be, given the long hours and the low pay. Lisa had heard that working for Trammel was like doing a medical residency, except these guys were lawyers and could be making good salaries elsewhere. The payoffs for those who succeeded, though, were enormous. Junior partners were given major financial stakes in the projects they headed up. If the projects failed, they dropped to the bottom rung, giving every waking hour of their lives for the opportunity to try again. But if they succeeded, the junior partners were suddenly buying their own BMWs and being catered to by their own interns. It was a gamble most married people with families couldn't take.

"Robert, give the lady your copy of the contract, would you?" Trammel said without looking at the man, who seemed almost hurt by the request. He glared at Lisa darkly as he complied, unsnapping his briefcase, and digging through the papers until he found it. She couldn't help staring at his face. It was long and narrow with a light mustache. And he was pale—an unhealthy kind of pale—like someone who spent too much time in the office and too little time sleeping. He thrust the contract at her, and Lisa grabbed it, quelling the urge to do a victory dance. This had turned out better than she had hoped.

"You'll get it eventually anyway, and it's a done deal. I don't know why the IDA is holding out on you. The deal is good for us and it's good for the city. With the riverfront and these gorgeous old brick buildings, this place will be a tourist destination. And this is just the start. There's no end to what we can do here."

Trammel took one last look around before he got into his car. The junior partner, Robert, was last to leave. He focused on the road ahead as he eased his vehicle away from the curb, but Lisa could tell he was still fuming from his stiff neck and jaw and his hard grip on the wheel. She didn't blame him. Trammel had a dismissive way of treating his employees that was almost humiliating. He could just as easily have asked the guy to email or fax her a copy. This was about power. Making him give up his copy was a way of putting him in his place.

She stood there on the sidewalk for a few minutes after they'd all gone, enjoying the quiet that followed. It was an interesting transition from Iron City Heights and its abundance of vacant buildings to the heart of the city. If she walked even a mile farther east, she would reach Toast and Roast, an espresso bar by day and a wine bar by night. Its neighbors included a small independent theater and a vegetarian restaurant. The walk would become even livelier as she continued east, with customers frequenting a dry cleaner, a vacuum repair shop and other such businesses—the mom-and-pop kind of places. Eventually, if she kept going, she would reach the newspaper building, the courthouse and the offices of Trammel and others like him, along with all the upscale restaurants, bars and delis that profited from the various hungers of their employees. From vacant to bustling in only about a five-mile stretch. The two worlds seemed so far apart.

There was still life in Iron City Heights beyond the squatters. The area was home to a few scattered businesses—warehouses for stores located elsewhere, a couple of auto shops, a small mattress factory—but most of those were on the western fringe of Iron City Heights, where the landscape transitioned to highway and then to the more blue-collar suburbs. Here, at its center, closer to the riverfront where Trammel had held his press conference, Iron City Heights was hollow, empty and broken. The homeless took shelter in some buildings at night, cats roamed the streets at all hours and money and bags were exchanged from the open windows of passing cars. Where would they all go when the rich moved in, Lisa wondered as she walked back.

Lisa hadn't bothered to lock her black Toyota Camry, the same car she'd driven for the past six years. One look at the odometer and even the dumbest of criminals would choose to walk instead. It had one hundred and sixty thousand miles on it from her drives all over the region for interviews and breaking news, and it was full of discarded food wrappers, old newspapers and ponytail holders in case she needed a spare. She was determined to at least clean it before the summer's end, though it seemed that was a resolution that kept rolling over from year to year. Still, she wasn't surprised when she noticed the back passenger-side door was slightly ajar. She'd left a handful of change on the console, more than a dollar, probably. To desperate addicts, every penny counted, and there were probably more than a few people squatting in the old factory buildings here.

She slowed her pace as she approached her car but could see no one inside. She knew better than to catch a drug addict in the act. Addicts could summon amazing strength when their weakened bodies were desperate for more. Lisa steeled herself for the mess she might find—slashed seats, an empty glove compartment, radio wires bulging from the dashboard—and pulled the door open. Then she screamed, dropping her notebook as she raised her hands to her mouth. On the floor was a man—small, curled up and filthy. She leaned in for a better look and, for a moment, she thought he was dead. His fingers were deformed and covered with bloody, swollen gashes. His lips were blistered and dry. His cheekbones protruded from his dark skin. He was thin and drawn. Then he looked at her with dull, pleading eyes and put a finger to his lips, a movement that seemed to drain his last bit of energy.

Lisa was so shaken she hadn't even noticed the gold sedan that had come around the corner and was now stopped before her, or the driver who had rolled down the window and was asking whether she was okay. His shouts grew louder, and Lisa faintly heard them through her shock, and pulled herself out of it. The man on her car floor was trembling now.

She saw then what was going on and she should have said no—that she was not okay. She should have done whatever was necessary to get that man out of her car. But he was pitiful, he was pleading and he was sick, and the man in the sedan, who had gotten out and was standing inside his open door, was too well-dressed in his expensive golf shirt and silken slacks. For whatever reason, the man hiding in her Camry was afraid of the other guy. His fear should have persuaded Lisa to stay out of it, but she couldn't do that to him. She would always wonder, always fear, what had become of him, and living with that guilt would be far worse than anything else she could imagine.

"I'm sorry," Lisa said, trying to still her shaking hands. She silently vowed to call an ambulance and the police as soon as the driver disappeared. "There was a bee in my car and I'm allergic. I freaked out for a second, but it's gone. I'm fine."

Lisa slammed the door shut, picked up her notebook and walked around to the driver's side. She expected the man in the sedan to keep moving, to drive away. Instead, he got back in his car, leaned out his window and looked Lisa up and down. His hand rested on the window frame, and he drummed his fingers as he watched her, tapping a thick gold ring on the metal. She was suddenly conscious of the fact that she was almost as overdressed for the neighborhood as he was, even though she wore jeans and had pulled her long brown hair into a simple ponytail. Her jeans were too expensive, and her hair was too smooth. Her boots were Italian.

"Not a good idea for a lady like you to be hanging out here."

The driver smirked. It was the kind of smirk that told her he was used to getting his way, especially with women. She was tempted to show him just how effective her daily runs, her pushups and her kickboxing routine were against men like him. She was nearly killed covering a story two years ago—twice. She wasn't going to let that happen again, and she would have loved to practice her own moves on him. Instead, she pulled herself together and gave him the flirtatious smile he was looking for. Better to play the game.

"I'm a reporter. I was here for a press conference, but I'm leaving now," she said. "Maybe you'd better get out of here, too. That's a nice car you're driving."

"I would, but I'm looking for a man," he said, his expression more serious now. "Maybe you've seen him. He escaped from Oakwood, the psychiatric hospital, and might have gotten into a fight with some local guys. He's probably beaten up pretty bad. He stopped taking his meds and he's dangerous. You know, they're unpredictable when they do that. He's a Black guy. Not too tall. Skinny. The last we heard, he was wandering around here."

Liar, Lisa thought. She'd done enough time on the crime beat to know that if the guy hiding in her car really did escape and really was dangerous, there'd be a patrol car or two looking for him as well. She hadn't seen any cops in the neighborhood except those who were assigned to the press conference, and they had left the second it ended.

"I haven't seen him and, like I said, I'm leaving now." Lisa climbed into her car, turned the key and started the engine. The stowaway's stench almost drove her back out—a mix of sweat, blood and rot. She worked hard to keep a straight face and look forward, but the sedan did not move. This driver was not going to leave until she did. So she did. Lisa left Iron City Heights with the interview in her notebook and a near-corpse in her backseat.

Chapter Two

By the time she'd driven out of Iron City Heights and through downtown Seneca Springs, Lisa had become accustomed to the odor. She debated whether to go directly to the hospital, but she knew that would take longer than simply finding an empty parking lot and calling an ambulance. Besides, she would likely get stuck in the emergency room, feeling guilty about leaving the guy there. She would want to stick around to see how he was doing. It would be easier to watch an ambulance take him away.

When she was sure the sedan and Iron City Heights were far behind them, Lisa pulled into the lot of a strip club, where the few daytime patrons had been savvy enough to park in back. The side lot was empty. She opened her back passenger door once again and found the man just as she had left him. He looked scared, even more scared than when she had first seen him. But at least he was still alive.

"Look, I'm not going to hurt you, but I think that other guy was. I've got my cell phone. See?" she said, holding it up. "I'm just going to call for an ambulance. They'll be here any minute. Just hang in there for me, okay?"

Lisa started to punch in the numbers but stopped when she heard a low groan of protest from within the car. The man stretched his neck and licked his lips, allowing them to part more easily. His voice was a hoarse whisper.

"No. Please. No police. They'll kill me."

The man had raised his head slightly in the effort to speak and was trying hard to sit up. It must have taken all his energy to get into Lisa's car, she thought. All his hope. He beckoned with his damaged fingers for Lisa to come closer. She started toward him, but then stopped. What if this was a trick? Maybe he wasn't so weak after all. Maybe he had a gun or a knife.

"I'll hear what you have to say, but I'm not coming near you. I don't know who you are or why you look this way, but it doesn't make me feel all that safe. Who are you and what happened? Why would the police want to kill you? I know these guys. Every police force has a few power-hungry jerks, but those aren't the cops I know."

"The last guy, he went to the cops," he said. Lisa had to draw a little closer to hear him, but she never took her eyes off his hands. "They brought him back and hung him in front of us. I don't know what happened, but it's not safe. They'll hang me, too."

He was working his way up now, carefully lifting himself from the floor and sliding onto the seat. But it took everything out of him. As soon as he managed to hoist his body up, it slumped to one side. He landed in a half-sitting position with his head resting against the door and stayed there, saying nothing for a moment. His t-shirt was torn and stained, and he wore thin cotton pants that were equally filthy. On his feet was a pair of cheap flip-flops.

"She said to say her name. She's the only one who knows where we are, what city this is. She was a mistake. They couldn't smuggle her out because too many people were looking for her. Chandra Bower. She said to say her name and that people would listen. But no police. They'll move the whole operation, and they'll kill her, too."

For an instant, just an instant, Lisa allowed excitement to course through her body. Chandra Bower had disappeared seven years ago and was presumed dead. Her parents—college-educated and successful—had raised her in the poorest neighborhood of the city, a predominantly Black neighborhood, as a statement of sorts. They had grown up there and they wanted to prove that Black and poor didn't mean dangerous or stupid. They wanted to revitalize the neighborhood and empower the local Black community. But they also wanted to prove to the neighborhood that good parenting could triumph no matter what the statistics showed about their schools.

Their daughter attended the lowest-scoring school in the district and emerged just shy of her eighteenth birthday with near-perfect SAT scores and a full scholarship to Boston University. And then she disappeared. Just like that. She had a cold and had walked to the drug store for some decongestant. Police found her purse in an alley. Nothing more. No other evidence. No sightings. No leads. Though the case was considered cold, her parents, Lisa and at least two investigators still jumped whenever the body of a young Black girl surfaced. Closure. That was all anybody had come to hope for. But alive? That was too much and too impossible to believe. Lisa let the excitement drain out of her and stared at the man. Why would he lie about Chandra Bower? Maybe he really had escaped from Oakwood. Maybe she had made a huge mistake.

"What about Oakwood? That man said you escaped from Oakwood," she said.

"That's what they called it." He didn't turn toward her this time. He couldn't. He was weakening again. She had to get him somewhere, fast. How would she explain a dead man in the back of her car in a strip club parking lot?

"It's not the same Oakwood. It's not a psychiatric hospital," he said. His words were beginning to slur. "It's a sweatshop in a basement. She works there. We talked. We weren't supposed to talk. They whip you when you talk. I need a drink. I'll be okay if I have water. They haven't given me anything to drink in two days. Please. Some water, and then I will leave. You can forget me. I'll figure it out on my own."

Lisa had promised her daughter she would stay away from all things dangerous from now on. This was how she had gotten in trouble last time. She had insisted on investigating the murder of Bridget's father when she'd been warned to leave it alone and had put the lives of her daughter and her best friend, Dorothy, in danger, too. But how would it be dangerous to give this man a chance? Bridget was supposed to spend the next two weeks at Dorothy's newly opened artists' retreat, helping her cook and clean to earn some extra money for college. She wouldn't be home. The man was too weak to take Lisa down and she would pat him down for weapons before letting him in the house. She would get him water, listen to his story and then call the police before he got his strength up. But she needed help.

"I'm making a phone call," she said, "but not to the police. I don't want to be alone with you and you need some medical help. I know somebody who can look you over who will be discreet, but you're going to have to trust me."

The man was quiet, almost listless, now. He was too sick to argue, regardless of where she decided to take him. She would leave it in Toren's hands. If he agreed to examine the guy, she would bring him home. If he declined, she would head for the hospital. Lisa hadn't spoken with Toren since their last date more than two weeks ago. It didn't end badly. It just didn't end well. The chemistry wasn't there, as much as they both had wanted it to be. Toren was a former family doctor who had become disillusioned with the costs of the medical malpractice insurance and the apathy of his patients. So he started working for the local hospice group, where the patients were more agreeable and not as likely to sue. He'd been its head doctor now for five years and claimed no regrets. He said he found it rewarding, to help people leave the world in peace and without pain.

Lisa shared his cynicism, and he made her laugh, but that was it. He was friend material, and she knew Toren had come to the same conclusion about her. But they were in that awkward stage. They'd seen each other naked. They'd had breakfast the morning after, both knowing that the passion of the previous night had been fueled more by deprived hormones than by true physical attraction. Toren was only the second man Lisa had slept with since she'd gotten pregnant with Bridget at fifteen years old, and she had been the first for Toren since his breakup with his live-in girlfriend a year earlier.

Four rings and no answer. That was the sign she was looking for, and with it came relief that this man would not be her burden. Relief and disappointment. She would take him to the hospital and maybe try to talk to him about Chandra later when he was better—if he didn't discharge himself and run away. Lisa was about to hang up when Toren answered, breathless from a run. He agreed to meet her at her house without asking more than a few basic medical questions. Quite an icebreaker, Lisa thought, shutting the car door again. Would you mind risking your license so I can get an interview? And, by the way, this guy's running from a sweatshop owner who might kill us all if he finds us. She tried to focus on the road and keep the

11

Chapter Three

Just yesterday, Lisa had told another reporter how much she missed Bridget and how badly she hoped to find her curled up on the sofa when she got home, watching television or reading a good book with her earbuds in, listening to some new song Lisa didn't know. Lisa had never been home without Bridget for more than a night or so and it had been three days since she'd left. She missed her terribly and wanted her back. Now, she dreaded the possibility that she might return.

The sofa had been too small for the man, whose name, Lisa learned, was Saul Jenkins. She and Toren had moved him to Bridget's bed, where Toren hooked him up to some intravenous fluids and antibiotics. His biggest problem was dehydration, Toren said. He was too thin, but only on the edge of malnourishment. Toren cleaned and treated the cuts on his fingers, which appeared to be deformed by arthritis. Saul had fresh welts on his back, which he said were from whippings. He told Toren and Lisa that the people who ran the sweatshop whipped them often, but always tried to leave marks that would eventually fade. They wanted to punish their captives, but at the same time, they needed to keep them in good health, and they wanted to leave as little evidence of the abuse as possible.

"We were forced to call the guards 'master,' but we called them a lot of other things when they couldn't hear us. Everything they did, they treated us like slaves—like African slaves," he said. "They shackled us when we acted out, they herded us, they fed us the same food every single day for every meal. They enjoyed it, the power thing, humiliating us, especially the new guards. They were the worst. Most of us were Black. A few were Hispanic or Asian. They were all white. Some of them didn't get into it as much as the others, but the owner, he was sick and he got worse over time. It must be some movement, some domestic terrorist group. It has to be. They are crazy. It blows my mind to think that a whole group of people could think that way. They said the nation had made a wrong turn and that they were going to correct it."

Lisa wanted to believe him. He sounded so sincere, but it was all too overwhelming and too over the top. She had read about sweatshops and the brutal treatment of their slaves or supposed employees, but Saul's story almost seemed more insane than plausible. Masters, whippings, shackles. Maybe he really was mad, and he had become obsessed with white supremacy. It was terrifying, the rise of white-supremacist groups in the United States. She could see how thoughts of their continued existence and growth might drive him over the edge, especially given the most recent incidents. Just last spring teenagers in a Texas high school held a fake slave auction on Snapchat, auctioning off their Black classmates. A year earlier, students in a Michigan high school recorded a video in which they discussed their ideas should they ever become president. They wanted to bring back slavery, brand Blacks, burn them and send them back to Africa. These kids were disciplined for what they said, but would that change them? Not likely. It probably made them martyrs among people who thought like them. Maybe Saul read about Chandra in the newspapers or had seen her story on the news. Maybe he honestly believed he had seen her and spoken with her. It was always possible that he knew her before her disappearance. But his injuries…how could he have inflicted those upon himself?

Lisa ducked into her office to look for an empty notebook and a pen that worked while Toren slipped off Saul's clothes and dressed him in some baggy sweatpants and a t-shirt that Lisa had given him. She had instructed Toren to seal the old clothes in a garbage bag and put them in the shed. She didn't dare throw them away. What she was doing, hiding him, was bad enough. She didn't want to ruin an investigation by disposing of evidence. Saul could use a shower, but that would have to wait until he was stronger. Fresh clothes would eliminate most of the odor.

She lingered a little longer than necessary to give Saul some privacy. The office had been Dorothy's bedroom for nearly ten years. Her artwork—abstracts with a unique blend of earth tones and natural brightness—covered the walls, bringing balance to the otherwise drab furniture and the only other décor, a laptop, a phone and an assemble-it-yourself pressed-board bookshelf. Without Dorothy, Lisa could never have balanced a career like journalism with single parenthood. She had been about to give up when Dorothy came into their lives and became grandmother to Bridget and best friend to Lisa. Now they were all outgrowing each other. Bridget would leave for college in the fall and Dorothy had finally opened her own artists' retreat, a dream she'd had since her husband and son died and left her with the old farmland they had once shared. Dorothy would have been happy to see Toren in the house today. She liked him, even though she'd only met him twice. She was openly disappointed when he and Lisa stopped seeing each other.

"Lisa?" Toren's voice pulled her back into the living room and then into Bridget's bedroom with its lavender walls, vanilla aroma and white down comforter. Saul was stretched across the comforter with a fleece throw partially covering his body. He looked different in clean clothes, less surreal.

"He wants to talk again," Toren said, waving a hand in his direction dismissively. "I told him it could wait, that he needed to get some sleep and let his body recover a little, but he wouldn't have it. He's got some kick left in him. I think he's going to be okay."

Lisa set her voice recorder on Bridget's nightstand. She didn't want to miss a word of this. Then she flipped open her notebook and sat on the chair near the edge of the bed. Saul spoke quietly and steadily, taking breaks now and then to rest his voice. He was clearly not used to speaking so much. He asked Lisa to be patient with him. Too many lives depended on him, he said. Saul said he was grabbed off the street in 2011 on his way home from a restaurant in Cincinnati where he was working as a bartender, probably around two in the morning or so. It was almost winter, late fall maybe. The exact date had become fuzzy for him, but he remembered the season because it was cold, but he hadn't brought a jacket along when he left for work. He was still in denial that summer had passed. He thought he heard someone behind him, but before he could turn to look, an arm came around his chest and a moist cloth held by a tight grip covered his face. He thought he was suffocating. It felt like death, but then he woke up. When he came to, he was bound and blindfolded with his face pressed against the cold metal floor of a truck. He had no idea how much time had passed or where they were taking him. They took the blindfold off when he arrived and he'd been here ever since, he said.

Until he talked to Chandra, he didn't know that "here" was Seneca Springs, New York. The guards referred to the basement as Oakwood. The operation had moved only once during his time as a slave—when Frank Tomey escaped. The owner—or Saul assumed he was the owner—brought Tomey into the new place just hours after the move and lynched him, using a rope dangling from the overhead pipes, right in front of all the workers. They left his body on the workroom floor for four days, letting the maggots feast on him. The sight and the smell were unbearable until they weren't anymore. The guards wore masks over their noses and mouths, but the workers had become numb to it all. They had no choice. Then they made Saul and another man wrap Frank's body up and throw him into the back of a pickup truck. Selfishly, Saul had hoped to see stars that night. It had been a long time since he'd seen stars, but it was cloudy. No stars. Not even a little rain.

Those were the only times Saul had been out of the basement workshop—when the operation moved and when he carried the body. When they moved, he was blindfolded again, and then knocked out as soon as he sat down. He awoke in a similar basement to see the guards bringing others into the room. It took two guards for each slave—one on each side supporting their unconscious or semi-conscious bodies around their waists with the slaves' limp arms draped over their shoulders. They let the slaves' legs and feet drag across the concrete. Saul remembered feeling the sting then and looking down to see a mess of blood and shredded flesh on the tops of his own feet. He did not know how long ago that was. He had lost track of time, regained it when Chandra came, and then lost it again. Tomey was lynched before Chandra's appearance. He knew that much. There were seven guards in all—the owner and six others. They were all men and they worked two per shift. Sometimes, another man and a woman came for a short visit. They seemed to make the owner nervous. Saul assumed they were investors, or maybe they were his bosses and he wasn't the owner after all.

The IV fluids had given Saul a sudden burst of energy, but he faded just as quickly and fell into a deep sleep. Toren said he would be much better in a few hours, especially with some food. Lisa's legs had long since fallen asleep from the way she leaned forward in the chair to hear him better, but she'd been too immersed in Saul's story to shift her weight. She stood slowly, shaking her legs as the pins and needles worked their way through. What would Bridget do if she walked in on all this, she wondered.

"This is not smart, Lisa," Toren said as he packed up his supplies. "You got some information from him. Now call the police and let them handle it. Just contact somebody you trust on the force and tell them what happened to that Tomey guy. There's no way they'll turn him over to those people, not when they know you're on the case."

But Lisa had been through this before, and she had a history of poor judgment. She trusted someone she shouldn't have, and it had almost gotten her killed. She wasn't going to be that ignorant again. If any cops were involved, they'd find a way to kill Saul and they might just come after Lisa, too. Even if they weren't involved, something had gone wrong when Frank Tomey had taken that path. He had gone to the police and ended up back where he'd started. Instead of freedom, he found death. Most likely, no one had believed Frank Tomey. What if the police didn't believe Saul? What if they could find no evidence of the sweatshop? They'd turn him loose and wish him good luck. That would likely have the same results—Saul would be killed, and Lisa might become a target. Lisa needed to do more research. She had to at least find out whether the police had any records of Tomey's report and research Saul's disappearance. Somebody must have reported him missing.

"I really appreciate your concern and your help, Toren," Lisa said, "but I've got this. I won't let him stay long, just long enough to check out a few things.

I'm begging you, though, to keep this between us. If word gets out that he's here or that I have anything to do with him…It just wouldn't be good. I know you're taking a big risk, treating him privately and not reporting this. I know it could cost you your license. But I promise to keep this between us, and I doubt Saul is lucid enough to remember your name or what you look like. You don't have to see him again. You don't have to be involved with him at all anymore."

"Lisa." Toren raised a hand as if to block her words. He was gorgeous—tall, lean, fit, the chiseled cheekbones of a *GQ* model. Why wasn't she more attracted to him? He dropped his hand to his side and sighed—deep and heavy.

"I'm not worried about myself, and I'm not going to do anything you don't want me to do. I'm worried about you. I know things didn't work out between us, you know…that way, but I really like you. If he agrees to stay and you decide to let him, call me and I'll follow up tomorrow. He needs to be followed up on. I'd find him someplace else to stay though. He might be a victim, but he's still a stranger. Do you really want him alone in your house while you're at work?"

"Good point," Lisa said. She had not thought that far ahead. She was thrilled just to hear he wasn't dying. "I'll figure something out."

"And go easy with him on food. He's not malnourished, but they didn't feed him much. No telling what good fresh food will do to his stomach and his intestines. I'd start him off with some broth and maybe some toast, and just keep things light and bland for the first couple days."

Toren turned to leave, but Lisa tapped him on the shoulder. She gave him a quick hug and was a little disappointed to find that she still felt nothing. It just wasn't there. "Thank you. You're amazing. It's not fair of me to drag you into this, but you came anyway, and you came right away. That says a lot."

"I love hospice, but it's not exactly exciting. Don't think I won't be harassing you to find out what you uncover. I could use a little adventure in my life." Toren smiled, and then his smile faded. "If what he says is true, Lisa, what difference does it make if I lose my license helping him? I can find another job. It's all about perspective. And I think I believe him. You really get to know people in this line of work—the crazies, the liars, the storytellers, the wishful thinkers. He's not any of those. He's sincere. I can tell."

Lisa followed him to the foyer and softly closed the front door behind him. She was alone—really alone—with Saul Jenkins and the rhythm of his breathing, which seemed to reach her even in the foyer. She closed her eyes, grateful for the sound of that breathing. Grateful that her actions, her decision to bring him into her home, had not cost him his life.

She fell into the recliner in the living room and wondered, once again, whether she had made a wise decision. The driver of the sedan had seen her, and he knew she was a reporter. If she started asking questions about sweatshops and escapees, he might hear about it, and he just might put two and two together. She would have to come up with a plan, a more discreet approach. But her mind was tired, and her thoughts were too jumbled—a blend of worries about Bridget, Saul, the daily story she still needed to write and where Saul could safely stay. She needed a sounding board. She needed Dorothy. That's when the solution came to her. She called her editor and said she wasn't feeling well, but that the press conference was uneventful. If he insisted, she could write something from home, she said. Thank god for disasters. Between a house fire with injuries, a high-speed chase that ended in a crash and a feature on a man with breast cancer, he had little room anyway. She was off the hook.

So she picked up her phone and called Dorothy.

Chapter Four

Whoever invented fire-starter bricks deserved an award, Dorothy thought. A huge one. She bent over and lit the edge, watching the brick catch and immediately produce a steady flame with flecks of deep blue heat among the yellow and orange. The flames licked at the wood above until finally, the logs were burning as well.

Dorothy had never been good at building fires, and these people expected a roaring one every evening, even during the hottest days of the summer. It was all about the nuances. Her guests this week had come from New York City, White Plains, Binghamton, Chicago, Florida and Detroit. Good artists can paint anywhere, but sometimes distractions melt away when the scene is appropriately set and they can act the stereotypical parts.

Dorothy's guests craved that scene. They imagined themselves after a full day of intense internal focus and creativity winding down in leather chairs before a good fire while nursing a glass of wine, a fine scotch, or Hefeweizen drawn from the keg and with the perfect head and a slice of lemon served in an authentic German stein. She could give them that, especially now that she had discovered fire-starter bricks. She threw another log atop the flames and poked at the fire, arranging it just right. Most of the guests took short hikes after dinner, but they would return soon, in pairs, in groups of three or alone, depending on the chosen path, the mood and the weather.

Dorothy's own art had suffered when she first opened the doors to her retreat more than a year ago, but she eventually developed a groove and carved out time for herself in her studio overlooking the hills and valleys of Central New York with glimpses of tea-colored streams and ponds in the distance. She worked early in the mornings while her guests slept off their evening indulgences, sometimes pausing to watch a bear and her cubs emerge from the woods to scavenge for their breakfast among the herd of deer that regularly grazed in the bordering field. She usually managed to find an hour or so in the late afternoon as well, after the lunch dishes were done and dinner was prepped and ready to go. With Bridget's help, she had even stretched a few sessions an extra thirty or forty minutes this past week.

She was fortunate. She believed that, though a part of her felt unsettled lately and that restlessness was seeping into her artwork. It wasn't a bad thing, from an artistic point of view. Her more recent paintings were attracting higher prices and enhancing her reputation, but it disturbed her. The idea that great art required a certain amount of immersion in misery and suffering was bull, she thought. Great artists drew from deep within their experiences and translated the rawest of emotions and sensations through color, shape, texture and form, but it was not necessary to relive it all. Or at least, it shouldn't be. Her son would have turned thirty-two last month had her husband not shot him during a hunting accident thirteen years ago. She could have shared her sorrow at this missed milestone with her husband had he not shot himself in his grief. So there she was, unable to control herself as her grief spilled out onto the damned canvas and she mourned them all over again. She wanted to paint other things. She wanted distraction, but when she tried, her paintings failed.

Then Lisa called, needing her.

Dorothy set the poker into the wrought-iron rack with the other fireplace tools and tidied up the hearth. The fireplace was fully aglow now and the great room, with its Native American rugs and hand-crafted exposed timbers far overhead, was immediately cozy and inviting. Bridget was already at the bar, setting up for the evening. Dorothy had changed the sheets in the spare room in her private portion of the house for the man who was to arrive tonight and had moved Bridget into one of the guest rooms.

She and Lisa agreed that it was safer for Bridget to sleep among the guests for now until they learned more about Saul Jenkins. Bridget knew only that the man was sick, a crime victim and homeless, and that he needed a private place to recover. That was enough for now. She understood the need to keep his presence quiet, but Bridget made it clear that she wanted the full story as soon as possible, reminding her mother of what had happened last time she tried to keep her in the dark.

Dorothy wanted the full story, too, but Lisa had been reluctant to tell her over the phone. Lisa had warned Dorothy that too much knowledge could be dangerous in this case, and that taking Saul in could be unsafe as well. But that was just what Dorothy had been looking for. Already, she was beginning to feel a bit like herself again, getting her edge back. She had to fight the urge to grab her bow and go shoot some targets. Dorothy preferred to practice with her handgun, but she learned early on that her guests were offended by what seemed perfectly safe and acceptable to her. Dorothy had been handling guns since her twelfth birthday, but she needed practice. It was an obsession, and she realized that, but she had no desire to put an end to it. It was her therapy. She wanted to be sure that she was always sharp, that she could recognize her target, confirm it and hit it in an instant with keenness and without hesitation. She wanted to hit her marks with no mistakes and no accidents. Ever.

By the time Dorothy heard the tires on the gravel drive, the sun was beginning to set and the guests had already started exchanging opinions and advice on everything from gardening to politics to sex, trying hard to one-up and impress each other more aggressively than they should with their inhibitions weakened by alcohol. This pattern of behavior had worried Dorothy in those first few weeks, but she soon learned that most of her guests enjoyed intense social interactions after a full day of isolation with their art, and that those who didn't were content to remain quiet and watch the show. It was just another part of their experience, enjoyed even more so by the knowledge that the guests would not likely ever see each other again.

Bridget ran straight into her mother's arms when she walked in through the mudroom door, forcing her to drop a bulging backpack and a duffle bag onto the kitchen tile. She was such a contrast from her mother in some ways, with her long dark curls and her olive skin, but they were both built the same—long and slim—and though Lisa's eyes were gray-blue and Bridget's brown with a hint of hazel, they both had that way of boring into people like they could see inside their souls. While Lisa held Bridget tight, a figure emerged from behind them. Bridget released her mother when she saw Saul Jenkins and stepped back, her mouth slightly open but silent. He was so thin, and pale despite his deep-brown skin. Dorothy grabbed the bags and beckoned him in.

"You're blocking the door, Lisa. Let the poor man through."

Lisa stepped aside and then offered Saul an arm, which he took, leaning heavily on her. He attempted a smile, but it did not come easy. This man needed food more than anything, Dorothy thought. She could do that. She had a feeling he wouldn't be picky.

"Why don't we go into my living room?" Dorothy said. "I think it'd be best if you stayed entirely in my quarters for now until we get you a little healthier and I figure out a way to explain you to the guests. I've got a small kitchen, a bedroom, a spare room, an office, and a full bath. That should be plenty of space for now."

With effort, Saul stood straighter and took his arm back from Lisa. He extended a hand to Dorothy, who took it without hesitation despite its obvious damage. Dorothy tried to hide her shock at his gnarled and cut fingers, but Bridget wasn't quite as capable. She had still said nothing and had failed to close her gaping mouth. Her eyes took in Saul's hands and seemed unable to let them go.

"I greatly appreciate this," Saul said in a strained voice. "I know you're taking a lot of chances, all of you. But I'm not the only one you're helping. I'll be out of here as soon as I can, but I'm no good to them if anybody finds me. Not just yet."

"You'll be safe here," Lisa said, offering support again just as he started to sway, and leading him through the kitchen toward the entrance to Dorothy's quarters. Dorothy nudged Bridget with her elbow and urged her to follow, awakening her from her daze. "Dorothy's got a keen ear and good aim. She's a tyrant though. She never let me get away with anything, so watch yourself."

Lisa settled Saul into a soft chair with broad cushioned arms and asked Bridget to get him some water. The bag and backpack were filled with a few things she'd picked up at Target while Saul hid in the car—toiletries, clothes, underwear, socks and sneakers. He would need a bath or shower as soon as he had enough energy, she said. He was so weak. If this was how he looked after a night's sleep and some nutrients, Dorothy hated to think how bad off he'd been when Lisa found him.

"He needs to drink at least every half hour or so, even if it's just a few sips. Toren gave him an IV and that helped, but he's still a little dehydrated. He said to go light on the food for a few days, too. Saul's been confined to a basement for more than a decade and fed next to nothing, so he might need to build up to the good stuff," she said. "I gave him soup and dry toast just before we left, but he could use something else within the next hour."

When Bridget returned and everyone was seated, Lisa began. She told Dorothy and Bridget how she'd found Saul, what he'd told her, and what she'd discovered during her internet search while he slept. Saul leaned back and closed his eyes, but Dorothy could tell he was listening to every word. Bridget looked like she wanted to be sick, but she was trying hard to keep herself together. She was growing up, Dorothy thought, growing up too fast.

A Google search of Saul's name turned up only a judgment against Saul involving his former landlord. Lisa called the landlord, pretending to be another landlord checking Saul's credentials, and got an earful. Saul had never paid his December rent that year and didn't answer his phone, the door or his mail. When the landlord finally used his key to get in, he found Saul had left all his stuff—mostly junk—behind. The garbage hadn't been emptied in weeks and it reeked. The fridge was full of food, most of it expired or rotten.

Lisa turned to Saul.

"He said to tell you that he kept the valuables—stuff like your photo albums and your Social Security card—and that if you want them back, you'll have to pay up. He sold everything that was worth money, but still didn't make back the rent. It was clear he didn't know you'd been kidnapped. It was too late to call the police and find out whether a missing persons report was filed. I'll try that in the morning."

"Don't bother," Saul said without opening his eyes. "When I lived in that apartment, I had just been laid off from my job at a technology startup and I was bartending here and there. I'd moved to Cincinnati from Chicago for that job only a few months earlier, so I didn't know many people there. Turns out the company was a financial and organizational mess. I never should have agreed to move for them. I didn't have a girlfriend at the time or kids and my parents were already both dead. My only relative is a half-brother, and I hadn't talked to him in at least five years. He was my father's son, and my mother didn't like me talking to him. I had friends in Chicago, but no one especially close. Not then, after nursing my mother through cancer and the breakup with my girlfriend. No one close enough to call the cops."

With a slight lift of his hand, Saul motioned that he needed a moment. He swallowed hard, and then continued. "That's why I could escape. The others—they knew that if they ran away, these guys would kill their families. They told Tomey just before they killed him—they told all of us—that his wife and two kids had already died in a house fire. Natural gas leak, they said. The whole house exploded while they were sleeping. He was from Minnesota. St. Cloud, I think.

"I don't think they know about my half-brother. They would have thrown that at me by now if they did. They did that to people. They gave them updates on their families, told them about birthday parties and graduations and weddings. They wanted them to know that they were watching them, keeping track. It didn't matter whether it was true. It was the thought of it—knowing that these people could hurt their kids, their spouses, their parents if they wanted to. That's what scared the others."

Bridget couldn't take it anymore. She stood up, holding her hand over her mouth, and ran to the bathroom. Dorothy could hear her retching through the closed door. Lisa started after her but then sat down again and turned to Saul, her eyes shifting from him to the bathroom door and back again. Dorothy understood. It was clear that Saul was struggling to stay awake and to talk. If Lisa went after Bridget, she might return to find him deeply asleep or without the energy, too hoarse to speak.

"Can you tell me more, Saul? Anything?" Lisa asked.

He took a sip of water, sat a little straighter and spoke.

"I'll try, but I don't know how much it will help," he said with a sigh.

He had escaped at night through a boarded-up, quarter-sized basement window in the bathroom that he'd been working on prying open for months. The bathroom was off the room they slept in, and it reeked, so the guards paid no attention if their captives got up to pee in the middle of the night. As far as they knew, no one could get out of there. He carefully replaced all the wood he'd loosened each time. When he'd finally mastered the art of taking it off in one piece and covering the window up again, he started working on the window itself. It wasn't hard. They had locked it from the inside, but not from the outside. The trick was getting it to slide open despite years of swelling and rust. For that, he used needles, picking away at the window frame until he'd freed it.

The window opening was narrow, but Saul had saved every bit of oil he could from the sewing machines, and he was skinny, lacking muscle and fat. He took off his shirt, oiled his shoulders, his chest and what he could reach of his back and slipped though, pulling his shirt back on again when he got outside. He had an advantage. He had escaped soon after the others had fallen asleep. Other than a hard rap or two on the door, the guards rarely responded to those who screamed or called out to loved ones in their sleep. It happened too often to bother. He found himself in an alley that smelled strongly of paint and gasoline and started moving, but he was disoriented. He paid no attention to signs or any other landmarks. He just wanted to hide himself as far away as he could. He knew he had only a few hours. They never got to sleep much, just long enough to give the guards a break, he figured.

He woke up the next morning on the second floor of an abandoned building to the sounds of voices and vehicles. When he looked outside, he saw the television crews setting up their cameras in the street below and people in dress shirts and slacks gathered around. It was too much for his senses. The light hurt his eyes and he knew his voice was unused to speaking in more than a whisper. He feared he'd be shooed away like a homeless nuisance if he tried to approach anyone, and then he'd be vulnerable again. So he waited. He had seen Lisa go back to her car for something before the press conference began and he saw her talking to a photographer with her notebook in her hand, so he knew that the last vehicle remaining belonged to a reporter. He sneaked downstairs and waited until everything was quiet. He had been in the car for only a few minutes when she opened the door.

"I'm sorry," Saul said, dropping his head into his hands. "I didn't mean to scare you, but you were my only way out."

Bridget came back into the room, carrying a wool blanket, her face somber and pale. Maybe this wasn't a good idea, Dorothy thought. Bridget was so young, and she'd been through so much already. Sometimes Lisa needed that second pair of eyes to see things she couldn't, like the possibility that this was too much for her daughter to handle. But then Bridget approached Saul and gently draped the blanket over his lap.

"Whatever you need, we're here for you," she said with a smile.

Chapter Five

If the sweatshop did exist, it couldn't be located in one of the buildings included in Trammel's project, Lisa thought. Members of his team had at least walked through every building. They would have noticed a bunch of underfed slaves sewing clothing in a dirty basement. According to Saul, the workers sewed everything from leather purses to designer jeans to silk scarves. The repetitive movements, the rapid pace and the lack of any safety equipment were what damaged Saul's fingers. He told Lisa, Dorothy and Bridget he had worked through broken bones and sprains and was forced to suck on his fingers between stitches whenever he cut himself so he wouldn't get blood on the fabric. The punishment for bloodstains was severe, he said. If his sewing machine broke, he had to keep up until it was repaired or a new one arrived. If he was lucky, a backup would be available. If not, he kept sewing manually, knowing he would likely sleep with his hands shackled to a pipe that ran along the ceiling and his feet barely touching the floor that night. The thought of it made Lisa shiver as she slipped her pass card through the slot that unlocked the newsroom stairwell.

Lisa took the steps slowly, trying to picture the layout of Iron City Heights once again. She would have to check the tax maps for the entire area and figure out who owned what. She couldn't think of any businesses currently operating on the eastern side, in Trammel's area. The closest was probably a shipping company that stored large wooden crates in an old warehouse in about the center of the neighborhood, on the western edge of Trammel's development. A guy who did powder coating for the military on contract leased a building a few blocks farther west. She had interviewed him once years ago about his involvement with equipment headed for Afghanistan. In the building next to him was a body shop for large vehicles like buses and delivery trucks. These were all companies that didn't need attractive storefronts. There was enough activity in some areas, especially on the west side, that an occasional van or truck full of fabric wouldn't necessarily be noticed or questioned. The sweatshop must be somewhere on the west side. It was the only place that made sense.

The building that housed the sweatshop would have to include a garage or warehouse with wide doors, someplace for the guards to park their vehicles or load or unload merchandise and supplies. They couldn't do business from the curb or a driveway. That would attract attention. It could not have been easy to move the whole operation in one night, the night Tomey escaped. They must have been well-covered. After all, they had to move people— prisoners—discreetly. How many buildings would be available that met the criteria? Did they move within Iron City Heights or was that the move that brought them here?

They might have been operating in some other section of the city before Tomey escaped, but they might also have been based in another city entirely. Saul said the lynching occurred before Chandra joined them. Chandra told him he was in Seneca Springs. He had no idea where he was before she came along. Then again, Saul said the guards had always referred to their location as Oakwood. From her encounter with the sedan driver, Lisa guessed the owner wanted to ensure that escapees were mistaken for patients of the psychiatric hospital of the same name. That reference didn't change when they relocated after Tomey's escape and Oakwood was located here in Seneca Springs. So, both the old and new locations were likely in or near the city. She needed to know what police department Tomey sought help from, whether it was city police or one of the suburban departments. That would tell her more.

She would find out soon enough. Before she left home, Lisa called a cop who once worked in records and had a soft spot for Lisa. Her first story as a member of the projects desk was an investigation of the records department and the officers who were assigned there. She found nothing wrong with the day-shift assignments. Just the usual complaints. For the most part, the people who worked in the dingy fourth-floor office from eight a.m. to four p.m. had the required skills and wanted to be there. Every now and then, Human Resources assigned someone who needed light duty because of a medical condition, but those people weren't around for long. They either returned to their regular assignments when they recovered or quit or went on disability.

But at night, the back room with its stale, dry air and cracked beige walls became a dumping ground for certain misfits and castaways. Lisa had visited the fourth floor each night as part of her duties on the night-crime shift. She'd come to know these people and their stories. One was a skinny, effeminate guy whose heterosexuality was constantly challenged by certain cops even though he was married to a woman and they had five kids. Another was a female cop who had turned in a sergeant for intentionally targeting a gay bar during an underage drinking sting and making threatening and disparaging remarks to the patrons as he swaggered through it. After her complaint, the sergeant was removed from the unit and investigated by Human Resources, but the results of the investigation were sealed. His punishment, if any, was never publicly revealed and he remained on the force in high standing. Another records officer was openly a lesbian and probably would have sued, but complaints had piled up in her personnel file about insubordination and extended breaks—allegations she denied but couldn't fight. They all had one person in common: Elizabeth Fromley, the assistant director of Human Resources.

Lisa's investigation showed Fromley was a member of several anti-gay organizations and had lost a previous job because she was so outspoken about her beliefs. Her former employer had withheld the information from the city for fear of lawsuits and had given Fromley a decent recommendation in exchange for a quiet departure. Lisa's front-page story got her fired from the Seneca Springs PD and led to a shakeup. Surprisingly, a handful of officers wanted to work in the records department at night. So jobs shifted, and Lisa earned a few new friends within the police department, including Lydia Houston, the lesbian cop whose negative personnel record was expunged.

She was back on the street working daytime patrols, but she was more than happy to search a few records for Lisa.

It was ten a.m. when Lisa entered the *Sun Times* newsroom. Phones were ringing. Keyboards were clicking. A planning meeting involving most of the assignment and section editors was taking place in the glass-enclosed conference room on the other end of the hall, giving some reporters and copy editors the green light to ease up a bit and converse. Lisa took a detour through the Lifestyles department, hoping to avoid anyone who might distract her. Her new desk, assigned to her in a recent redesign, was in the back of the newsroom, away from the fray. She could almost call it an office compared to her former cubicle. Lisa's space had two corners for computers, allowing her to work alongside another reporter when necessary. The corners were linked by a long rectangular countertop where she could spread out documents, maps and other cities' newspapers. It was shielded from the rest of the newsroom by a tall divider.

The privacy was convenient for Lisa, but also for other reporters and editors who didn't want their phone conversations overheard. Lisa never knew who she would find when she peered around the divider. Today it was Fred Macki, arguing with his wife over yet another night out with the girls. Last night was apparently her second of the week and he was growing suspicious. From the sound of it, he should be. Fred was a nice guy, and it would be easy to think he was the type of reporter people could walk all over. But his demeanor was deceptive. Lisa had seen him in action recently at the courthouse when a sheriff's deputy tried to bar him from jury selection, believing it wasn't a public procedure. Fred smiled, turned around and started pushing buttons on his cell phone. Lisa tried to intervene, but Fred pulled her back gently, thanked her and told her to stick around for a bit. Within ten minutes, the sheriff himself was in the hall along with the judge, who had called a recess. The deputy's pale skin had reddened significantly, and he was stuttering as he tried to explain. The judge threw an arm around Fred's shoulder and walked him into the courtroom. The sheriff apologized as Fred passed and nudged the deputy, who apologized as well. Fred's wife was an idiot to mess with him this way. He looked up when he saw Lisa and handed her a Post-It note with Toren's name and number scribbled on it.

"Look. We'll talk later," he told his wife. "I've got to go unless you want me to pull the whole newsroom in on this."

He hung up, conjured his usual smile for Lisa and left. Fred's wife probably thought she'd convinced him to back off, but from what Lisa knew of Fred, she guessed he was already en route to his lawyer's office. His wife wouldn't know what hit her until long after it did. This was the kind of thing Dorothy and Bridget needed to see when they pushed Lisa to date more. Age did not automatically bring about maturity in relationships. Lisa was picky. She knew that, and she intended to stay that way. She was attracted to men who took risks, who were passionate about their jobs and about life, but she had always tried to keep her home life stable for Bridget. Risktakers were not stable. They were dangerous. Maybe that was why it didn't work out with Toren. He was too nice, too safe. She just couldn't do it even though, logically, he was good for her.

Lisa returned the call to Toren, who said he would stop by Dorothy's later in the day to examine Saul again and redress his wounds. He tried to express disappointment in Lisa's decision to keep the police out of it for a while, but his excitement was obvious. She just hoped she could trust him to keep quiet. For the moment though, she had to push all that aside and get a story written. At the very least, that meant calls to the heads of the city and the county IDA's office and a sandwich from the cafeteria at her desk.

Chapter Six

Dorothy could not hide her shock when she returned to her quarters after cleaning up from lunch. She found Saul in her own little kitchen, washing the coffee cup she had left behind that morning and wiping her crumbs off the counter. His shoulders were not slumped. His feet did not drag. His skin was an even deeper brown with a softness she hadn't noticed before. He had showered and was wearing a t-shirt and a pair of basketball shorts Lisa had bought him. His thin legs were lost in them.

"Saul, you're alive," Dorothy proclaimed from the doorway.

Saul jumped at her voice, banging his hip on the counter, and Dorothy chastised herself for walking in so quietly. Of course he would jump. He'd just spent a good decade in a basement getting beaten, whipped and shackled. She'd have to remember to announce herself more subtly, with a cough or the scuffing of her feet on the floor, to give him some kind of quiet warning.

"I admire your energy, but you don't recover in two days," Dorothy said. "You sit down and let me get you some lunch or some breakfast or whatever it is you want. I'm going to brew us a big pot of coffee and we're going to spend some time just being human beings. We're going to sit and we're going to talk. Okay?"

"Yes," Saul answered quickly, placing the cup in the dish rack with hands that shook. "Sure. I mean—okay."

His voice still had that raspy, unused quality, but it was stronger than before. Dorothy had planned to sneak in a little painting time this afternoon. Lunchtime cleanup went much faster with Bridget around. But Saul was far more intriguing, and he looked so lost, like he didn't know what to do

33

with himself. Dorothy couldn't resist picking his brain a bit, and he seemed to need some direction. Freedom was obviously new to him. Dorothy had never been a prisoner, but she knew that lost feeling. She couldn't function for a long time after her son and husband died. Not really anyway. Her routine was gone, her own direction.

Despite her announcement, Dorothy stayed mostly quiet while Saul ate in an armchair in the living room. It was fascinating to watch, the way he focused on his food with such intensity. With each bite, he seemed to battle desires to shovel it all down and to keep the food on his tongue, savoring the flavors and the texture with all his senses. But as soon as he finished, she started in.

"This is a retreat for artists. Every guest here paints, draws, whatever. They come here for the solitude, so they can think and create because creating is actually hard work. So if you're going to stay here, I'm going to ask that you work," she said. She stood up and grabbed a pad of paper off an end table and a long thin metal box. Then she gently tossed them on his lap and sat back down in a chair across from him.

"Here's a sketchpad and a set of pencils. Don't tell me you don't know how to draw. I don't care. Scribble if you want to. Just do something and have something to show me at the end of each day. If you want to go outside, stay on my screened-in porch for now. Don't go on the wraparound and don't go for walks. We'll wait until you're a little less skeletal looking and then I'll come up with a reason for your being here. I have to tell you that even after some sleep and some food, you're kind of scary looking. People will ask questions. We've got to get some meat on your bones. Now, tell me about you. Who were you before all this?"

Saul's gaze rested on his lap and his fingers fiddled with the pencil box. He released a long breath and then lifted his face to look Dorothy directly in the eyes. The steadiness of his stare surprised her. There was strength in those eyes, in his ability to connect.

"I'm not sure I know how," he said. "I mean, I think about those days a lot, but I haven't dared to speak about them. They were mine, you know? The memories. That was one thing they couldn't take away from me. I knew who

I was, and I knew I was no slave. Even now, I worry. What if they come back for me? What if this is just a dream, an illusion, and what if I do it? What if I speak? I saw what can happen. One man, he talked about his son and about taking him to the pool in the summer. The guards—they used that. They tortured him with that memory, with images of the boy drowning in that pool because his father didn't produce enough or missed a few stitches or screwed up the pattern. They told him exactly how drowning kills, described it in detail. I remember thinking thank god I didn't have kids. I don't think I could have survived that, mentally, I mean."

His eyes dropped back down to his lap and the room grew quiet. Dorothy didn't know how to respond. Saul had good reason for his fear. His captors had not been arrested or even identified. In fact, no one else was looking for them. Only Lisa. Police weren't even aware a crime had been committed. If his captors found him—she couldn't even bring herself to think about it. She shouldn't have asked such probing questions so soon. She should have left him alone. She was about to get up and leave him to his thoughts—come up with a polite excuse so she wouldn't make him feel bad—when Saul spoke again.

"There was a girl," he said. "I almost married her, and I probably would have if my mother hadn't gotten sick. I thought about her a lot. Her smile got me through some of the worst times. I hope she's happy now. I hope she's married and has a couple of kids. I'll tell you about her. Her name was Donna."

Chapter Seven

This time, Lisa parked on the west side of Iron City Heights, where the streets were slightly more alive, though not with pedestrian traffic. There was little reason to travel by foot in this area. Most anyone who had business here drove a delivery truck, a tow truck or a pickup with a large metal toolbox attached to the bed. They either came to work and stayed for the day or did their business and got out. She knew she would attract attention, so she decided her best cover was honesty—sort of. She would tell shop owners she was a reporter writing a feature about the businesses that thrived on the west side and how they might be affected by the development. It wasn't a bad story idea, really. She might even write it, she thought.

Immediately, Lisa made some interesting discoveries. Tucked away in a squat three-story building shielded by taller structures was a large open-floored staging room for a florist. Stems and Petals was a popular downtown stop for last-minute bouquets and small expensive gifts. Lisa knew they did some large events, like weddings, but she had never thought about where all the displays were arranged, wrapped or tied. She was pleasantly overwhelmed by the scent of fresh-cut stems and a rush of cool air when she opened the door. Three people were inside—a man and two women—pulling flowers from large round bins and carrying them to the appropriate tables. They chatted as they worked and were thrilled to welcome Lisa. This was one of the perks of being a reporter, the excuse to step into and out of other worlds that she might never experience otherwise. The fragrances remained with her when she left.

Next, she found a workshop for a wood sculptor. It was a small space compared to the florist, but more than large enough for his stacks of logs, his worktable, his equipment and his finished products—dozens upon dozens of bears, deer, raccoons, birds, all kinds of wildlife along with gnomes, totem poles and spiritual figures. Some were painted, like the bald eagle with its outstretched wings and its talons clutching a rock. Others were perfect as they were, like the angel that reached out gently, offering comfort and safety to those who passed through the buyer's gate or front door. He fascinated Lisa, the way he worked so precisely, so quickly, with a chainsaw. Figures emerged immediately with what seemed like little effort, their features surprisingly accurate and alive. The air in the workshop was thick with sawdust and smelled like fresh pine, like Christmas year round. Once again, she found the scent itself difficult to leave behind.

A few doors down, she found a warehouse for a company that sold rain gutters and, across from that, a large-vehicle repair shop. Farther in, Lisa found a company that made bicycle parts for sale in Japan. But each time she stepped back onto the street, one particular scent pulled her a little farther east—a little deeper into the center of Iron City Heights—eventually overpowering the gasoline and paint, the pine and even the floral scents that still lingered in her memory. It was the smell of baking bread. Lisa followed it until she came upon a storefront attached to a long narrow building, with a sign over the door that read, "CMD Baking Company." Adjacent to the building was a single-story warehouse with four sets of garage doors. A white van pulled in front of one stall as she watched from across the street. The door opened just long enough and high enough to let the van in before it shut again. Lisa was curious, but she was also hungry. She had skipped breakfast and barely touched lunch. This was clearly a commercial bakery, but she would buy a dozen loaves if she had to.

She turned the handle on the heavy wooden door and walked in, but before she could announce herself, a man emerged from behind a Formica countertop. He wore jeans and a clean white t-shirt stretched across a broad chest. Lisa guessed by the slight lines near the corners of his eyes and the lack of silver in his thick light-blonde hair that he was in his late thirties. He was taller than Lisa by a good five inches and she immediately noticed his clothing lacked any flour residue or spots darkened by shortening. Perhaps he'd worn an apron. Or maybe he was the bakery's accountant. But something about him was out of place.

"What can I do for you?" he asked.

His eyes immediately found the bulge in Lisa's front pocket, where she had tucked her voice recorder. She pulled that out only if she was sure sources would be comfortable with it. The man came closer until he was just a few feet away, right on the edge of Lisa's personal space. He crossed his arms over his chest and then smiled brightly, contradicting his stance. The smile threw Lisa off. She stammered a bit as she introduced herself, but then recovered and asked to speak with the manager or owner. As she spoke, Lisa focused on relaxing. A reporter writing a feature would not be suspicious of a good-looking man in a bakery. If anything, she would be attracted to him. She had to remember the role she was playing and push thoughts of sickly men and women crammed in a basement, sewing until their fingers bled, out of her head.

"I'm the owner," the man said. "But I'm not interested in a story. We have plenty of business as it is. More than we can keep up with. We're a commercial bakery. We wouldn't want to draw in disappointed individuals, would we? Good luck to you though."

The man reached behind Lisa and opened the door for her, but Lisa couldn't leave yet. She had to find a way to stick around a little longer. She put a gentle hand on the man's arm and gave him her own best smile. As expected, he pulled away from her touch and from the door, allowing it to swing shut again.

"Hey, forget the reporter stuff," she said, stepping back to give him space and reclaim some of her own. "My dad is thinking of opening a deli. You know, he's close to retirement, and he's tired of the whole office scene. I don't suppose I could buy a loaf or bun off you and get your card? It smells so good in here. Your bread must be awesome."

Lisa didn't mention that she'd only talked to her father once in the past eighteen years and that once was enough. Her father didn't have the money or the motivation to open a deli and never would. He wasn't even man enough to come after Lisa when she ran away at fifteen years old, or when her daughter's birth announcement appeared in the weekly paper a few months later, or when her name showed up as a byline in the city newspaper a few years after that.

"Like I said, we don't really need any new business, but how about you give me your card and I'll call you if our situation changes. I'll trade you a dozen rolls. You just wait here, and I'll be back." He kept an eye on Lisa as he moved behind the counter again and disappeared through an open doorway into a back room.

Lisa slid closer to the counter and peered through the opening. She couldn't see much—just a sliver of steel countertop and a few empty bakery racks. She heard voices. The man's voice was low and hushed. The other voice, another man, sounded impatient and irritated. She couldn't make out the words and drew back when she heard him coming again. He shoved a white paper bag full of rolls at her and, again, asked for her card.

"Oh, I'm sorry. I should have gotten that out while I waited for you. Could you hold on a second?" She hadn't brought her purse, but she always kept a few business cards in a holder in her back pocket. She intentionally fumbled for them, hoping to stretch the time out just a bit more. "So, who are some of your clients? You must deliver to Brody's and some of the other bigger places. Their bread is fantastic."

"Yeah, Brody's and a bunch of others," he said, still holding the bag out. "Look, I've really got to go. We've got a couple batches in the oven and a few more deliveries to make before our day is over. It's been a long day and I'd like to get out of here at some point."

Lisa couldn't stall anymore. She gave him the card, took the bag and left. But she left with more than rolls. This bakery definitely did not deliver to Brody's. Pete Brody made his own bread in ovens located in the back of his shop. He was famous for it. Anyone who knew anything about the local restaurants and eateries knew that. Lisa reached into the bag and pulled out one of the rolls as she walked. She was starving and, despite her suspicions, she was looking forward to its softness. Her teeth couldn't even pierce the crust. It was both over-baked and stale.

She wanted a better look at the place, but she couldn't just stop in the street and stare. So Lisa walked the half-mile back to her car and threw the rolls onto the passenger seat. She would cruise by slowly and at least get a better feel for the layout. But just about fifty yards from the bakery, her car started vibrating strangely and Lisa felt her body lean slightly to one side. She pulled over, got out and looked. A flat. She could see two nails jutting from the rubber. And worse, she'd forgotten to replace her spare after the last time.

She was about to call AAA when she heard a garage door open and realized she'd landed in front of an auto restoration shop, one she had not yet visited. A short man with thick arms, dark curly hair and grease-stained coveralls approached, introducing himself as Harley. He looked over the damage, went back into the building and returned a few moments later with a jack. Harley said he could take off the tire, patch it and put in back on within a few minutes. But he warned her that the fix wouldn't last long. She would have to go right to a tire shop and get a better patch job or a new tire.

Lisa thanked him profusely and tried to strike up a conversation while he worked, but she was grateful to find that he preferred not to chat. The silence allowed her to focus instead on the bakery building, which was just down the street on the opposite side. She couldn't have planned it better. The more she studied the building though, the more confused she became. The bakery itself might have a basement, but it would be a tiny one. Probably too small for the kind of operation Saul had described. The basement was not exposed in the front, but the land sloped along the side and revealed an increasing amount of concrete brick. It was possible there was a bathroom window in the back facing what looked like a small alley between the bakery building and the building behind it. The garage appeared to be set on a concrete pad with no foundation. For all her suspicions, she wasn't sure it would work. She would need to study it more on Google Maps and maybe walk around back sometime when it was closed.

Harley never offered Lisa a place to sit inside, despite his graciousness, so she leaned against her car and watched the bakery's doors for a half hour. Nothing. No movement, no visitors, no action whatsoever. Finally, Harley told her she was free to go. She tried to pay him, but he refused. She gave him her card instead and asked him to have his boss call for inclusion in the story. After all she'd seen, she decided she would do something with the day's interviews. Iron City Heights really was full of treasures, but they were not the buildings the head of the IDA had spoken of.

Lisa drove past the bakery and turned right, figuring she'd stop at the Firestone dealer about two miles west to get a new and safer tire, when she saw something that made her slam on her brakes. The gold sedan she had seen the day of the press conference had passed her traveling in the opposite direction. The same man was behind the wheel, but he was focused on the road and didn't seem to notice her. He turned left, the way she had come.

Lisa did a quick three-point turn in the narrow street and tried to follow him, but she was too late. By the time she'd turned around, the car was out of sight and the bakery's garage doors were still closed. Harley had already cleaned up his tools and his garage door was on its way down. She could barely see his feet. He would likely not have noticed if the car turned into the bakery, and how would she ask him anyway without explaining her reasons? But at least she knew she was in the right neighborhood, or close to it, and she was sure that somehow the bakery fit into all this, even if it wasn't the site of the sweatshop. Perhaps there was an underground tunnel that connected with the building behind it. Maybe it was simply their headquarters. She would have to find out more. She had printed out PDFs of the tax maps for the areas closest to Trammel's development before she set out and they were in the backseat. They would make for excellent reading over a sandwich from Brody's after she got that new tire.

Chapter Eight

L isa needed more from Saul, anything at all he could remember—sounds, smells, anything. The tax maps hadn't been much help. The bakery building was owned by the city, probably leased to the company by the IDA. Chances were slim that the owner of a sweatshop had signed a city lease in exchange for a tax break. So the bakery was probably legitimate. Maybe she'd been too on edge, looking too hard for something suspicious or amiss. She would have to get access to IDA records to find out who ran the bakery, and, from her recent experience, she guessed that would take a while. The online records were often several months to a year out of date.

The auto restoration shop was owned by Crown, Inc., which also owned a few of the vacant buildings in the area. The large-vehicle repair shop was owned by a corporation she recognized, Complete Auto Services. They had a couple of garages throughout the city and one used-car lot. Several vacant buildings were owned by the city, or by banks that had foreclosed on them. The florist owned its own building, as did the rain gutter company. There were a few empty city-owned buildings on the street the car had turned down and it probably would be easy enough to squat in their basements, but squatting would be a huge risk for such a long-term operation, especially if it was that close to Trammel's project.

Maybe the sedan didn't pull into any of those businesses. Maybe the driver had rounded another corner and gone elsewhere. Lisa had been so focused on the bakery that she hadn't even thought to keep driving around. But she knew enough of the neighborhood now that the little details, the observations Saul might otherwise overlook or think irrelevant, might be helpful. Besides, she wanted to see him again. He was still so frail when she saw him last that sometimes it was difficult to convince herself he would pull through.

It was just after dinner when Lisa eased her car up the mile-long dirt road to the two-story timber-frame perched on top of the hill. The sun was beginning its descent and Lisa knew that in an hour or so, its rays would frame the house with colors so intense, any artist who tried to realistically portray it would be accused of exaggerating. Only two years before, she and Dorothy had picnicked at this spot, imagining what her artists' retreat would be like. Now, here it was. Dorothy's dream had come true. She was happy for Dorothy, but she missed her, and she missed her cooking. She hoped leftovers were still available.

Dorothy was scrubbing pans in the main kitchen when Lisa arrived, a job that was supposed to be Bridget's. The dishwasher was running, but Tupperware containers of chicken cordon bleu, wild rice and orange-spiced green beans still sat uncovered on the counter. Dorothy caught her staring and nodded toward the food.

"Go ahead," she said. "It's not like I can serve them leftovers and your new friend still doesn't eat much."

Lisa hadn't realized just how hungry she was. She quickly filled a plate and leaned against the counter to eat, watching as Dorothy rinsed the final pot with the sprayer, dried her hands on a dish towel and then squirted lotion into her palm, rubbing it vigorously into her hands. When Dorothy pulled off her chef's apron, Lisa noticed she was dressing better these days, probably in response to her new role as hostess. Gone were the paint-stained jeans and loose white t-shirts, her usual work clothes. Tonight's jeans were free of colorful splatters and, though she still wore t-shirts, they were of higher quality and bore designs that reflected her tastes—Native American symbols, earth-toned tie-dye or some kind of original design from an artist she had come to know.

But, no matter how she dressed, Dorothy still had that look of someone much younger than her sixty-four years with arms more buff than Jennifer

Lopez's and a long, thick braid of gray hair down her back. Rarely did Lisa think of their age difference. It seemed irrelevant, except when Bridget was involved. Dorothy had a way of calming Bridget that Lisa did not, a patience that seemed to come with age, a grandmotherly tolerance that had earned her the title years ago. Lisa had expected Bridget to come in from the dining room any moment carrying coffee cups or wine glasses or a rag that she'd used to wipe down the table. The entirety of dinnertime cleanup was supposed to be her job during her two-week employment, but her daughter was still nowhere in sight.

"Where's Bridget?" Lisa asked when she'd finally slowed down enough to speak.

"She's in my kitchen eating with Saul. I thought it'd be good for both of them," Dorothy said, pulling an oversized bottle of red wine from one cupboard and two glasses from another. Lisa stopped eating with her fork in midair. She did not want Bridget spending time alone with Saul. What if he was crazy? What if this was all a hoax? What if Bridget grew fond of him, and these guys came after him and he was killed? Two years ago, Bridget lost a father she'd never had a chance to know. She had nearly lost Lisa to her father's killer. She had been threatened herself. Lisa could not bear to relive that.

"I can feel your pulse racing from here. Never mind. She's fine. I've spent some time with him. He's as gentle as they come. But this is something I wanted to talk about," Dorothy said, handing Lisa a near-full glass of merlot. "You can't come here anymore. You can't even call, not even to talk to Bridget. Not until Saul is gone. If someone hears you're looking into this, all they'd have to do is tap your phones or follow you, and Saul, Bridget, all of my guests and I will be in danger. I can't have that."

Lisa swallowed hard, put down her plate, and then took a long drink of her wine. Dorothy was right, of course, and she should have thought of that. Saul was safe only if he was completely disconnected from Lisa. Still, no contact with Bridget? Could she do that? So far, she had discussed Saul and his story with no one but Toren, Dorothy and Bridget. Even if she'd raised suspicions in Iron City Heights today, no one would have had time to follow her yet. They were probably safe today, but she had to agree. No more visits. It would be too dangerous.

"What if I called from someone else's phone?"

"No," Dorothy answered without hesitation. She downed her own wine in three large gulps. Then she refilled her glass and topped off Lisa's. "Did I ever tell you about the work I did for a domestic violence program? I oversaw security. That's why I learned to shoot something smaller than a hunting rifle. Nothing more dangerous than a disgruntled man who believes you've stolen his most valuable property. We covered our tracks in all kinds of ways. Still, every now and then, one of them would succeed in finding a safe house and we'd have to move a family. Keeping locations confidential is tricky business. This sweatshop has been operating for at least a decade without attracting attention. Who knows what kind of technology they have? Maybe they can trace cell phones. Maybe they have GPS tracking devices and will attach one to your car. I can't take that chance, not with all these people in my care."

Lisa's wine went down too quickly. This time, she filled her own. If nothing else, the situation was incentive to work fast. The sooner she found some evidence to back Saul's story—anything—the sooner she could go to the police and turn this whole situation over to them. Her daughter had only a little more than a month before she left for college. Lisa didn't want to waste even a minute.

"I get it," Lisa said. "I guess I'd better make the best of this visit and start talking to him now. I've got some questions."

Lisa put down her wine and pushed open the adjoining door. She was taken aback by what she heard from the kitchen. Laughter. Bridget had apparently just told a story and Saul was laughing. He had a pleasant laugh. Warm and smooth. How long had it been since he'd used it, she thought. Bridget leaped up from her chair at the table when she saw her mother and threw her arms around her neck. Lisa hugged her back tightly and kissed her through her mass of curly hair. She would miss that. She would miss that so much when Bridget left for college. So many moms complained that their children distanced themselves from them in their teens, wouldn't accept hugs anymore. Bridget didn't just accept hugs; she offered them, and regularly.

"Mom," Bridget said, "come sit with us."

Lisa explained the situation to Bridget, telling her she'd like her to stay put at the retreat until further notice. She didn't want Bridget coming by the house and leading someone up here. Bridget whined for just a moment about needing a few other articles of clothing and forgetting her favorite lipstick, but she put up almost no fight. She was enjoying the intrigue of Saul. She asked Lisa whether she could at least call her boyfriend, Ben, to let him know she wouldn't be able to meet him for a late dinner the next night. He would be upset, but he was busy, too, trying to work a few extra shifts before he left for college. If she gave him enough notice, he could get in a few more hours. Her biggest concern was for Lisa.

"What about you, Mom? What if somebody finds out you're poking around and comes after you? Who's going to keep you safe? I don't like it." Bridget brought her long thin arms around herself, enveloping her body, the way she always had since she was young, when she was scared or unsure.

"Bridget, I want you to take this seriously," Lisa said with a sigh, "but not that seriously. Nothing is going to happen to me. I don't plan to knock on doors in Iron City Heights asking for the sweatshop. But it's not just me, you and Dorothy we have to worry about. It's Dorothy's guests, too. We have to go that extra mile, take extra precautions for their sake. Do you understand?"

Bridget nodded but still did not relax. Lisa turned to Saul, who sat quietly staring at his plate. She knew what he was thinking. "Saul, this isn't just about you, so don't go getting all apologetic here. Other lives are at stake, including Chandra's. I need your help. I need you to think with your senses and tell me everything you can remember about your environment, especially during those few times when you were outside, especially when you escaped."

Saul looked up. Lisa couldn't believe the physical changes in him in just a few short days. His lips were beginning to heal and the dark shadows under his eyes were fading. His skin was looking less opaque, less ghostly—becoming richer in its color. She couldn't have guessed his age when she first found him, but now it was much more obvious. According to her research, he was thirty-four years old. If he had been this healthy when she first saw him, she would have guessed mid- to late-thirties.

"I wasn't paying much attention when I escaped. I just wanted out. It was all so unfamiliar." Saul shook his head like he was trying to clear his mental vision. "Dumpsters. I remember that much. There were two large dumpsters along the side of a building. They were dark colored, probably green, but it was nighttime, so I don't know for sure. They didn't belong to the building I escaped from. They were alongside the one kind of in front of it, adjacent to it. I came up in a bit of an alley. The window was on the end of the building, sort of in the middle of the alley, and the dumpsters were kind beside it. I didn't run in the direction of the dumpsters though. I turned the other way because it was darker there. I thought I could hide better. I didn't want to find help right away. I wanted to be careful.

"I tripped on a storm drain that had lifted from the street. That was after I came out of the alley, somewhere in the same block, I think. It made me look around. I was in the street by the curb with a wide-open driveway on one side and the street on the other. That made me realize I was too exposed. After that, I stayed in or between buildings. Man, I was just so scared. All I smelled was fresh air. It was just so different from down there. Down there it was stale, almost oily. I wanted to just stop and breathe, but I couldn't."

Saul's eyes looked past Lisa now. He rubbed his hands nervously under the table.

"Everything I passed looked the same, probably because I wasn't really looking. It was a warehouse or a garage or just some old factory building. Sometimes, there was a vacant lot. It's all still a blur. I finally stopped in that building where I watched you. I figured they'd think I'd keep on running and find myself a cop. Staying put seemed like the right thing to do for a bit. Then I saw you and your car. I didn't know if I could do it, haul myself out to your car. I put all my energy into getting in your backseat without being noticed. That's about it right now. That's about all I can remember. I'm sorry. It was just overload for me."

Lisa tried giving him some triggers. She described the bakery and its smells.

She described the block surrounding it and the other blocks as well, where the florist, the rain gutter business and the functioning warehouses were. She showed him the tax maps and pointed out the buildings, including the one he hid in. It was no use. He kept trying, but Saul couldn't come up with anything else.

"What about the sweatshop itself?" Lisa asked. "Do you remember anything about how they operated? Where they got their materials? Who their customers were? Any names? Cities? Companies? Did they ever talk in front of you?"

Saul sat up straighter, looked directly at Lisa and raised his eyebrows.

"They did. Not a lot, but sometimes. We talked about it—all of us—trying to put the pieces together. There wasn't much else to focus on, so we shared what information we had when we were able to. We know they smuggled the materials across the Canadian border so they wouldn't leave a tax trail. Some guy—Rousseau, they called him—owns property on both sides just west of a place called Trout River, but under two different identities. That keeps the border patrol off his case. If he owned both parcels in his own name, they'd suspect him. The boss would go off on him a lot to the other guys—cursing, yelling, picking one of us out for a random beating when he was really angry. This guy Rousseau knew how to play him. He smuggled for other people, too, but he didn't want to draw too much attention. So sometimes our operation would either have to wait for a shipment or pay more to get bumped up on the list. A lot more, apparently. The boss made up the cost by taking a few slaves across every now and then for other sweatshops and some sex operations. People from other countries. Asians, Mexicans, Russians. He kept them locked in a separate room until somebody came to fetch them. Then he sent someone down to get them. They were never there long, he said.

"From what we could tell, our owner was the only one who used Americans. The others—there were at least four other sweatshops that we knew of—used foreigners, which makes more sense to me. I mean, they don't know where they are, and they can't speak the language. No one in the U.S. knows they're missing, so who would be looking for them here? Sometimes, the boss and the others said something about a port on the St. Lawrence Seaway, where vehicles are shipped to the U.S. I never understood the connection there. Maybe they stowed stuff on the ships, or transported slaves on them? I'm not sure. It was never clear. But that's it. That's about all we learned in almost ten years of trying. They didn't talk much around us, but when they did, we listened. Sometimes, I think they really believed we were animals, that we were too dumb to care or that we couldn't understand what they were saying."

Saul took a deep breath and sank back into his chair.

"We were running low on materials for designer purses, and we had a deadline to meet," he said. "There should be another shipment coming through soon, probably within the week. There would have to be."

"Saul, that's great stuff," Lisa said, scribbling in her notebook. "I know the area you're talking about. Just west of the Adirondacks, between the Seaway and the Canadian border. There are plenty of unguarded dirt roads up there that straddle the border into Canada and it's heavily wooded. When I was growing up, I knew kids who would cross that way to get Canadian beer for parties because the drinking age there was only eighteen, but they couldn't get it through customs unless they were twenty-one. No one ever got caught. If these guys have a property owner ushering them through on each side, it's got to be a breeze."

Lisa stopped writing and looked up at Saul.

"We'll get them, Saul, one way or another. If I can't find the sweatshop on my own, I'll find the smugglers and follow them over. I have a name. There can't be too many Rousseaus living along the border in that particular area and I'm betting at least one of the properties is in his real name. I won't quit. I can't."

Saul smiled, but he was clearly struggling to keep his eyes open. She'd pushed him far enough. It was time to go. Lisa stood and hugged each one in turn, saving the biggest and longest hug for Bridget. Dumpsters and a broken storm drain. That could describe any number of buildings in Iron City Heights. But the rest of the information—the smugglers, the Seaway—that was something she could work with. It wasn't much to go

Chapter Nine

After all the events of the past few days, Lisa was feeling restless, unsettled. She had neglected her physical needs—sleep, food and exercise—and she craved all three. The pavement vibrated with the beat of the music as she stepped out of her car and approached Rick's Gym, located in the middle of a small worn-out plaza that included takeout pizza and a thrift store. A blast of music and instructions hit her as she pulled the door open.

"Left, left, right, left! Come on. Keep it moving!"

When Lisa first got hooked on kickboxing six years ago, it was as part of a self-defense class. Ricky, the studio owner, had agreed to take her on as a student, teaching her to kick and punch with force and precision while stressing the importance of flexibility and anger management. He worked her hard, pairing her up with other students to spar and bringing definition to her twig-like arms for the first time in her life. He gave her a physical and mental confidence she'd never had.

But on this Sunday afternoon, his studio was filled with women and a few men, arranged in rows before a wall of mirrors, imitating Ricky as he stood before them, punching, jabbing the air and throwing kicks at imaginary opponents to his left and right. None wore gloves or kickboxing shoes. It looked more like a eighties aerobics class than any form of martial arts, but Lisa knew from experience that it was one tough workout.

Ricky spied Lisa in the mirrors and offered her a wave. She set her duffle bag down in a corner and pulled out her wraps, gloves and kickboxing shoes. As long as she did her own thing, Ricky didn't seem to mind if she came and punched a bag on her own once in a while, and today she really needed the release. What she'd learned during her research on Saturday disturbed her deeply and had kept her up for much of the night. Sleep was becoming elusive, and she needed to sharpen up.

Lisa had spent most of Saturday researching modern slavery and sweatshops. Saul's situation was not unique, she learned. Nearly three decades ago, in 1995, police raided an apartment complex in El Monte, California, where seventy-two undocumented Thai immigrants were kept in bondage for seventeen years, sewing clothes for some of the country's top manufacturers and retailers. Seventeen years. It was sick. They were paid seventy cents an hour for eighty-four-hour workweeks, and they had to pay heavily inflated prices for their keep. They were never allowed beyond the razor wire and chain-link fence that formed their borders. They lived in crowded filthy conditions and armed guards ensured they kept working. Seven people were arrested and convicted.

For seventeen years, these people had been dead or lost to their families. During that time, babies grew from infancy to early adulthood, spouses had probably remarried, homes had likely been abandoned for newer quarters, relatives had died, more relatives had been born into their families, all without them. For these people, time had stayed unbearably still. Horribly still. Life had gone on without them. How had their captors kept them hidden? How could something like that last for seventeen years? How many people suspected something horrible was going on, but didn't want to get involved?

That same year, in Honduras, United States investigators found teenagers as young as thirteen sewing clothing for Kathy Lee Gifford's Global Fashion plant. They were paid from nine to sixteen cents a day, forced to work overtime and allowed only two bathroom trips per day. Just like in the California case, armed guards intimidated them, forcing them to work faster on machines that were old and prone to accidents. Walmart was among the retailers that sold the clothing these teenagers made, though the company claimed ignorance to the situation. The United States cracked down on sweatshops within its borders more than twenty years ago, but they simply reopened overseas.

In other cases, immigrants were prohibited drinks while working on U.S. farms and were forced to pay their bosses for damaged goods. They were docked pay for slow production and charged for the small tents they shared with at least half a dozen people, leaving them in debt to their bosses. They had been given fake work visas and their bosses threatened to have them deported if they tried to leave or told anyone. Young immigrant girls and women were sold to homeowners as housemaids or nannies in the United States, prohibited from ever leaving the houses in the gated communities they lived in. Some were malnourished and had suffered constant beatings.

But the worst was the sex slavery and trafficking. That Lisa couldn't even think about. Girls as young as ten. Boys, too. The people who traded told investigators it was easier and more profitable than drugs, especially in the poorest and least stable countries. The dealers either lied to the parents, promising to send their kids to school in exchange for light work, or they simply took them outright. Compared to them, the others had it good. Lisa had stared at her closet for a long time that night, wondering who had suffered for her designer jeans, her tailored shirts and even her sweat-wicking running clothes. The items she'd bought in bargain basements didn't seem like such bargains anymore.

Lisa had done some research on that Rousseau guy, too. It was almost too easy. There were only three Rousseaus who owned land along the border and two of them lived closer to Quebec. The third owned land in the woods northwest of the Trout River State Forest. Earlier this morning, she'd called an old friend in nearby Malone, just south of the Trout River area, who was always looking to earn some money. She'd met Dewey years ago when she was covering the hunt for a couple of escapees from a prison in Dannemora in the same general area. The escapees had broken into local hunting camps, and Dewey knew several of the people who owned them. He drove her around so she could call in updates without slowing down and he introduced her to some of the camp owners, who gave her details no one else had. When one of the escapees was shot and killed in Malone, Dewey contacted her immediately with information no other journalists had and that she was easily able to verify.

Dewey was an alcoholic and he was useless when he was drunk, which had cost him plenty of full-time jobs, but he was reliable when he was sober, and he could go for long stretches without a drink. For fifteen dollars an hour, he agreed to look for a driveway or road that accessed Rousseau's land, which was on the U.S side, stake it out, and to call her immediately if he spotted any kind of delivery truck or van leaving. He would keep following it and she would pick it up as it neared Seneca Springs. It was a long shot, and she knew he couldn't stay there night and day, but it was something. It was a chance.

After breakfast, Lisa had parked at Toast and Roast and gone for a run through Iron City Heights. She weaved through the area Burt Trammel would soon develop, thinking about how each building would change, yet retain its character, giving the appearance of something old when it was almost, in reality, entirely new. She envisioned women in their high heels and manicured nails sorting through clothing in high-end boutiques, never thinking about who cut that fabric or sewed the labels into those blouses, dresses and slacks. She couldn't fault them. She had never bothered either. Lisa's focus had been entirely on quality, style and price—not on whether slaves had made the sweater that flattered her figure and brought out the blue in her eyes. Such thoughts had never crossed her mind.

Lisa had been hitting and kicking the bag in Ricky's gym for so long and so hard, she hadn't noticed the gym had emptied until she saw Ricky standing behind her bag with his arms folded and his sweaty brow pulled into a frown. He held a hand up and she stopped, suddenly sore and out of breath. Sweat dripped into her eyes. She wiped her forehead with an equally drenched arm.

"You're going to break my bag," Ricky said. "When I tell you to focus, that's not what I mean."

Ricky was somewhat small for a man—about five-foot-eight—but well-built thanks to all his training. He had twice won national titles in his early twenties, but then he tore a ligament in his knee and bowed out of competition, opening the gym instead. Despite his smaller stature, he could easily take on a man a hundred pounds heavier and six inches taller. She had seen him put a few cocky clients in their place over the years. Ricky's father was American, but his mother was Japanese, giving him the ethnic credibility many of his clients required. He and Lisa had often laughed about that. Though Japanese, his mother was raised in the United States and had taught him very little of her native language and culture. This was the melting pot, and she was determined that both she and her two sons would blend in. He learned kickboxing from an American—a lily white, Irish-English American.

"Well, I guess the bag won because I'm hurting," Lisa said, pulling her gloves off.

"It's okay to just burn some energy sometimes, but you have to remember to keep your cool if ever your opponent is the kind that bleeds," Ricky said. "The second you lose focus, your opponent or your attacker wins. That's all it takes. You've come a long way, though. I'm not sure I want to spar you anymore, not if anybody's watching. It wouldn't be good for my reputation."

Ricky grinned and gave the bag a few hits with his bare knuckles before he retreated to his office to make some phone calls. Lisa peeled the wraps off her moist hands and threw them in her duffle bag. She took a quick shower in the oversized bathroom Ricky called a locker room and left, hollering goodbye to Ricky, who responded with a reminder to ice her shoulders tonight.

It was getting late by the time she left, almost dinnertime, and she was hungry. She knew she had to go home, but she was dreading it. She had managed to stay out of the house all day today and most of yesterday. This weekend had been especially hard, and not just because of the situation with Saul. Lisa had woken up alone in her house many times since Dorothy moved out more than a year ago, and she knew she would have to get used to it. As Bridget grew older, she was gone more and more often. She'd become an avid camper ever since she and Ben took a trip to the Catskills last summer, and now spent a lot of her free time camping with Ben and their friends in the Finger Lakes or the Adirondacks. She'd even grown to love winter camping and backpacking. That was hard enough, but soon Bridget would be leaving for Arizona State University in Tempe, where she would spend the next four years. Lisa planned to fly out for Thanksgiving and take her on a mini vacation to Sedona or the White Mountains, but Bridget would not return to her bedroom until Christmas. Even when she was home, Lisa would have to share her with Ben and the friends she'd left behind.

Lisa wasn't sure she would ever become accustomed to that moment in the morning when she climbed out of bed, made coffee and realized there was no one upstairs in Bridget's room. No one to harass about eating breakfast. No one to share strange dreams with. No one to discuss the plans for the day, even if those plans differed. On days like this, when she felt particularly lonely, she would usually climb into her car and head for Dorothy's retreat, but she couldn't even do that tonight. She missed Toren, or rather the idea of him. She missed having someone her age to spend time with—to go out to dinner, the movies, maybe a baseball game with. But Toren wasn't the one, and she didn't have the energy right now to go looking.

As she drove through her neighborhood, she noticed kids playing under sprinklers, runners passing walkers on the sidewalks and a few people grilling in their yards. She had chosen well when she bought her house. This neighborhood, with its mix of Craftsman houses, was mostly middle class and relatively safe. It was more ethnically diverse than most neighborhoods, and that meant Lisa could find anything from Indian to Italian within a five-mile radius. The corner grocer carried garam masala, masa and linguine, along with good old Wonder Bread. A food truck rolled through on Saturdays, selling Southern barbeque.

Lisa had always felt comfortable letting Bridget walk alone to a friend's house in this neighborhood, at least once she'd turned nine years old, but maybe it wasn't so safe after all. Maybe nowhere was safe. What if someone grabbed Lisa off this street right now? What if some man hijacked her car and took her with him? Who would stop him? That was how it happened to Saul, wasn't it? He was simply walking home one night when they snatched him. He'd had no warning, no signs that he could look back on and berate himself for ignoring. Nothing.

She'd been nearly 18, about Bridget's age. And Chandra. She'd been sick, miserable with a cold, looking for relief. She was on her way to the drugstore, the same store she had visited alone so often throughout her childhood for everything from candy bars to tampons, when she disappeared. S. Her worries about being approached by strangers were supposed to be over. Her parents had raised her in one of the city's poorest neighborhoods, a neighborhood stigmatized not only because it was poor, but also because it was almost entirely populated by people who were Black. Chandra had defied the stereotypes, only to be stolen by outsiders. The resulting effect on the community was the opposite of what her parents had intended. Many people assumed that someone from the neighborhood had kidnapped and killed her. For them, it just reinforced the very stereotype they had attempted to disprove, that the combination of poor and Black inevitably bred crime. Never mind any of the statistics that proved differently.

Lisa had raised Bridget to be a loving, caring, responsible, level-headed adult. She had spent Bridget's lifetime trying to defy and disprove the stereotypes that defined single teenaged moms and their offspring. She had thought she would be relieved when Bridget reached adulthood, that she would finally be able to relax in her parenting role, but she couldn't. There were too many other sources of parental stress. The worrying hadn't ended. And now, she knew, it never would.

She was tired when she pulled into the driveway—the kind of tired that made shifting her legs out of the car and onto the pavement difficult, like moving lead—and thinking about ordering pizza. But it didn't seem right to order pizza for just one person. The thought was depressing. So when she trudged up the porch stairs and saw the manila envelope at her door, she was tempted to leave it there. Probably Jehovah's Witnesses again, she thought. But she bent down and gathered it up anyway, flipping it over to find her name scrawled on the front in pencil.

Before opening it, Lisa kicked off her sandals and curled up in a corner of the sofa. Summer weekends were the only time those sandals got any use. Lisa would prefer to wear leather boots every day, year-round, but she couldn't quite pull it off with shorts. Bridget often teased her about her boot collection, but boots with low or no heel were so convenient. They dressed up everything, from slacks to jeans, and they were good for most any terrain. She used to wear pumps occasionally in warmer weather, but one day, she found herself at the site of a small plane wreck in the foothills of the Adirondack Mountains, half a mile off the road with no trail to follow. She returned to the newsroom with blisters all over her heels and toes. Lisa quit wearing anything but boots after that.

The envelope was sealed with both a clasp and tape, but it opened easily. Lisa slipped the documents out and felt her adrenaline returning. Inside were bank papers belonging to a company called Fantasy Works. They were evidence of a corporate account that showed regular deposits of five thousand dollars—one every three weeks for the past five months. Attached to the statements were copies of cancelled checks written out to the company and signed by Burt Trammel on behalf of Trammel Enterprises. Incorporation documents were included as well. Fantasy Works was an LLC owned by David S. Glass, head of the IDA, who was its only officer. His signature was on the page.

This was the break she'd been looking for. Solid evidence that David Glass was taking kickbacks from Trammel in exchange for a sweet deal on the Iron City Heights property. This was big, and the story was hers. There was so much potential for abuse in these tax deals, so much temptation, and David Glass had fallen prey to it. How many other projects had Trammel bought from various government leaders and employers, she wondered. In her mind, she was already creating a checklist. Phone calls, interviews, documents, Freedom of Information requests.

But as quickly as Lisa's adrenaline had climbed, it began to fall. Something about this was suspicious. Everything was here—plenty of evidence for the state police, city police, FBI, anyone to launch an investigation. Usually, if someone slipped Lisa documentation like this, it was incomplete, or it had been ignored by agencies that might have done something. Sources contacted her because she could dig up the remaining facts and get people motivated with the threat of public exposure, or because they had simultaneously given it to the appropriate authorities and wanted to ensure they would follow through. The second motive was a possibility, but why would David Glass be this stupid? Why would Burt Trammel be this stupid? Both were smart men, yet they left an obviously marked trail of corruption that anyone could find and follow.

It could be legitimate, but she couldn't take the risk that she was being played. She needed more proof, another set of eyes. She needed her uncle, Lee Vickery. Who would do this? Who would benefit from setting up both the head of the IDA and Burt Trammel? The envelope proved to be a good diversion. Regardless of whether the documents were legitimate, there was a story in it. A good one. Suddenly, she wanted that pizza, a large one. She could freeze the leftovers and save them for the next time she had a craving. Pizza, wine, and a mindless movie. That was what she needed. She picked up the phone and dialed, feeling at least a little content for the first time in days.

Chapter Ten

Refreshed from sleep and food, Lisa was waiting at her Uncle Lee's office door the next morning when he arrived. He amazed her. Despite a high-pressure job and long days, he always looked like he'd just come in from a nap on an ocean beach. His face, his shoulders, everything exuded relaxation. Even his reddish-brown hair fell with ease, always slightly out of place, but never disheveled. And he had her mother's eyes, which Lisa shared as well—a kind of gray that had seemed steely and cold when her mother looked at her but were soft and soothing on Uncle Lee. Somehow, on him, they looked more blue than gray.

Lisa had only just reunited with Uncle Lee two years ago, after he'd read a column she wrote for the newspaper and had put her name together with their shared family history. Before then, Lisa had not seen him since childhood, not since her parents had turned to drugs, her father started drinking more and he turned his back on all of them. Uncle Lee had spent the past two years catching up and apologizing. He hadn't realized it was that bad, he'd said. He didn't know Lisa's parents had driven her away as a teen. He didn't know about Bridget, and he didn't know her mother had walked out, following the drugs to better sources. As much as he loved Lisa, he was an FBI agent then and he couldn't risk the association even early on when they were just dabbling in pot.

"Morning, kiddo," he said, dropping his briefcase to the sidewalk as he pulled her into a huge hug. His hugs, big and bearish, always took the breath out of her, and when she buried her head in his chest, the scent of him instantly brought back some of the few good childhood memories she had.

"What brings you all the way out here on such a beautiful morning? You should become a sports reporter. Less dangerous and more time in the sun."

Uncle Lee's name was painted in black on the thick opaque glass window of the door, along with the names of two other lawyers. Federal law was his expertise. He was a civil lawyer and so was one of his associates, but the other practiced criminal law. Together, there wasn't a federal-level case they couldn't handle. Lisa was too young when he disassociated himself from the family to have remembered his last name. She'd known her mother's maiden name was Vickery, but it had held no importance for her then. She'd never had any desire to look for relatives on either side. So she was surprised to find that she had been working just a few blocks away from him for so long with their names sometimes sharing a front page—hers as a byline and his as a source in another story.

"I've got something I'm hoping you can look at for me. Got time for coffee?"

Uncle Lee always came to work at seven a.m. He worked best when the office was empty, and his wife was a late sleeper, so early mornings worked best for him. Unfortunately, Lisa had spent most of her years on the city desk working the night-crime shift well past midnight, and her body had not adjusted well when she moved to projects. This hour required coffee, the strong stuff, and lots of it.

"Anything for you," he said with a grin. "Let's head down to Starbuck's. It's all takeout at this hour. We should be able to find a quiet table."

He was right. Despite a line that snaked out the door, most of the tables were empty. Lisa claimed a small round table in a corner where she watched with amusement as a woman ripped open one packet after another of Sugar in the Raw, pouring each one into her cup. She stopped at seven by Lisa's count, and she licked each of her fingers on her ripping hand in turn when she finished. People like that always made Lisa curious. They added a little flavor to days that often were as serious for Lisa as bold coffee served black.

Though Uncle Lee said he had all the time in world for her, Lisa knew he didn't, so she pulled out the envelope as soon as he returned to her with lattes and scones. He scanned them quickly at first and commended her on her suspicions. "Not everybody understands the way the FBI works. A lot of it is simple accounting, and this doesn't add up. We'd have been all over this in an instant. It's almost too easy, and it is definitely too obvious. There's no reason for anyone to bypass the FBI with this one and go right to the press."

Uncle Lee studied the documents silently for about ten minutes, taking a sip from his cup and a bite from his scone now and then without ever shifting his eyes from the papers. Then he cocked his head and frowned, looking up at Lisa.

"You know what? The signatures of David Glass and Burt Trammel almost look too much alike. It looks like someone tried to make them different by using longer, squatter letters in one signature than in the other, but there are some telltale handwriting traits here. Look at the way the letters loop. It's the same for both. I have a buddy, a handwriting expert, who testified for me a few times. I'll get him to take a look. Do you have any other papers from Trammel or the IDA with their signatures on them? Anything you know is legitimate?"

"The contract between the IDA and the city," Lisa said. "I've got that."

"Good. Get it to me as soon as you can so he has something to compare it to." Uncle Lee slipped the papers back into the envelope, put them in his briefcase, and sat back in his chair. He said nothing as he fiddled with his near-empty coffee cup. For the first time since they'd reunited, Lisa saw him grow tense, the muscles in his jaws tightening in a way that was unfamiliar. She caught a glimpse of what he must be like in the courtroom, relaxed and approachable for the jury's sake, but on guard. Very much on guard. She was suddenly uncomfortable, anxious to leave. It was very effective and intimidating.

"If these documents are forged, someone went through an awful lot of effort and spent a bundle of money to ruin these two guys, probably with the goal of putting a stop to this Iron City Heights deal. This is a big investment. You have an excellent reputation. You wouldn't run a story without knowing for certain that the account exists, that the transactions occurred, and that the money is there. Never mind that it would be nearly impossible for a layperson to get verification given the privacy laws regarding banking. This person is clearly not smart enough to know that. So there is likely a bunch of money in that account they know they can never reclaim without getting caught. They obviously expected you to bypass the police, fly with the evidence and write a front-page story. When they see you haven't done that, someone is going to get angry."

He leaned forward and looked directly into Lisa's eyes. His eyes caught hold of her, taking her breath momentarily away.

"People like this—people who do this sort of thing—do not like to be cheated out of their money. They get mad, very mad. I know. I've arrested some of them. I'll get my guy on this as fast as I can, but be careful, Lisa, and I mean it."

Just as quickly, Uncle Lee's smile returned. He picked up his coffee cup and scone wrapper and tossed them into a nearby garbage can without leaving his chair. Lisa urged him to go ahead while she got a refill. She wanted to stay for a few minutes and let the coffee do its thing. She had a long week ahead and she knew it. They stood and hugged one last time and Lisa watched him as he walked down the street, swinging his briefcase just a bit. It felt good to have family, real family besides her daughter. She hadn't known until he came back into her life just how much she had missed it.

Chapter Eleven

The small red light on her landline phone was flashing when Lisa finally reached her desk. With all the renovations, the new technology, the addition of up-to-the-minute online reporting and video blogging, despite all these changes and modernizations, the *Sun Times* had yet to replace the old phone system, the one that had already been on Lisa's desk for a decade or more when she started at the paper. She punched in her retrieval code and was thrilled to hear the voice on the recording. It was Lydia Houston, and she'd found the information Lisa was looking for. A two-page report, she said. Pretty simple. Tomey had come to the front desk, wild-eyed and crazy, claiming he'd escaped from a place called Oakwood, where he was a slave. He called his keepers "masters" and talked about being shackled and whipped. The officer called Oakwood security, who confirmed he had escaped and sent two men to get him. He was held in an interrogation room until they arrived. Then he was removed in restraints. The report was waiting for Lisa in an envelope at the station front desk. Before Lisa could even hang up the phone, the envelope landed in front of her. She turned to see Fred Macki, who greeted her with a nod.

"Thanks for keeping quiet about that phone call yesterday. A lot of people around here live for that kind of stuff," he said in a low voice. "I was at the police station this morning and saw this sitting on the front desk with your name on it. I convinced the officer to hand it over. Thought I'd beat you here, but you're early."

"You're awesome, Fred," Lisa said, ripping open the envelope. He brushed her off with a wave as he walked away.

In the report, Lisa found what she needed—names, including the name of the security officer the front desk officer had called. She was relieved to learn the police likely had no ill intent in returning Tomey to his owners, but someone at Oakwood was involved. That much was clear, and his name was right there in front of her: Earl Weinstock. She started by asking the newspaper's librarian for everything she could find on him. She wanted to be fully armed before she confronted him. Unfortunately, all requests for library information, especially driver's license data, had to be approved by an editor. That stuff cost money. So Lisa wasn't surprised when the managing editor called her into his office on her way back from a trip to the restroom.

"What does Earl Weinstock have to do with Iron City Heights?" Joe Theodore had his feet up on his mahogany desk. He leaned back in his swivel chair, locking his hands behind his head, settling in for her answer. Santa Claus came to mind whenever she saw him, Santa before he went gray and gained so much weight. Joe was stocky, but stocky in a muscular kind of way, with a full beard and mustache. He had a habit of twirling the ends of his long brown mustache when he was thinking, sometimes resulting in the handlebar look. His voice was deep, and it blasted throughout the newsroom when he was angry, but his laugh was just as powerful. When he laughed, it seemed everyone stopped to listen.

"Come on, Lisa. You always come up with some good ones. Just make it believable this time."

Lisa stayed in the doorway, leaning against the frame, hoping he would sense she was in a hurry and let her off easy. "I've caught wind of some illegal activity down there and he might be involved. I just want to know everything I can about the guy before I go nosing around. If you think about it, no one has paid much attention to Iron City Heights in a few decades. I'm sure it won't just be the squatters who are displaced when this development rolls in. Where is a criminal to go?"

Lisa had hoped a little humor would distract Joe and she'd be done with him. No such luck.

"What kind of illegal activity? I want you focused on this project. The first stories are scheduled to run before Trammel Enterprises breaks ground.

That's only a few weeks away. If this thing is big, I want to know about it now. If it's not, forget it for now and move on. It's not worth your energy or our money until after these stories run. So tell me more about this Weinstock guy and Iron City Heights if you want that information. And get out of the doorway. You're not going anywhere until we're done."

Joe leaned forward and placed his folded hands in front of him on his desk. He stared right into her eyes, waiting for an answer—waiting for any shift in gaze, any squinting, anything that would indicate she was hiding the truth. He was good at that, way too good. She would have to give him something. Lisa released a long breath and dropped herself into a chair directly across from her boss.

"I have a source who says a sweatshop is operating in one of the buildings. He's a good source, definitely reliable. But I can't tell you anything more about him without putting several people in danger, including myself. I just need to nose around quietly a bit and see if I can find any more evidence, something I can give the police. I don't want to blow it by reporting on it too early and then have them pack up and move in the middle of the night. From what I hear, they're pretty good at that."

"A little danger is necessary—healthy even—in this line of work. We'll never uncover the good stuff if we're always afraid of taking risks. But a lot of danger is stupid, really stupid. Have you learned yet where to draw that line? I can't afford to lose one of my best reporters to weeks of disability again."

Just the mention of disability brought back the pain in Lisa's once-dislocated shoulder. She rubbed it instinctively. "I know, I know. I'm just checking it out and I'm still working on the other stuff. I finally got the IDA contract and I'm looking into the payment-in-lieu of taxes deal. I've been down there interviewing shop owners. There are a lot of mom-and-pops in those parts that rely on the low rents to keep their businesses financially afloat. I think I'm going to do a piece on them. You know, investigate the impact on similar businesses in other communities that have done this kind of thing."

Joe released his fingers and drummed them on his desk. "I'll tell you what.

I'll approve your request, but I want that small-business story on my desk in a week. No exceptions. I need you to focus. I want to be kept up to date on this sweatshop thing, too. If it heats up, you back off. We can always brainstorm. Remember, you're not alone here. You've got a whole team of people to back you up."

Logically, Lisa knew that, but she'd been betrayed by a coworker before, and though she had spent months in therapy, she knew she would never regain that old level of trust. She could still see his face, the calm in it, as he held the knife to her throat in the hospital room and explained his jealousy like it was the most normal, natural thing. Jacob was in prison now, where he would remain for a long time. She understood he was insane, an exception to all the rules. But she didn't know about his darker side before the knife. What guarantees did she have that another Jacob was not lurking among her colleagues, especially now that she had the projects job? There were plenty of coworkers who didn't understand her position, the stress of it. They believed she had it easy with few daily deadlines and stories that were often promised spots on the front page long before they were completed. She knew she was fortunate to get the job, especially since there were other reporters who worked just as hard and were equally qualified. She would be jealous, too, if she were on the other side of the cubicle.

But she had deadlines, plenty of them. And she had expectations to meet, high expectations that she would find the stories that mattered, turn up the right information, get the right interviews, get all the supporting facts without flaws—ever—and then organize it all in such a way that it was more than informational. It had to be compelling, so compelling that when her stories ran, people noticed. Her projects had to lead to change—big change. With each story, her job and the whole concept of a projects desk were on the line. One screwup would be all it took. She would be back in her tiny cubicle, making rounds to the police department twice daily, searching through the reports for briefs—if she were lucky.

When she got back to her desk, Lisa scanned the IDA contract and emailed it to her uncle. The contract had several signatures on it, including those of Glass and Trammel. She knew she should wait—wait for the information on

Weinstock and the results of the signature comparisons, wait to hear from Dewey. But she couldn't stay here. She couldn't sit still. Chandra and the others would suffer for Saul's escape and for the fact that he had not yet returned. Her stomach turned when she imagined the possibilities, what they would do to those people, how they would pay.

Lisa grabbed her purse, cell phone and notebook. She owed the mechanic a thank-you, maybe a gift certificate from Bob Evans. Who wouldn't appreciate a good omelet? The visit to the garage would give her a chance to eye that bakery again. The familiar sedan had apparently passed it by, but something was going on there. She could feel it. They were baking rolls. That much was true. It was obvious by the smell. But the slice of kitchen she had seen was too clean for a commercial bakery, and her brief conversation with the owner left her feeling he knew little about the business. Maybe the sedan went around back to another entrance. Anything was possible.

As Lisa pushed through the side door of the newspaper building and stepped onto the sidewalk, she felt a sudden urgency, like she should run. People could die. The phrase kept going through her head. People could die even as she walked to her car. Running, she knew, would only raise questions from colleagues who caught up with her later, questions she didn't have time for. So she quickened her pace, fearing any lost seconds could mean another crack of a whip, too much time in shackles, starvation, dehydration. She couldn't bear it. As soon as she started her car, she turned the radio up full blast, hoping to drown out the morbid thoughts in her head.

Chapter Twelve

D orothy was sorting through bills when Toren came into her office. The retreat was doing well, better than expected, and she was fully booked for the summer, but last winter had been so slow that she had decided to cancel all reservations from October on and close until early spring. Fortunately, she already owned the land, which was free and clear of all liens, and the money she and her husband had saved for their retirement, along with profits from the sale of their former home at the bottom of the hill, had paid for the timber frame. But it cost a lot of money to heat this place and to keep up with the maintenance.

She wanted to stay open year round from now on, but if she was going to make this work, she would need to figure out how to bring in more business during the slower times. Right now, she was booked only a few weeks into the fall, apart from a couple reservations scattered throughout the upcoming winter. She feared catering to one guest at a time during the winter months, which would not only diminish profits, but would probably not create the kind of atmosphere her guests wanted. As much as they craved the solitary work time, they also enjoyed socializing during their down time.

"Why so serious?" Toren asked as he stood in the door with his medical bag at his feet. "The way you're acting, you'd think you had a fugitive living with you who's being sought after by some highly dangerous people."

Dorothy smiled. Toren had a way of lightening the mood no matter what the situation.

"Just finances," Dorothy said. "We artists are not known for our management capabilities. Thank goodness for the business courses I took last winter when I was closed. At least I know how to keep the books. I should have taken a marketing course though. I loved having free time to paint last winter, but I can't afford to close down again, and this social media stuff is all new to me."

"It'll happen, Dorothy. Word will get out, but it takes time."

"Thanks, Toren. I know that, but I'm an old woman. I have a right to be impatient." Dorothy closed her books and offered Toren a seat, motioning toward a mission-style rocking chair across from her desk. "How's Saul?"

"Amazing," Toren said. "He's fully hydrated again, but he really needs a solid physical with blood tests and maybe a peek at some of his internal organs. He's still weak, but you've been feeding him well. I had him step up on your scale again today and he's gained two pounds. That's wonderful. But I can tell he's not sleeping."

"He's up off and on all night," Dorothy said. "The poor guy. We all have nightmares, but it has to be much worse to know that your nightmares were once reality."

"Well, I'm giving you some sleeping pills for him. Make sure he takes them. And try to keep him busy. It's not good for him to sit around and think so much. Hopefully this will be over soon, and we can get him some professional psychological help. How are you holding up with him here? It can't be easy."

Dorothy thought for a moment. "You know, I'm doing fine. I don't know what it is about the guy, but I like him. He's been a good distraction for me and a good experience for Bridget. At least Bridget can't claim it's dull around here."

Dorothy found herself surprisingly protective of Saul, even more so than she had been of Bridget. Her thoughts drifted less often to her own past. How could she possibly dwell on her losses, as terrible as they were, when Saul and the others had suffered so much and for so long? Her son had lived a good life, as short as it was. He was loved and he had never suffered, not even in death. The shot had killed him instantly. She still ached for him, and she knew that ache would always be there. She didn't want it to go away. But the pressure was easing a bit. It wasn't quite so encompassing. Sometimes perspective is all we need, she thought.

"There's not much more I can do for Saul without taking him into a clinic or a hospital, but I'll come back to check on him again in a few days. He's in no immediate health-related danger, but you might want to keep a close eye on him anyway. If he becomes too much for you...well, don't put yourself at risk. He's been through a lot of trauma, and you never know how that will exhibit itself. Maybe we can find a way to get him into a safe residential setting somewhere where he can also get treatment. Somewhere out of town."

"Don't even think about it," Dorothy said. "I can handle him."

"I have no doubt," Toren said with a smile as he rose to leave. "I'm going to stop by the kitchen and say hello to Bridget, see if she has any messages for Lisa. Get some sleep yourself. You look tired. Not that you don't look great. It's just that, well—"

"Oh, get out before you ruin a good moment," Dorothy teased.

Toren slipped away, leaving Dorothy on her own again.

He was right. She had not slept much, but she would survive. Saul had not become violent or disruptive. He had shown no signs of any psychosis. But his mind and his memories were full of ten years' worth of terror, and he had every right to release that at night or whenever he felt the need. Who was she to complain? At least Bridget was in one of the guestrooms, so she didn't know the full extent of it. So far, none of the guests had even noticed his presence. As long as she could continue to keep that balance, to care for him and keep the guests safe and unaffected, he was welcome here.

Dorothy lifted her ledger and slid it back into its drawer. There would be time later to worry about finances. Maybe she needed to take out a few more ads or hire some marketing firm to help, but artists were a tough group to reach. They were everywhere and they were nowhere. It was hard to know where to advertise and when. Word of mouth was helpful, but not good enough. She would need another strategy. Maybe she'd even have to give in to this social media branding thing Bridget kept talking about. But not today. Right now, she wanted to see how her guests were doing and whether they needed anything. Then she wanted to pull out her own easel and paints.

She was in the mood to paint something different today, something that had interested her previously down the trail near the pond, but that she had not been in the mood to work with at the time.

It was a tree that was full on the bottom, fuller than most. Its bottom limbs were thick and sturdy and curved beautifully upward like arms lifted to the sky. As she followed the trunk toward the clouds, she noticed the branches became slimmer and finer, but not weaker. They were not dead or leafless. Rather, they knew their place. They rested comfortably in arms of the lower limbs, tapering in perfectly until the branches from each side were so small that they met at the very top. She wanted to use more warm tones today and avoid too much abstraction. She didn't want to interpret this tree. She wanted to paint it realistically and bring the tree and its limbs out into the world for others to interpret themselves.

It didn't need anything else.

Chapter Thirteen

The day had grown dark and muggy. Thick, gray clouds hung low, threatening to burst at any moment—not with thunderclaps, lightning, and downpours, but with a hard, steady, rain, the kind of rain the hot summer air lifted off Lake Ontario and carried inland. Eventually, the load would become too heavy, and the skies would be forced to let go. The streets were empty of the homeless. They usually came at night after a day of begging or stealing food or drugs in the busier parts of the city and settled into the vacant buildings after dark. These were the loners and the mentally ill, the kind of homeless who couldn't abide by shelter rules or didn't want to. They were the kind of homeless that people insist they want to help until they learn helping might mean a long-term commitment. Lisa felt that if she hollered, her voice would echo off the clouds, the buildings and the concrete, and keep echoing through the emptiness until finally it gave up and faded away.

Lisa parked her car in the wide commercial lot in front of the bay doors of the restoration shop. The pavement was cracked and stained with decades of oil. In some areas, chunks of pavement were missing, and the gaps had been filled with gravel. She had not researched the shop, so she didn't know how long it had been in operation, but the building had probably housed similar businesses since the introduction of motor vehicles to central New York. Some of that oil was probably as old as the first Model A Fords.

Despite the heat and humidity, the bay doors were closed. Their glass was opaque and impossible to see through even when Lisa cupped her hands around her face and leaned into the windows in hopes of spying movement.

She could not tell whether lights were on inside. Perhaps they weren't open every day, she thought, or maybe they had all gone to lunch. She approached the service door to the left of the bay doors, where a sign next to a small black button instructed her to ring for help.

She rang twice and waited each time for a good three minutes. Lisa was about to give up when the door opened. It was Harley, the man who had fixed her tire, but he wasn't smiling this time. His face was hard, and his eyes darted about, searching the street and parking lot behind her. He seemed impatient. She had probably caught him at a bad time, but maybe it was something more.

"What can I do for you?" he asked without inviting her in.

"You helped me out the other day when my tire was flat. I just brought a bit of a thank-you." Lisa reached into the back pocket of her jeans and pulled out the Bob Evan's gift card. "It should be enough for at least a few of you depending on your appetites."

Some of the tension left Harley's face and his lips lifted into a near-smile.

"Sorry," he said. "This can be a tough neighborhood. Lots of drug addicts and squatters. Most of our work is done by appointment, so we get a little nervous when somebody just shows up at the door. It took a minute for your face to sink in."

He stepped back and opened the door widely, allowing Lisa inside. The shop seemed bigger inside than it had looked from the parking lot, and despite the darkened windows, it was bright. Large fans cooled Harley and the two mechanics who worked with him. Only one car was on a lift, a BMW that looked to be at least thirty years old. An old Chevy pickup with its hood open occupied another bay. What looked like a new engine sat in a corner of a third bay and a few tires leaned against the garage walls. It was unlike any garage Lisa had been in—much cleaner and less cluttered—but then she had never been in a shop that focused strictly on restoration. The two other mechanics didn't seem all that busy. One was jotting down something on a clipboard. The other was examining the engine, which looked too new for either of the vehicles. Then again, Lisa knew nothing of cars. Maybe the engine was old and had been restored to its original gleaming beauty.

"Wow," Lisa said, looking around and taking in her surroundings. "Nice place for such a lousy neighborhood."

"Yeah, well, we like to keep a low profile. People think we're a repair shop. If we locate any place busy, they'll keep stopping by wanting us to fix this or that or change their oil or something like that. To them, a garage is a garage. They don't get it. Nobody bothers us here. We don't usually patch tires either, but I couldn't leave a woman like you stranded on a nearly empty street in a neighborhood like this."

"Well, I appreciate it greatly," Lisa said. "Did you, by any chance, talk to your boss about a story? The shop would be part of a bigger story on businesses that are thriving in this area, part of a larger look at the potential impact of the new development."

Lisa would not push hard, she decided. The bakery was not visible from inside the shop, and she couldn't find much reason to do all of her interviewing in the parking lot. Still, the shop would be a good addition to the story, especially with the owner's need to maintain a low profile clashing with Trammel's desire to bring tourists in. And it would give her an excuse to come back one more time, to maybe go over notes in her car or listen to a recorded interview while keeping an eye on the place. She would have to find a reason to go back to the bakery, maybe push one more time for an interview.

Before Harley could answer, another man came out of an office toward the back of the shop, walking quickly and confidently, and approached them. This man was slightly taller than Harley and better dressed, with black pants, a white button-up shirt and polished leather shoes. His close-cut hair and his skin were dark, much like Bridget's. He was trim and showed no signs of gray in his hair even though he appeared to be in his fifties. The man extended a hand to Lisa—a hand with no oil stains and few calluses—and introduced himself. Lisa's first thought was public relations, but that wouldn't make sense for a small auto restoration shop.

"Forgive me," he said, shaking her hand firmly. "I am James, James Greene, the owner of this shop. I understand you would like to do a story."

Now that they were face to face, Lisa could see the flaws—the slightly crooked teeth, the acne scars that pitted his cheeks, the sweat stains forming under the arms of his shirt from the day's work. The other mechanics had stopped working. They were watching him. She instantly relaxed. This was a man with a history, hopefully a colorful one worth writing about. Lisa was intrigued.

"Yes. I'm not sure how much Harley has told you, but I'm working on a piece about the businesses in Iron City Heights and how they might be impacted by the new development. I was hoping you might be willing to give me a little of your time. Harley says people often don't understand the difference between repair shops and restoration businesses. Maybe this will help. You can educate people."

Greene smiled. Harley stood to the side of his boss with his eyes focused on the concrete floor and his hands in his pockets. He rocked back and forth on his heels, like maybe he was nervous. She hoped she hadn't caused trouble for him. Perhaps his boss frowned on him helping strangers with flat tires when he was supposed to be working.

"He probably also told you we don't like a lot of attention. We have enough work as it is. This is a selective business. We do only a few vehicles at a time." He paused and Lisa prepared her argument in her head. He would not be easy to persuade. If he didn't need the PR and he didn't want the attention, there wasn't much in it for him.

"I don't mind if you include us in the story. I can't say I'm thrilled about the new development. We'll probably have to move eventually and that will cost money, if I don't retire first. But we would rather not be a main focus. And no photos. We don't want any photos. Some of our car owners like to keep their vehicles under wraps. They don't like the wives knowing how much they're spending on these classics."

"Got it," Lisa said. "No photos. That's fine with me. We'll have plenty of others. I didn't bring my notebook with me and I'm due elsewhere soon. Can we arrange a time, maybe close to the end of the week?"

"Friday. Two o'clock," he said. "I'll give you fifteen minutes. Harley will show you out."

"Great. Thanks." Lisa paused. "Hey, have you had much contact with the people who run that bakery across the street? I tried to talk them into participating in the story and the owner was pretty rude about it. Have they been here long?"

"I don't pay much attention to our neighbors," Greene said. "They've been around at least a few months, but I've never interacted with any of their employees. The aroma sure is distracting though. It's making me hungry even now."

He smiled again, but this time it was clearly forced and impatient. Harley looked up at his boss, who nodded, and then motioned to Lisa that she should start walking toward the door. He followed her and escorted her outside. The rain was just starting. A few heavy drops had hit the pavement, forming dark splotches that instantly disappeared, soaked up by the heat. Harley opened Lisa's car door for her, and she got inside. He paused like he wanted to say something. Then he looked back toward the shop and seemed to change his mind.

Lisa wished he would go. She wanted to stay for a moment, to pretend to be getting organized so she could observe the bakery for a bit and decide what to do next. But Harley shut the door, and then stepped back, waiting like a gentleman for her to drive away. It would be too awkward to roll down the window and explain that she wasn't ready to leave. So she had two choices—go to the bakery with no plan or do some research first.

With the rain starting to fall thickly now and Harley already drenched, Lisa decided to drive away—to look up the incorporation papers, the bakery's DBA, the sales tax filings, whatever she could find. A few months of operation wasn't enough, but maybe the bakery had been some other business before. Maybe the sweatshop owners had to change the exterior business now and then to avoid detection. She already knew the bakery owner was lying, but she needed more. She wanted documents to give the police or the FBI and to back up her story for the newspaper. Chandra was here, somewhere in this neighborhood. She knew it. She couldn't afford to act too quickly and screw it up now.

Chapter Fourteen

Lisa was too wired to go home for dinner, and she knew she couldn't go to Dorothy's. Takeout in the newsroom didn't appeal to her either. So, despite the rain, she parked her car in the newspaper lot and walked three blocks to Fletcher's, a diner known for its soup. She ordered chicken noodle and a roll and chose a booth in a corner where she could dry off while she stared out the window and tried to think. There was no time for a trip to Albany, the state capital. She would have to make some phone calls and ask them to search the incorporation filings for her. She never trusted that the online files were up to date. She'd started a small business of her own once and it took months to show up in the system. She'd stop by the IDA offices first to see who was leasing the space in case the bakery name was just a DBA. It was possible the bakery site had been leased for years to the same person or company but had changed "Doing Business As" names.

The rain had settled into a light drizzle by the time Lisa left and she walked back slowly, enjoying the cool, misty air. It was a relief from the heat of the previous days, and it was nice to think just for a moment about the way it felt on her face and arms. Her boots, her clothes and her hair were still damp, but she wasn't uncomfortable. She breathed in the smell of the wet concrete mingling with the aromas from Fletcher's, the pizza place next door, and the BBQ ribs from the restaurant across the street. It was a Tuesday evening after rush hour, so only a few people walked the streets, mostly men and women in business attire, taking clients out for an evening of persuasion or grabbing a bite before heading back to their near-empty buildings for a few hours more of work.

The newspaper building was on Lawrence Boulevard, a four-lane road with a thirty-five-mile-an-hour speed limit. It was not a tall building—four stories—but it was impressive, with a large bird-bath-like fountain to the left of the entrance and wide tiered stairs approaching from three sides. Lisa had been in the front entrance only once in all her years at the newspaper, for her internship interview just before college graduation. Since then, she had always used the side entrance, like most other employees. The side door was protected by a security guard and required a card swipe for entry, but it lacked all formalities. No receptionist. No ID. One swipe and she'd be through.

The light at Lawrence Boulevard and Gifford Street had just changed, prompting the "walk" signal to appear on the post next to the newspaper building. Lisa stepped into the road, thinking she'd type up some of her notes and then head home for a good book and maybe a glass of Pinot Noir. Maybe she'd even stop by Ricky's gym first for a quick workout. She'd have to check his schedule, see if he would be open for an evening class. As she walked, her hand reached for her purse and the pass card inside, but her fingers touched her thigh instead. Her purse was gone. She had left it in the diner.

Lisa turned on her heels, but instantly froze. A car had come careening around the corner from Gifford Street and was heading right toward her—crossing the center line and aiming for her. Her feet refused to budge. Only her mind seemed to function, shifting into high alert, registering every color, every person, every movement as if in slow motion. The car was dull maroon, she noticed, old with no front license plate, a little rust on the bumper and dead bugs on the headlights and the grill. She could see the driver. She guessed it was a man, but the driver wore a hood and sunglasses. There was no way to know for sure. Even as her feet began to move again and she flung herself toward the curb, she found herself writing the story for the next day's paper in her head. It would be a brief in the local section unless she died. Then it would be a story—a lead one. An irrational part of her laughed inside as her body hit the concrete.

She felt the concrete shred the blouse off her arm and shoulder like coarse sandpaper and shave off a layer of skin as she slid across the sidewalk. She felt the air move by her feet as the car swung close to the curb, and then veered back into its lane, peeling away. She felt the jarring of her brain as her head hit the sidewalk, the blow softened by the fact that she had landed on her shoulder first. Then there were people around her—only one or two at first, and then three or four. Her eyes caught those of a man standing on the curb across the street wearing a baseball cap and a golf jacket, despite the warm air. He looked like he was about to cross, but he turned and walked in the other direction. A pickup truck pulled over and she heard someone ask the driver whether he had a cell phone. He jumped out and offered to call 911. A woman checked to see whether Lisa was conscious and tried to put a man's rolled-up suit jacket under her head. But Lisa forced herself to sit up, catching a glimpse of her bloody shoulder as she did, and protested.

"I'm okay," she said. "It was just a stupid accident. I don't need the police."

"That was no accident. Call 911."

Lisa was screwed. It was Joe Theodore, the managing editor, and she knew that look on his face. She'd seen it before. He was angry with Lisa and worried about her at the same time, but mostly angry. She remembered the lecture he'd given her two years ago, about the fact that this was a job, a business, and no story was worth putting her life on the line. But she disagreed. Some stories were not just stories. Some stories changed lives. Some stories saved lives. He knew that as well as she did, but he had a job, too, and part of that job involved helping his reporters and photographers achieve a balance, pushing them to take chances and pulling them back when they'd gone too far. He was going to tell Lisa that she had exceeded the limits. She'd gone too far. She would have to tell him something more. They would have to reach a compromise. She couldn't drop this story, and she wasn't ready to leave Saul at the mercy of the cops.

"No ambulance though, okay? I just need to stand up for a minute and I'll be fine."

Lisa started to stand, but Joe squatted down and put a firm hand on her good shoulder. "You were walking back to the building, probably going back to work. You were on the newspaper's dime and that makes you my liability. From a legal standpoint, I can't let you go. Stay put and wait for the paramedics."

Then suddenly they were there—a police officer asking questions of Joe and the others who had gathered, and the paramedics, checking her blood pressure, flashing a penlight in her eyes and cutting off the ruined portion of her cotton blouse to get a better look at the damaged skin. One paramedic asked her to stand, and she did, taking just a moment to get her balance. She needed to focus. The ground was moving, shifting, but she couldn't let him see that. She took a deep breath and it stopped. The world was normal again.

"Well, it looks like just a few scratches, a cut-up and bruised shoulder and bump to the head. No signs of concussion so far," the paramedic said, looking at Joe as if Lisa wasn't capable of taking it in. "She really should go in for observation, but she's refused, and we can't force her. Concussion symptoms can show up even a day or two later. We'd feel more comfortable if someone stayed with her."

Lisa lied.

"My daughter will be home in an hour and she's an adult. She can stay with me. I'll have her pick me up and leave my car here. I don't need to go to the hospital. I'm fine. Really, Joe."

Joe said nothing for a moment. He simply stood there with his hands on his hips and his head slightly cocked, looking at her. Then he stroked his beard and sighed. "Fine, but I don't want to see you in the office tomorrow, and we're going to have a talk when you come in the next day. I want to know everything, and you will tell the cops everything before you leave this sidewalk. Maybe it was an accident, but I swear that car came right at you from the opposite lane, and it swerved when you turned back in the other direction. I saw it. Now come on. I'll walk you inside."

"Don't worry. I've got this," Lisa said, waving him away. "And thank you. I really do appreciate your concern, but I have to go back to the diner and get my purse and I'll have my daughter pick me up there. This was partly my fault. I turned back in the middle of the road. The driver was probably trying to avoid me, thinking I was going to cross all the way."

"Don't do this to me, Lisa. I've got two night editors out sick and I've got to pitch in for the first two editions. I can't walk you to the diner. Just come in with me. We'll call the diner and have them hold onto your purse. We can go get it when I'm done."

"They'll be closed by then, Joe. I'll be fine. I promise. Just go."

Joe released another heavy sigh.

"Okay, but call me when you get home. Call my cell phone. Don't go calling my desk phone when you know I'll be running around the newsroom and then pretend you couldn't reach me."

A police officer with a notebook gestured to a bench off the sidewalk, and Joe left as soon as he saw them sit down together. Lisa told the officer, a young guy with fair skin and a freckled face, what she knew—that she had been crossing the street when she realized she'd forgotten her purse, and that she had turned around abruptly. Next thing she knew, the car was headed right toward her. She tried to describe the driver, but she wasn't much help. The sunglasses were aviator-style, or maybe not. She couldn't be sure. The hood was dark, probably blue or black. It looked like a jacket, not a sweatshirt. She couldn't see his face. Skin color? Height? Age? She had no idea. It was possible the driver meant to hit her, but it was equally possible the driver thought she was going to continue across the street and had swerved into the other lanes to avoid her, she said. Anything was possible.

"Running me down with a car is a little cliché, don't you think?" Lisa said with a laugh. The officer smiled in return. That was a good sign. He wasn't taking this too seriously. When he asked whether anyone had reason to want her dead or injured, she played into his sense of humor.

"I'm a journalist. Isn't that enough?"

He laughed again. Then he closed his notebook and stood.

"Still," he said, "keep your eyes open and let us know if anything else suspicious happens. There are some whackos out there, and it's not the big stuff that gets them worked up. It's the little stuff, you know, like calling their hair 'silver' in the newspaper when they really believe they have no gray. You'd be amazed how mad people can get. Then they call us instead of you guys, thinking we can do something about it."

"Believe me, they call us, too, and email and comment on the website," Lisa said. "The same people, just about every day. I know most of them by name."

Lisa remained on the bench while the officer got into his car and jotted down a few more notes. The paramedics were long gone by the time he turned off his flashing lights and pulled away from the curb. Lisa was a mess, and she knew it. The rain had stopped completely, but her normally straight hair had started to frizz as it dried, and one sleeve of her blouse had been replaced by bandages. Her jeans, her favorite pair, were torn as well. But she had to go back to the diner. She needed her purse.

Once there, she decided to recover with a cup of hot chocolate, which the owner declared complimentary after she explained away her bandages. She waited another thirty minutes until she felt less jittery, and she was sure Joe would be hunkered down at the city desk on deadline. Then Lisa headed for the parking lot to get her car and drive home. She felt terrible lying to him, but she would need her car tomorrow.

Joe had said not to show up at work, so she would not. Lisa would work from home. She had no reason to stop by the office except to check her mail, and she was not expecting anything earthshattering. That would give her time to figure out just how much to tell Joe to convince him that the risk was worth the story. Now though, all she wanted was to be on her sofa, watching a stupid sitcom with that glass of Pinot Noir. Maybe two glasses. Maybe three.

That driver was trying to hit her. Joe was right. She was glad now she'd had an alarm system installed in her house last year, and that Joe wanted her to call when she arrived home. It was nice to know someone would notice immediately if she didn't make it through the door. And if all that failed, she had another system: a semiautomatic that she planned to sleep with until this was over.

Chapter Fifteen

Lisa was groggy when she stepped into the shower the next morning, but the sting from the warm water hitting the scrapes on her arm and shoulder left her wide awake. Someone had tried to run her down, so she was close. She had to be. It was frightening and comforting at the same time—frightening, because someone had tried to take her life or, at least, take her out for a while; comforting, because she was on the right track, closer and closer to finding Chandra and the others. But how could they know she had Saul? Maybe the sedan driver, the man who was looking for Saul on that first day, knew she was lying. She had told him she was a reporter. It wouldn't be hard to figure out who she was, and then start following her. Then again, there was always the chance this was about the documents she had found on her porch. Even if she'd fallen for it, even if she'd thought they were legitimate, did anyone really think a story would appear in the paper this quickly? Maybe someone had seen her give the papers to Uncle Lee. It was all so exhausting to think about.

She had wanted to wear sleeves, to hide the scrapes from curious eyes. She didn't have time to answer questions. But the rub of the fabric over her roughened skin was too much, even with bandages covering them. She would have to go sleeveless for a day or two until scabs formed and new skin began to generate. Her entire body ached as she pulled on light khaki pants and a loose lavender, double-layered tunic, not her usual work clothes, but more suitable for the IDA offices than jeans, and cooler, too.

Lisa pulled her long smooth hair into a tight ponytail, and then slipped on her boots. As she left her bedroom, she nearly tripped over her running shoes, a worn pair of Brooks that she had tossed carelessly aside after her last run, before her accident, before Saul, before any of this. Everything had changed so quickly. What if she had left the press conference earlier? What if she had locked her car door? What would have happened to Saul? Lisa moved the sneakers into her closet. She usually started her mornings with a run, but she had been too preoccupied with research to run these past few days and she didn't feel up to it today. She promised herself a good hard one tomorrow after twenty-four hours of Tylenol.

It was nine a.m. and Lisa was about to head out the door with a bagel in her hand when the home phone rang. She wanted to ignore it, but she was never good at that. Unanswered phone calls ate away at her. Even now that Bridget was an adult, Lisa worried. Today she was glad for that maternal instinct. It was her boss, Joe Theodore, checking up on her and reminding her that she wasn't to come into work.

"Your car is gone. Don't think I didn't notice," Joe said. "And you never called me last night."

"Okay, so I drove home. I intended to leave it there, but then I got thinking. What if I had an emergency? I didn't drive right away. I went back to the diner for a while and had some hot chocolate. My head was clear when I left. I'm sorry I didn't call though. No excuse there. I was just tired and I forgot."

"We're going to sit down at this time tomorrow," Joe said. "I want to know everything, and then we'll decide where to go from there. You have to learn to trust other people, Lisa. This is one of those times. Don't be stupid. And don't go anywhere. I'll be calling every now and then."

"What about the drugstore?"

"Not even the drugstore."

"But—"

"But nothing. It's a paid day off. Stay home, stay safe and recover," Joe said, hanging up before Lisa could say another word.

Lisa didn't hesitate. She would have to be back before he called again, but she would tell him everything tomorrow. That much she had decided. He was right. She had to start trusting people, and this was a big story. It wouldn't hurt to have some help. Joe didn't get where he was by being conservative or cowardly. He would agree to pursue the story, but he would look out for her, and she needed that now. It wouldn't help Saul, Chandra or the others if she wound up dead. The trust thing would have to wait another day though. She felt bad lying to him, but she didn't have time for a day off. Lives were at stake and whoever was behind this thing was getting antsy. There was no way of telling what they might do to their captives now.

She grabbed her keys, her purse, her notebook and her cell phone and headed for the driveway, tearing off bites of her bagel while she struggled to keep hold of the rest. She was about to throw all of it into her car when something caught her eye and she stopped. She dropped her armload onto the driver's seat and picked up a photo that had been left on the passenger side. It was an image of her in midair, just inches from hitting the concrete, and the car that had tried to hit her. A note was scribbled in black marker across the bottom.

IS HE WORTH IT?

Her first thought was that she had locked her car last night. She remembered because she rarely locked her car. She was being extra careful because of Saul. Whoever did this had jimmied the lock. She shuddered and felt her pulse quicken. Someone had been here in her driveway, inside her car while she slept. That same person had been standing nearby when the car came at her, or at least close enough to zoom in on her. But this wasn't a threat. It was more like a warning. Or was it a threat? It was hard to tell. She thought of the man she'd seen across the street. Something about him was familiar, but he wasn't holding a camera. Maybe he had one in his jacket pocket, or he used his cell phone discreetly, but she doubted it. This picture seemed professional, clear, probably taken from a distance using a camera with an excellent zoom lens. Not something that would fit in a golf jacket pocket. Whoever took this photo knew that car would come at her and had planned the shot. The driver and the photographer were working together. They had to be.

Lisa took the photo back inside, laid it on the small table near the front door, and walked upstairs into her bedroom. She opened the nightstand drawer and pulled out her gun and its waistband holster. Carefully, she slipped her belt through the slits in the leather hostler, refastened her belt and tucked the gun in its place. . Then she draped her tunic over the bulge. The gun was small—a Berreta Nano—but it still felt awkward. She didn't have a permit for carrying a concealed weapon, or for owning any weapon at all. She had never thought she'd really need the gun two years ago when Dorothy gave it to her. But if the time came to use it, would she really care about a bit of paperwork? Would anyone?

The rain from the previous day had cleansed the air of its humidity. The sign at the bank showed a temperature of seventy-eight degrees already, but it was a comfortable seventy-eight degrees. Still, Lisa felt her body heat rise as she approached the door to the city's municipal building. The photo and the note had baffled her for a while. Why threaten her like that? Why not keep quiet and try to kill her again? But now she understood. If they believed she had Saul and they killed her, they might never find him. They wanted to scare her, not kill her, to force her to give him up. But it was too late for that. She was in too deep. These people, whoever they were, were probably watching her now.

The sweat on her palms made her hands slip on the door handle on her first try. She wiped them on her pants, hoping the dark stains would dry quickly, and tried again. The building had its own café near the entrance. Instead of going directly to the elevator, Lisa grabbed an orange juice without taking her eyes off the door for more than a split second, handed the cashier a five-dollar bill and told her to keep the change. Then she took a seat facing the doors and waited. Twenty minutes later, her orange juice was gone and so was her patience. No one had followed her in as far as she could tell. Everyone who entered got right on the elevators or stopped for a coffee and then went on.

Lisa tossed the orange juice container, waited until the doors were about to close on an elevator full of people and lunged for it, using her body to stop the doors' progression. Her move elicited a group moan from the elevator's occupants, but she was certain she had succeeded. If someone had followed her, they didn't get on this elevator, and they couldn't know where she would get off, not even if they took the stairs. The stairs were on the other side of the lobby.

The IDA office took up only a small corner of the fourth floor. It was musty with the smells of old files and books that hadn't been opened in years, but it was bright. Monica, the secretary, greeted Lisa with a genuine smile as she walked in.

"I was just about to call you," she said, holding out a manila envelope with Lisa's name on it. "I've got the copy of that contract you requested. Sorry about the delay, but these things have to go through the IDA lawyer, and he's been out of town. Mr. Glass asked me to apologize on his behalf as well. Hey, what happened to your shoulder?"

Lisa was tempted to push the envelope away and tell her she no longer needed it, but she stopped herself. Better to be gracious when asking a favor. It couldn't hurt to have another copy anyway. Instead, she took the envelope, tucked it under her arm and smiled in return.

"I stumbled on a curb," Lisa said. "It's been a tough week. Thanks so much for this. Could I ask you one more little favor though? I'm a little behind on a feature story I'm doing about existing businesses in the Iron City Heights neighborhood, and I need some information about a bakery that is apparently leasing space from the IDA. I talked to a manager, but I need the name of the owner to verify some of the information. I called back there today, but I got no answer and I'm really on a tight deadline."

Lisa felt bad lying to Monica. She looked like her mother would have if she hadn't gotten hooked on drugs and run off with some strange guy all those years ago. The secretary's face was aged with pleasant lines fanning out from her eyes, and others arching smoothly around the edges of her mouth. She had her mother's sandy blonde hair and slight curls. Only the eyes were different. Monica's were a bright blue in contrast to her mother's, and her own, steely gray. Interesting, Lisa thought, that on driver's licenses, one of our most widely accepted forms of identification, each would list her eye color simply as "blue" when in reality, their hues made them different colors entirely.

"Sure. Why not?" Monica said, pushing her chair away from the desk to stand. "Got the address?"

Lisa handed her a slip of notebook paper with the address and the bakery name scrawled on it, and Monica began searching on her computer. She frowned, pushed her chair away from the desk and disappeared into a back room. She reappeared after a few moments with an empty open file in her hands and a puzzled look on her face.

"Are you sure you got the address right? I can't find a physical file for that building and there's no new information in the computer. Well, I have a file. This one right here. But it's empty."

"I think I did," Lisa said. "Let me check my notebook."

Lisa read the address aloud and Monica confirmed it against the note in her hand. Then she compared it with a large rectangular survey map that covered most of one wall. It was eye-opening to see Iron City Heights from this perspective. The area marked for development took up only about an eighth of the map, starting with the land that bordered the downtown area of Seneca Springs and fanning out from there. But there was so much more. Lisa had tried using Google Maps with its satellite views and street views to look for the dumpsters and the basement window Saul described, but the task felt impossible. So far, she had only eliminated a few streets and the less dense areas on the fringes. The search was time-consuming, and many of the alleys were too dark to see on either view. She would have to walk down the streets she couldn't eliminate in person rather than virtually and, looking up at this map on the way, she almost wanted to give up. If it wasn't located near the bakery, how would she ever find the sweatshop? She ran her index finger through the streets of Iron City Heights until she found the bakery address.

"That's the one right here," she said, tapping the location.

"We definitely still own it, but you know how slowly things move here and we still can't seem to get away from paperwork. If someone bought it or is leasing it, it probably hasn't been changed in the database yet. I can ask the boss when he comes in this afternoon and keep my eyes open for the paper file. I'll call you as soon as I find it though. It has to be somewhere."

Suddenly, Lisa felt overwhelmed and tired. This was not what she had expected. She needed more, something to go on. She thanked Monica and forced herself to move quickly out of the building. She had to get home before Joe called again. The phone was already ringing as she pushed the front door open. She ran for it, leaving the keys in the lock, but she was too late. She picked up the receiver to hear only silence on the other end. A few "hellos" later and she heard a click. Joe had probably taken the phone away from his ear and missed her greeting.

Lisa quickly entered her code into the alarm system, shutting it down before it could sound off, and pulled her keys out of the lock. She closed the front door and sank into the recliner. The photo had changed everything. It made the whole situation that much clearer, that much more urgent and far more real. Just as she was starting to give in to the softness of the recliner, the phone rang again. This time, Lisa jumped up and caught it just after the first ring, hoping it was Dewey with some news. She'd given him all three of her numbers—home, work and cell. But it was Joe.

"Oh, Joe, sorry I missed your call a minute ago. I was in the bathroom, and I couldn't get to it in time." Her third lie of the day. Joe didn't deserve lies, but Lisa couldn't afford to waste an entire day. A day lost was another day of beatings, of near starvation, of all kinds of things Lisa didn't want to imagine for those people Saul left behind.

"That wasn't me who called, but I'm glad you're there. Look, obviously, I can't legally order you to stay home. I was being a bit of a jerk. But I don't want you working on this story anymore, not until after we meet tomorrow, okay?"

"I'm not driving anywhere right now, Joe. That much I can promise." And she meant it. She could check her office voicemail from home and call the Department of State from anywhere. "Can I call you right back on my cell phone? I think my battery is dying on my landline. I left it off the base overnight."

Another lie.

"Sure, if you need to," Joe said.

Lisa hung up, grabbed her cell phone and some notes, and went for a walk, turning the security system on again before she left. She couldn't shake the feeling that someone was watching her, not after that photo, and that

90

made her wonder whether the house or the phone were bugged. She walked two blocks until she found a bench at a playground where three children were playing and two moms were chatting nearby. The women seemed so carefree. Lisa wondered whether she would ever feel that way.

She pulled out her phone and dialed Joe's number.

"Look, do you think we could meet this evening instead? Things are getting kind of crazy, and I need to tell you about it," Lisa said. "I wanted to wait until tomorrow, but I can't anymore. The situation has changed. I'm okay to drive and that will be a full twenty-four hours from the time of the accident anyway."

She paused a moment, not sure whether she should say it. "Joe, I think they're after me because I'm closing in on the sweatshop. I helped a guy who escaped. He was almost dead when I found him. He's safe now and doing much better. I can't tell you where he is, but they want him back."

Silence. Lisa wasn't even sure he was still on the phone.

"Joe? Are you there?"

"This can't wait, Lisa," Joe said. "I'll come there now. You don't have to drive."

But, despite it all, Lisa needed a few hours to sort things out. She wanted to be prepared, and she would feel better meeting him at the newspaper. Joe protested, but she assured him she was safe right now, and then she hung up before he could say anything further. Something was bothering her. It was that man, the man she'd seen across the street just after the accident. He was so familiar. His face had haunted her all morning. She'd seen him before. Lisa closed her eyes and reached into her memory, trying to block out the neighborhood sounds of cars, lawnmowers, and children. She drew in a deep breath. Bread. Rolls. The bakery. It was the man from CMD Baking Company, the man who had claimed to be the owner.

She had searched the incorporation records online and she already knew what she would find when she called the New York State Department of State to find out whether they had anything that was more up to date. Nothing. Just like the IDA offices. Of course they weren't paying rent. They had squatted in those buildings, or else they were paying kickbacks to someone in the IDA for use of the space. The two women were still there on another bench just a few feet from Lisa, and a third woman had joined them, towing two more children along. The kids were laughing, sliding and swinging. No creepy men lurking around. Lisa pulled out her notes, found the Department of State's number for records inquiries and confirmed what she already knew. No CMD Bakery existed. Not in their books.

Chapter Sixteen

Saul screamed in his sleep twice last night, keeping Dorothy on edge. It was getting better, especially since Toren had brought the sleeping pills. Toren was right. He could really use some professional counseling, she thought, but painting seemed to help. Painting and writing. His artwork was rough, but after the first two attempts, he started picking up a notebook whenever he struggled to explain a piece to Dorothy, and what he wrote painted clearer pictures than he could ever create with a brush. Disturbing pictures. Despite the horror, Dorothy couldn't help thinking that he was a talented writer. He painted with his words.

As it turned out, he was quite the chef too. Saul wanted to be useful, so he had started making special meals for Dorothy and Bridget. Sometimes Dorothy worried that her guests would smell the aromas coming from her quarters and turn up their noses at the food she offered them. Saul had been imprisoned for more than a decade and still, he remembered how to cook. It took a while for him to get used to the newer, more modern appliances, to remember how to sauté and baste and broil, but he did it, and he did it with the eagerness of a child let loose in the world's biggest toy store.

Dorothy was amazed.

But today, Dorothy had yet to see the occasional glimmer of delight. Saul seemed more agitated than usual, off-center. Sounds and smells were coming back to him along with snippets of overheard conversation, he said, but he could never remember them after he woke up. She found him on her private porch, the farthest she dared let him stray outside. Even there, she worried some of the guests might see him. He was still a shocking sight—so thin. But he craved fresh air and she couldn't bring herself to deny him that.

"Hey, Saul," Dorothy said before opening the screen door. She didn't want to startle him with any sudden moves, not when he was in this kind of state. It was like he'd been in shock since he arrived, a welcome state of shock that had protected him from the worst of the memories, of the fear. But that shock had already worn off in his dreams, and the numbness that had protected the core of his being, his very soul, during the day, allowing him to function, was beginning to peel away now, too.

"I brought you some iced tea."

Dorothy set two tall glasses garnished with lemon and fresh mint on the table between the pair of Adirondack chairs and sank into the vacant one. Saul attempted a smile but was otherwise quiet. They sat like that for a while, listening to the birds and the crickets. Dorothy knew Saul would speak when he was ready. He always did.

"I know I can help," he said finally, in a voice that no longer sounded weak. "I know I'm dreaming things that might be useful, but I—I can't seem to reach them after I wake up. They are so far away. Dorothy, I feel so helpless. It hurts to remember, to think about it, but I know I have to. That's the worst."

"Just keep trying, Saul. That's the best you can do. If you come up with something, I'll find a way to get word to Lisa. I know it's hard not knowing how she's doing with all this, but it's safer for you and my guests if she doesn't call us. I don't want anybody tracking you here. You've only been free for a few days. You need to give yourself some time…and forgive yourself for needing that time."

Saul was staring now, straight ahead at nothing at all, like he often did when his mind went back there. He held his chin high, and his hands rested on the wide wooden arms of the chair. Dorothy couldn't help watching him. His expression did not change as he spoke.

"One of the guards, he raped a woman one day. It wasn't the first time, but it was the first time the boss had heard about it. For some reason, their shifts were screwed up and the guy who did it—the rapist—ended up working with a different partner. I guess he thought this guy would cover for him just like the other guard did. It was forbidden by the boss. Lust was distracting and so was sex, he told them. But he did it anyway. He didn't care. He'd take her right off the line and drag her into the room where we slept. He didn't even bother shutting the door. After the second time, she didn't scream anymore. Then, when he was done, he'd drag her back and force her to work again, like nothing happened."

Saul swallowed hard. His voice was flat, level, like he didn't dare bring emotions into it. His hands betrayed him, though. They gripped the chair arms so hard that the knuckles of his dark hands nearly turned white.

"That's what he did that day, but when he came out of the room, the owner was waiting, and he had another guy with him. They took him out at gunpoint, and we never saw him again. But the woman, it was obvious she was pregnant. We were all so skinny, the slightest bulge showed. Three days later, they brought in a small fat guy with a briefcase. One of the guards led the woman into that room again. You should have seen her face. There was nothing left in her. She didn't even cry out. When the fat guy left, he was carrying a bulky plastic garbage bag. We all knew what was in it, but we couldn't say anything. What was there to say? We'd be beaten if we spoke anyway. She was still bleeding when they made her start sewing again. They just put plastic under her chair and a few rags. She complained two days after that of the chills and she was sweating like crazy. They ignored her, but they didn't make her work. A few days later, she was dead."

Suddenly, Saul released his grip and closed his eyes. As his body relaxed into the chair, he seemed to sink inside himself, looking for comfort there.

"Why? That baby couldn't have survived anyway on what they were feeding us. Why couldn't they just have waited a while and let her miscarry? She didn't try to escape. She didn't even scream or cry out after the first two times. She always went back to work just as she was told. She did everything she was supposed to do, and they killed her anyway. Her name was Kara. We weren't supposed to use each other's names, but, of course, we knew anyway. We were each assigned a number and that's what we were supposed to call each other. I was twenty-two. If you look at my clothes, the stuff Lisa found me in, it's written in permanent marker on the back of my shirt. At least they didn't brand us, probably because they were worried someone would see it and believe us if we ever escaped. Kara was number seventeen. We all said her name that night. We whispered it to each other before we went to sleep."

Why? Because they are evil, Dorothy thought. Horribly evil. Dorothy wanted so badly right then to call Lisa, to tell her to stop investigating, to keep herself far, far away from these people. The victims—the captives—were strangers to Lisa and to Dorothy. Dorothy had already lost her husband and son. Lisa was her best friend, but she was more than that. She was family, and she couldn't bear the thought of losing her. Dorothy knew it was selfish, but she wanted more than anything for Lisa to quit, to just go to the police and give up now. But she knew that was wrong. Lisa would do the right thing, and if she didn't, she wouldn't be the Lisa Dorothy knew and loved.

She hoped Lisa remembered all that Dorothy had taught her on the range. She hoped she would keep her wits about her and not take chances. Dorothy didn't plan to take chances either. To heck with her guests and their sensitivities. No arrows today. She needed to practice with the real thing. It would give them all something to talk about over drinks tonight. Dorothy took Saul by the hand and led him from his chair to the hidden drawer in the kitchen, where she kept her gun. She wanted to make sure he knew where it was, just in case, and that he understood what he was hearing when she practiced. She didn't want to scare him. Then she took the gun outside, stood several yards back from her target and started shooting.

Chapter Seventeen

It was seven thirty p.m. when Lisa walked into the newsroom. She needed a few minutes at her desk before meeting with Joe. Someone—probably an intern—had left an empty Lay's potato chip bag beside her computer along with a crushed Coke can. There were crumbs on her keyboard, her chair needed adjusting and her pencil supply had once again diminished. One day. She was gone one day. She threw herself down in her chair, picked up the phone and dialed the PIN for her messages.

Two callers were regulars, people who were against the IDA project and every other project, tax, program or purchase that involved any form of government. The florist had returned Lisa's call, agreeing to meet with her Friday morning for the impact story. She had already interviewed the wood carver, but he called to say he'd be happy to have a photographer come by Monday afternoon. Three calls were hang-ups with just enough dead air to record. The final call was from Uncle Lee. His handwriting expert was certain two of the signatures on the bank documents were created by the same person, he said.

"My friend wants to turn this over to the FBI and I agree. Someone is trying to set up the head of the IDA and Burt Trammel, and that's a felony or two. I'll keep you in the loop and make sure nobody gets the story until you do. You did the right thing, kiddo."

Uncle Lee wasn't getting away with that. At the very least, if he was going to take her story out from under her, Lisa deserved to know whether it appeared one of the two men forged the other's signature and, if so, which one. She made a note to ambush him Sunday at home, the one day he actually relaxed. Maybe she would even tell him about the bakery, about the lack of information on its incorporation and ownership. He might be able to help. The FBI wouldn't move that quickly though, especially since the forged documents put no lives in physical danger, so she knew she had time. It could wait a few days. Right now, she needed to review her notes on the sweatshop and prepare her case for Joe.

Lisa reached for a yellow legal pad and found a stack of printouts on top of it—the information on Earl Weinstock, the head of Oakwood security. Links to the information were included in an email from the librarian as well. It wasn't much. He was once quoted in a story about a couple who complained Oakwood had allowed their son to simply walk off the grounds when he was still in treatment. The boy was a teenager who was not considered a flight risk. He'd been playing softball with other patients when he disappeared and was reunited with his parents in a hospital emergency room six hours later. Apparently, the ball was scuffed up and worn from use. He had left to find a new one and had collided with a bicyclist when he tried to run across a road. Both he and the bicyclist were treated and released.

There were a couple of other mentions in the newspaper—one in a story about a new state-of-the art alarm system at Oakwood, a few about some charity events he attended, results lists from local 5K races he took part in. The one that interested Lisa most though was a real estate transaction. Earl Weinstock had apparently bought a home in the Claymore section of Seneca Springs for five hundred and sixty thousand dollars eleven years ago. He probably earned a decent salary as head of security, but enough to buy a house in the wealthiest neighborhood of the city? He sold a house about the same time for seventy-four thousand.

A state Department of Motor Vehicles search showed he was fifty-six years old and had always held a New York State license. He had received only one speeding ticket in all those years. According to DMV records, he pleaded guilty to a muffler violation instead, which was a common resolution for first-time violators. Nothing unusual there. He probably took a safe driving course, too.

Lisa took a closer look at the articles she'd spread out on the desk before her. Earl Weinstock didn't just attend those local charity events. He was often honored for his levels of donations. A five-thousand-dollar donation to a local private high school, where his nephew was a student, put him in some pretty influential circles. He also donated three thousand dollars to help build a psychiatric wing at St. Mary's Hospital and two thousand dollars to the United Way. The donations started about the time he bought the house. No charity-related mentions of him prior to that date in the newspaper.

She saw nothing about family other than the mention of his nephew. No obituary that might have led to a large inheritance, no marriage, nothing like that. It was always possible he had invested well. Maybe he'd hit it big with some start-up company. He seemed happy to show it off, regardless. Lisa noticed each of his donations was just enough to elevate him to that honorary level, the level that would get him noticed.

By the time Lisa looked up at the clock again, it was four minutes past eight. She grabbed the printouts along with the police report on Tomey and made her way to Joe's office. Joe was eating a sandwich when she walked in. He took a final bite and washed it down with coffee, motioning Lisa to sit down with one hand while he brushed the crumbs out of his beard and mustache with the other. She wondered whether he ever got a real meal. If Joe wasn't meeting with someone in his office, he was in a meeting. While he was in meetings, lines were forming at his office door again. That was one of many reasons Lisa never wanted to move into the editing side of journalism.

"So, how's the head?" Joe asked. He crumpled up his sandwich wrapper and tossed it into the garbage can beside his desk. "And your shoulder and your nerves?"

"I'm fine. Just a little sore, but...look. I have to admit that I think you're right. I think that driver was trying to hurt me." Joe leaned forward in his chair and started to speak, but Lisa held out a hand to stop him.

"Let me tell you why. Listen and let me finish though, okay? No questions until I'm done. There's so much to tell you and I'm afraid I'll get off track and not get through it. Do you mind if I close the door?" Lisa didn't wait for an answer. She got up and shut the door just as an assistant city desk editor tried to peek in.

"Lisa, I'll do my best. But you have to trust me. No leaving anything out."

"I am trusting you in a lot of ways, Joe. I'm trusting you with the information, I'm trusting you to believe me, I'm trusting you to keep me on this story, and I'm trusting you with a whole bunch of lives, including the life of Chandra Bower."

Joe sighed.

"Not Chandra again, Lisa. We can't do this to her parents. For god's sake, they won't even have a memorial service for her. They just keep clinging to that little bit of hope and it's cruel to feed that illusion. It's been seven years without a sign. She's dead. Even the police have given up."

"Not all the police believe she's dead. A few are still looking for her. Are you willing to hear me out or not? This is the kind of thing I was afraid of." This was a waste of time and a mistake, Lisa thought. She started to get up, but Joe motioned her back down.

"Fine, fine. I'll keep quiet. Tell me what's going on."

Lisa sat back down slowly, a little less confidently. Joe had been with the paper longer than she had. He was the city editor when she started as an intern, and she'd admired him even then. He'd always been willing to take stories to the edge, to hold presses for the breaking stories that he knew were bigger than they had seemed on first notice, to give them prominence online. She had to trust him, trust his instinct. If she couldn't talk to him, who could she talk to?

"It started after the press conference last week at Iron City Heights," Lisa said, and she told him everything—almost. She told him about Saul; Toren; Frank Tomey and the police reports; the slave-owner tactics; the bakery and the IDA and the lack of incorporation; Rousseau, the smugglers and Dewey; Earl Weinstock and his money; and finally, she showed him the photo with its warning to back off. The one thing she would not tell him was Saul's location.

"I have to protect the people who are protecting him," she said.

By the time she was done, it was dark outside despite the late summer sunsets. Reporters, editors and photographers who had hoped for a minute with Joe were long gone. The only employees left in the newsroom were a few editors, the night-crime reporter, a reporter who'd just come back from a meeting, a couple sports guys and an intern. Joe said nothing for what seemed like a long time. He simply stared at the photo of Lisa crashing into the concrete.

"You can't go anywhere alone and you're not going home," he said finally. "We'll put you up in a hotel—a big and busy one. Buy what you need to get through the next few days and expense it. I'll let you keep working on the story until Monday, but no visiting the bakery and you'll have another reporter with you during all interviews. This is dangerous stuff, Lisa, very dangerous, and I am not comfortable with you working on this story. But I think you're right. I think if we go to the police now without a positive location, we could really screw it up. If it's not the bakery and the cops raid it, two things will happen: the cops won't believe us even if we find the true location, and the sweatshop owner will likely up and move, either killing the people he's still holding captive or taking them along."

"Thank you, Joe," Lisa said, letting out a long breath. "Who are you going to stick me with?"

"You tell me. Who can you work with?"

Lisa had never been comfortable working alongside other reporters, and that was made worse two years ago when a coworker tried to kill her out of jealousy. He was clearly insane, of course, and he was in prison now, but it wasn't something she would ever get over. She should have trusted her intuition with Jacob. She'd known something was off with him from the first time they'd met, but she had ignored that feeling. This time, she would go with her gut, she decided. The name came to Lisa immediately. Fred Macki. He'd been a photographer and reporter for a weekly paper when he first started out, so he could pose as the photographer when he accompanied Lisa. He and Lisa had already developed a certain level of trust between them, and she appreciated his communication style. He came across as harmless, which would prevent people from shutting down during interviews with him around, but he was tough, and he was smart. She knew she could count on him to have her back.

"Then it's settled," Joe said. "I want to know where you are at all times, so check in with me on my cell no matter what the hour and keep me posted on your progress. I'll look at what Fred's working on and try to free him up. We'll meet here at nine a.m. and figure out which leads to pursue at this point, probably starting with Earl Weinstock. How's the Holiday Inn sound?"

"Great. Thanks, Joe," Lisa said. "For everything."

Chapter Eighteen

Toren should have arrived two hours ago. Dorothy poured another cup of coffee and took it out onto the porch, where she had a clear view of the gravel drive, lined with purple, yellow and orange meadow flowers and fully leafed trees. It wasn't necessary, this visit. Saul was doing just fine, and she wouldn't worry if not for the fact that Toren had called the night before to say he was coming. Maybe he had had an emergency—a hospice patient in pain, a family in crisis. She couldn't imagine what his world was like, how he could prefer the dying to the healing. But she was glad for him and for people like him. Hospice was there for Dorothy when her husband was dying, and her son was dead. She did not behave in a way that encouraged help, and she knew that. But the nurses and the doctor and the counselors—they all stood by her anyway. They held her up when she didn't know she was falling down.

Dorothy allowed her gaze to wander about the land that stretched before her. To her left, along the old tractor road where the hayfields turned to forest, the man from Long Island sat in a camping chair with a sketchpad in his lap. His right arm and shoulder seemed to move furiously, but steadily and with purpose. Two other guests, a man and a woman in their fifties, strolled hand in hand up the gravel driveway, carrying no supplies at all. They stopped now and then and bent over to examine something—a flower perhaps, or a toad, or maybe some kind of beetle. To some, it might appear they were lax about their art, but Dorothy knew they had been up well before dawn, trying to capture the colors that came with the day's awakening. By the time she served breakfast, they'd already put in a good three hours' work.

At the far right corner of the wraparound porch, a woman in her mid-thirties was setting up an easel, preparing to paint the landscape. She had sketched the basics the day before and taken a few photos to guide her once she returned to single parenthood in Binghamton. The woman was newly divorced with three young children. The week here was a gift from her parents, who were caring for the kids. She'd always had talent, she said, but her ex-husband had discouraged her, referring to her efforts only as a hobby. The woman wore colorful sundresses that fell loosely on her thin frame, giving other guests a seemingly innocent peek at her braless bosom. She left her long sandy waves untamed, despite the distraction when the wind blew. Anna was her name.

Dorothy liked Anna, but she couldn't find empathy for her situation. She seemed like the type who liked to try on identities, including those of wife and artist, and Dorothy guessed she probably quit whenever the role she was playing lost its attraction. Anna couldn't explain just how her husband had stopped her from pursuing her art. He might not have believed in her, but, she admitted, he never prevented her from spending money on supplies; he never insisted she get a "real" job; he only occasionally voiced his preference for a home office in the room that was her studio. Moral support is nice. Confidence from a loved one helps, but it is not vital, Dorothy believed. In all honesty, it sounded like Anna lacked talent or motivation or both, and her ex-husband was a convenient scapegoat for her lack of devotion to art and for a lot of decisions she'd regretted in her life. She'd find a new identity soon and move on.

Some of the guests were like that—full of excuses for their lack of productivity when they first arrived at the retreat. They were often the ones who benefitted the most. It was easy to pretend, to play the part of an artist without ever producing a thing, when they could blame life for getting in the way.

"I couldn't paint this week because of the kids."

"I couldn't sketch today because my boss made me work overtime."

"I had the flu."

"I was too tired."

"Christmas is coming up."

"It's raining and I never work well in the rain."

"My mother called."

"I just broke up with my girlfriend."

None of those excuses were valid here and, after a few days, most struggling guests discovered that for themselves. Art is work and it must be treated as work for those who want to succeed. Having a passion for it or the talent just isn't enough. Successful artists made time even if it was just once a week or once a month. The physical time spent painting or sketching or throwing clay was just a small part of it anyway. Most art takes place in the head long before the brush or the pencil or the charcoal touches the canvas or the paper. It was a way of thinking, an intellectual commitment.

At home, they could avoid the hard work with their excuses. Here, they were forced to discover their talents and weaknesses and to work on both. The differences in these guests from their arrivals at the retreat to their departures was part of what drove Dorothy. It was a rush for her to see someone arrive with no confidence and leave with a passion that could not be defeated. It gave her even more pleasure to know she had a hand in it.

Bridget had no interest in art, but Dorothy could see already that some of those lessons were taking hold. It showed in the way she talked about some of the guests, praising those who worked all day, breaking only to eat and to reenergize in the evening, and giggling at those who spent their days "preparing to work, looking for inspiration." These were yet another breed of guests, the wannabes—people who loved the idea of art, but lacked talent and skills. These people spent hours hiking the trails with their sketchpads, trying to persuade another guest or two to come along, lingering at the breakfast table, chatting with Dorothy and Bridget. They often left with addresses, phone numbers and lots of photos, but with little or nothing in their portfolios. That was okay though. Dorothy enjoyed some of those people, too. Even if they didn't produce art, most of them had a great appreciation for art in all forms. The arts community needed them, and Dorothy didn't mind helping them feel part of it. She still wasn't sure which category Anna fell into—the wannabes or the artists who needed a push.

Regardless, she had still not finished arranging her paints in the time it took Dorothy to finish her coffee.

"Is there iced tea?" she asked, turning to Dorothy. "I think I really need iced tea before I get started. It's dry out here today."

"Sure. Let me get you some," Dorothy said, rising from her chair.

"No, no. I'll get it. The break will do me good." Anna twirled from her easel and nearly skipped along the porch toward the door. Dorothy smiled. Just a few years ago—before Bridget, before Lisa—she would have scowled at someone like Anna. Now here she was offering her iced tea, actually appreciating her presence. Dorothy was contemplating pulling out her own easel when Bridget burst through the door onto the porch.

"Saul needs you," she said, gasping for air. "I think he's having some kind of meltdown. He's huddled in a corner, and I can't get him to move."

Dorothy followed Bridget into her quarters, where she found Saul in the bathroom, curled into a ball in a corner by the toilet. He was whimpering softly. He probably felt protected there, she thought, with walls on two sides. Dorothy squatted down a few feet away and softly said his name. Though she forced herself to stay calm, part of her was panicking. Her greatest fear in taking Saul in, besides the possibility that someone dangerous would come after him, was his psychological state. She wanted desperately to help him, and he deserved that, but she wouldn't be able to hide someone who was acting out from her guests. It would ruin her. They came here to get away from their problems, not to take on those of their host.

"Saul," Dorothy said again. "It's me, Dorothy."

Dorothy carefully reached over and lifted his chin, forcing him to look at her. She was so relieved, she laughed aloud. He was asleep. He was dreaming and he must have sleepwalked. Perhaps he'd taken refuge in the basement bathroom during his captivity and so now, when he was having a terrible dream, his body took him here. Sleepwalking often happened to people who were sleep deprived. Her own son was prone to sleepwalking as a child when his breathing difficulties regularly disrupted his sleep, before his allergies were diagnosed and treated. Dorothy stood and faced Bridget, who seemed horrified by her reaction. She had wrapped her arms around her body and

106

had backed away from the doorway.

"Don't worry. He's not melting down. He's asleep and he's dreaming. He'll be embarrassed though when I wake him up, so why don't you go and get lunch started for the guests? It's Monte Cristo sandwiches today with tomato soup. You've made that before."

Immediately, Bridget released her hold on herself and grinned.

"Yeah, he'd better be embarrassed. He scared the heck out of me," she hollered as she walked away. Dorothy waited until she heard the door click before she tried to wake him. Saul's strength amazed her. Despite all he'd been through, the nightmares were the only times she'd ever seen him lose control. Toren had given her only a few prescription sleeping pills for Saul and she was running out. She would have to ask him for more when he stopped by. Saul needed to sleep.

Saul complied, barely noticing the disruption as Dorothy placed her arms under his, helped him to a standing position and guided him back to his bedroom. From experience, she knew he would not remember the incident. Her son had once made a peanut butter and jelly sandwich in his sleep and ate it without waking or remembering. When Saul was settled, she called Toren. He answered neither his cell phone nor his home phone, and he had left no message for Dorothy. A chill moved through her. She hadn't known Toren long and she knew him mostly through Lisa, but this didn't seem like him. He was excited by anything and everything involving Saul. He should have shown up or called by now. Dorothy left a message but was careful to keep it simple.

"Hi. It's Dorothy. Call me when you can. I have a question for you."

Chapter Nineteen

Lisa sat on the bed of her hotel room and dialed. Once again, it went to voicemail. It was the third time Lisa had tried to call Toren at home and the third time she'd gotten his voicemail. She left the same message she'd left earlier: "Call me as soon as possible." Then she emailed him. She probably could have called Dorothy herself from the hotel phone and told her she was staying at the Holiday Inn. Chances were slim that anyone could have tapped that phone so soon even if they knew she was there, but hotels keep records of outgoing calls. Lisa didn't want to take the chance.

Lisa was fairly certain she hadn't been followed. After stopping at the drugstore, she'd driven around for about an hour, watching for any headlights that appeared continuously in her rearview mirror. There were none as far as she could tell. Then she took a last-second turn off the highway, turned right immediately off the ramp onto a block lined with tall buildings, shut off her headlights and pulled into an alley. She followed the alley around the building into a parking lot behind it, waiting there for twenty minutes before she dared to start moving again. Thankfully, it was familiar territory for Lisa. She'd once covered a murder that had occurred in that same parking lot.

When she was sure the coast was clear, Lisa pulled out again, careful to keep her headlights off until she was on the street. The room was reserved under Joe Theodore's name, and she registered as Amber Fleishman, the name of the author whose novel she was currently reading. Four more days of this. Lisa wasn't sure whether she had the energy or the creativity to pull it off.

Sleep was getting hard to come by, so Lisa took two of the Benadryl she'd bought to help bring it on. While she waited for the medicine to kick in, she laid out the tax maps of Iron City Heights across the bedspread. Warehouses didn't usually have basements, but it was always possible the bakery site had one. Or maybe the sweatshop was beneath the bakery itself. The building was small and narrow, but from what Saul said, his captors didn't give the slaves much room. They could easily cram a dozen or so people, each with a sewing machine, into a space that small and still have a separate room for them to sleep in, especially if they packed them in like animals. Only one side of the bakery was parallel to another tall building, forming an alley. That would have to be where Saul came out when he escaped.

She wondered how the guards could stand it. They didn't live in the sweatshop, but they spent at least eight hours a day watching over their slaves. It had to be nauseating—the stench, the lack of ventilation, the potential for disease. Of course, they'd have to be crazy to take part in this operation in the first place. This wasn't just any sweatshop. The place was run by the laws of white supremacy, and the people who lorded over the slaves would have to buy into that, or at least pretend to. That guy—the one who claimed to be the owner of the bakery—didn't look like someone who'd spent eight hours a day amongst sweat and filth, but there was something else about him. A watchfulness. A wariness. A sense that he was ready to spring at any given moment.

He was suspicious of Lisa from the beginning and annoyed by her, but she got the feeling he wasn't the boss. She wanted to stake out the bakery. She wanted to follow him, find out whether he had a home. She and Fred would have to find a place to hide themselves and a car. There were plenty of alleys on that block and a few empty buildings that would offer a good view, provided no drug addicts jumped them. Getting there without being seen would be the problem. She also had to find a way to get into that alley and look for the dumpsters and bathroom window Saul had described. She wanted to get in that building and explore, too. The sweatshop owner would have to turn out the lights at some point and pretend to be closed. If she could just get near enough to listen, to observe a bit, maybe witness a shift change. Maybe she could find a safe way in and locate the entrance or passageway to the sweatshop.

She had promised Joe, though, that she wouldn't go at it alone. So, once again, Fred would have to come. Well, that would be one way to get his wife's attention—spending the night with another woman. Maybe two or three nights. He could leave the circumstances a mystery and let her imagination wander. Joe had called earlier to say Fred had agreed to work with Lisa, and that Joe had assigned his beat to someone else for the next week. They had agreed to meet—all three of them—in Joe's office in the morning. But Joe had changed the deal. Fred was to be with Lisa at all times, not just during interviews. He didn't want her to be alone.

There was still the fact that the bakery had been around only a few months, according to James Greene, the owner of the restoration shop. Maybe it had been something else before. Maybe changing storefronts now and then was a way of protecting the sweatshop from too much attention or detection. Unfortunately, she still didn't have any IDA records that would tell her who was leasing the space, and an internet search for the address gave her no new information. She would have to ask around at each interview. Maybe someone would remember.

Lisa was starting to get groggy, so she removed her gun from her holster and placed it on the nightstand. The mall was already closed for the night when she ended her meeting with Joe, so she would have to wear the same clothes tomorrow and pick new ones up the next day. She saw no harm in stopping by the house in broad daylight with Fred. Fortunately, she'd found an oversized t-shirt from the drugstore to wear to bed, along with cheap new underwear. As Lisa closed her eyes in the queen-sized bed on the fourth floor of the Holiday Inn, with curtains drawn closed and all the locks in place on the door, she drifted into her first good night's sleep in nearly a week.

When she next looked at the clock on the hotel nightstand, it read 6:55 a.m., just five minutes before her scheduled wake-up call. A slice of daylight came in through the curtains where they didn't quite meet. Her cell phone was ringing, piercing her Benadryl fog with its tone. She grabbed the phone and flipped it open, expecting to hear Toren's voice.

"Lisa?"

"This is she," she said, pulling herself up to a sitting position.

The voice was unfamiliar.

"I'll get you for this, you bitch."

"What? Get me for what?"

The man hung up without answering. The number was blocked from her caller ID.

Chapter Twenty

Fred Macki was exactly the reporter Lisa needed. He was enthused, but not dangerously excited. He was professional, and he was happy to spend a few extra hours at work this week, especially odd hours. Lisa hated to take advantage of his personal situation, but that kind of dedication and availability was what she needed now. She could see that Fred's wife had pushed him across a line and that he had made a decision, a decision he seemed content with. She could feel the wall rising up from that line, severing him from that life he knew before. She had built a wall like that herself many years ago when she left home as a teenager, and she hated to see anyone follow her emotional path. But she knew it was a coping mechanism, and one that worked. Despite all he was going through, Fred kept his cool, kept his focus, and that gave Lisa confidence in him.

They had agreed that an interview with Earl Weinstock should be their priority. Lisa decided to play his ego. She called the Oakwood security office and told him she wanted to profile him for the community section since he was well-known as a local philanthropist. He barely asked any questions, not even when Lisa said she had an early deadline to meet. He invited her to come by at eleven a.m. Fred had brought his camera and equipment from home. He would act as the photographer.

In all her years at the newspaper and in the city, Lisa had never been to Oakwood. She had never even driven by it. But she had imagined the psychiatric facility as a long rectangular two-story Romanesque building with thick white columns and arched doorways. A winding drive lined with century-old maples would lead from the main road to its covered semi-circle drive and patients would be strolling about the lush green lawns with nurses in white caps or family members who had dressed up for the occasion.

Despite its stately appearance, the pillared building in her mind had secrets, cold basement rooms with sheetless beds housing patients who were not allowed to wear clothing "for their own good;" hallways full of moaning, groping people who were so heavily medicated, they couldn't tell anyone their admissions were mistakes; nurses who were crazier than the patients. All the stuff she'd seen in movies. Lisa had to admit, she was nervous, even though she knew her conception was fictional.

To her relief, Oakwood Behavioral Health Center was nothing like that.

Oakwood was comprised of two simple boxes—a squat one-story square entry building that probably housed the lobby and a few offices, and a four-story rectangle of slightly larger perimeter behind it. It was well-kept. The red brick exterior was clean and fresh. No obvious signs of fading, erosion or crumbling. No graffiti. Rosebushes full of pink and red blooms garnished the façade, while evenly trimmed evergreen shrubs, at least six feet high, lent privacy to large fenced-in side and backyards. Laughter drifted from behind those tall hedges. Then Lisa heard the crack of a ball hitting a bat, followed by more hoots and hollers. She smiled and relaxed. The nonfictional Oakwood reminded her of a college dorm.

Lisa and Fred signed in at a front desk and were asked to wait in a lobby full of private spaces—clusters of sofas and armchairs each with small coffee tables or end tables. In one corner, a woman in her sixties sat with another woman who appeared to be in her late twenties or early thirties. Both were dressed in shorts and t-shirts. The older woman wore sandals while the younger woman wore flip-flops. They bore a resemblance to each other, possibly mother and daughter, and they leaned into one another as they spoke, sometimes pulling back to laugh or chuckle. It was unclear that either was a patient until a nurse stepped into the lobby and motioned to the older woman. She hugged the younger woman tightly and they promised to visit again the next day. Then the older woman followed the nurse through a door marked with a sign that read "Authorized Personnel Only." The scene soothed Lisa until the younger woman turned and looked her way. The pain she saw in the woman's face before she dropped her gaze to the floor was almost unbearable. Though Oakwood was not the place of horror movies that Lisa had imagined, neither was it anything like a college dorm.

Nobody wanted to be here.

Earl Weinstock was smaller than he appeared in photos—not shorter, just smaller all over. He had the build of a football player with his thick shoulders and thick neck, but everything was in miniature. He was taller than Lisa, but only by an inch or two. His handshake was firm, but his fingers were short and stubby. His thick ash-colored hair was too long for his frame with bangs that drifted into his eyes, and the short sleeves of his button-up shirt nearly reached his elbows. His compactness might have been endearing except for his arrogance. It was evident from the moment he walked into the lobby, or rather, swaggered in. It showed in the way he looked Lisa up and down before he spoke as if she were ripe for consideration, and then ignored her, addressing Fred instead. He exuded it. Whatever his role might be with the sweatshop, Lisa was surprised they trusted him. People who were that arrogant were usually low on self-esteem. They wanted attention. They needed it. They made mistakes because of it, like buying houses that were priced well beyond their means and making large donations to charities.

Lisa seated herself directly across from Earl Weinstock when they reached his office while Fred remained standing, taking photos while they spoke. She started with the usual questions: his age; whether he had a family; his education and career; where he was born; where he grew up; what brought him to Oakwood. For several minutes, she focused on their shared passion for running, hoping to build trust and make a more personal connection with him. Finally, Lisa led him into stories of his time at Oakwood, a discussion of the challenges of his career.

"Does anyone ever escape? It looks like things are tightly sealed here, but then I noticed a patient was allowed to visit with a relative in the lobby. Doesn't that concern you?" Lisa asked.

"We have all levels of patients here," Earl Weinstock said, smiling once again in Fred's direction as if he had asked the question. "Our highest-risk patients are not allowed outside without strict supervision. Our lowest-risk patients can wander where they please as long as they stay either within the buildings or in the yard, and they stay out of restricted areas. Remember, this is not a prison. This is a hospital. A small percentage of people are committed here by the courts, but most are here by choice, because they want to get better."

"But has anyone ever escaped, anyone who was committed here?"

"Not while I've been in charge of security." He crossed his arms over his chest and tipped back in his swivel chair. "Well, I take that back. One guy climbed the fence in the middle of the winter with only his boxers on. He didn't get far. Maybe two blocks. He was just confused about why he was here. In the first week or so a lot of patients are classified as high risk. It takes a while for the medications to kick in and for reality to make an appearance."

"That's odd," Lisa said, pulling the police report on Frank Tomey from an envelope on her lap, "because I found this report about a guy who came to the police very distraught, going on about being held against his will in some place called Oakwood. Apparently, the police called you and you confirmed he was an Oakwood patient. It says here you sent two men to get him."

Lisa kept her eyes on Earl Weinstock while he took in the information. First, he paled. Then he smiled, but the blood did not return to his face. Deep inside, he was worried. He was concerned about what Lisa knew, why she had brought this up.

"Oh," he said, fighting to keep his voice neutral. Fred continued clicking, but Earl Weinstock had stopped posing. "Oh, that case. That was so long ago, I'd forgotten it. So I guess you got me there. Indeed, someone did escape under my watch. He was schizophrenic, I believe. A tough case. But we got him back and got him better."

"Mr. Tomey was schizophrenic?" Lisa asked.

"Yes, yes. He was. I suppose I shouldn't be telling you that, given the privacy laws and all, but it seems you already know a lot about him. Besides, he was doing much better when he left here, taking his meds regularly, responding to therapy, taking responsibility for his disease and its management. It was a long road, but we traveled it with him, as we do with all of our patients, and he succeeded."

"That's funny. I checked with your records department, and they have no file on him. None at all. An odd thing happened, too. About the same time he appeared at the police station—within a few hours—his whole family died. An accident, they say. And his family didn't commit him here. He had been reported missing years before. No one knew where he was. I have a copy of the article here if you want to see it."

Lisa had called Oakwood's records department before they left the newsroom, pretending to be Frank Tomey's daughter. Frank Tomey had been committed to another facility in Texas, she'd told the employee, and that facility needed all his old records. Lisa was surprised when the woman bought her story. It was rather frightening that it was that easy to get information on a patient despite the privacy laws. She reached into the envelope and pulled out another sheet of paper, a printout of an article. She held it out to him along with the police report. Earl Weinstock grabbed them quickly, but not so fast that Lisa couldn't see the tremor in his hand.

"Pretty tragic. A house fire. The whole thing just blew up out of nowhere, taking his wife and two kids with it. The fire investigator attributed it to a natural gas leak, but it just seems a little fishy to me. He tells the cops here in Seneca Springs that he's been held captive against his will for years. He'd been forced to work for no pay, beaten when he failed to meet his quotas, fed next to nothing, allowed no contact with the outside world. I think it even says here that he feared for his life. He calls the place Oakwood, which, combined with his outrageous allegations of whips, shackles and slave labor, leads the police to believe he's a psychiatric patient and inspires them to call you. He never shows up here or anywhere for that matter and, just about that same time, his whole family is wiped out. What do you think?"

"Maybe I'm wrong about his family committing him. Like I said, that was a long time ago. Often our patients abandon their previous lives and wander, living on the streets or in homeless shelters, doing drugs to self-medicate, stealing or begging for food. They're picked up by the police when they become a danger to themselves or others and are committed here. It's a shame, really. So yes, I believe that was the case with Mr. Tomey. I believe he was brought here by the police."

His words lacked the confidence and the rhythm they'd had before, but he clearly thought he'd pulled through this one. Earl Weinstock sat upright in his chair when Lisa had first mentioned Frank Tomey's name. Now, he was beginning to sink back into it again, relaxing the muscles in his back and shoulders that had tensed and stiffened.

"There are no other police reports on Mr. Tomey, nothing that shows he was arrested under the mental-health laws, and I have it from a very reliable source that the conditions he described were no fabrication. And, like I said, Oakwood has no records on him. No proof that he was ever a patient here. Yet you picked him up. Do you have another job? Could there be another reason you were interested in Mr. Tomey? Think harder, Mr. Weinstock. Was Mr. Tomey ever really here?"

"I think..." he said, pushing his chair back and standing slowly. "I think you have some wrong information, and I don't like your implications. If we don't have the file here, it's simply because it's old and it hasn't been entered into our new computer database yet. It's probably in transition. And I'm guessing that wasn't his family at all, that family who died in the fire. It was just a coincidence, another Tomey. I also think we're done here. I'm a busy man and you have plenty for your profile."

Lisa made no move to get up.

"I had your records person check that possibility, too. She said all the other files from that year are right there in your storage room in cabinets in alphabetical order where they should be and have already been entered into the database. But no file for anyone named Frank Tomey. But I guess if it were true, if he were not really a patient here, it wouldn't make much sense that you picked him up from the police station, would it? Why were you working at that hour anyway? According to the report, he arrived at the front desk at eleven at night. Pretty late for someone in your position. So, I'm asking you again: do you have another job? Is there someone else you work for on the side? Real estate records show you have an expensive house. How did you afford that on your salary?"

"All calls from police are forwarded to my cell phone after hours, regardless of whether I am working. I handle those cases personally, as would anyone who is in this line of work. And my housing purchases are none of your business. Look," he said, opening the door to his office and motioning for them to exit through it. "I said this interview is over. I don't like what you're implying, and I want you out."

"What am I implying, Mr. Weinstock? Why don't you tell me?" Lisa stood and faced him at the doorway. Fred was behind her and still as cool-headed as ever. He said nothing, but he didn't push Lisa to leave, and he didn't interfere, even as Earl Weinstock's veins began to bulge and his fingers curled into fists. Earl Weinstock was no longer addressing Fred instead of Lisa, or letting his gaze wander her body. He aimed his glare directly into her eyes.

"Out. Now."

"Well, you know where to reach me if you suddenly come up with the Tomey file, or if you just want to chat. Thanks for meeting with us." Lisa offered her hand but nodded politely instead when he refused to shake it. Fred nodded as well as he passed Earl Weinstock, who wasted no time slamming the door behind them.

"I hope you don't mind, Fred, but I suppose you're on their hit list too now," Lisa said as they made their way out through the lobby. "No doubt he's involved."

"I knew what I was getting into," he said, putting his camera into his shoulder bag as they walked, "but he's definitely not a big player in this thing. He's got to be a hired hand. He's too hotheaded and stupid to trust with much of anything. Man, they'll eat him up in prison. I doubt they'll care that he's in his fifties."

As they walked through the main doors, Lisa and Fred found themselves laughing at the thought of Earl Weinstock in prison—just a little too much, the way cops and firefighters sometimes do when they are overwhelmed at the scene of death or tragedy. Lisa had said more than she had intended to in there and, in doing so, had put both of their lives at risk. She hadn't meant to do that, to make Fred a target, too, and she could tell that despite his calm demeanor, he was nervous. But she got what she had come for. She knew now for certain that Earl Weinstock was involved, and she knew the police would find no file at Oakwood for Frank Tomey if they checked. Tie that in with the family fire, and they at least had reason to suspect him of wrongdoing.

When she returned to the newspaper, she would compile her notes along with Fred's and put them all in a file with the clips, the report, the notes from the interview and notes from her interviews with Saul. They would go in the safe in Joe's office with instructions to turn them over to the police should anything happen to Lisa or Fred, and the audio file from the voice recorder she'd been hiding in her purse throughout the interview would be stored on multiple servers.

This was the way they had agreed to do it. All evidence Lisa and Fred collected would immediately go into the safe. Only Joe and the newsroom secretary, Helena, knew the combination, what to do with the information and when. Lisa just hoped that she and Fred would be the ones to open that safe, that they would have a chance to write the story and turn the evidence over. She suggested he send his wife out of town for the weekend and book a hotel room tonight as well. He nodded and when he did, she saw the concern in his face. Unlike that wall she had built so many years ago, his had come down a little.

Chapter Twenty-One

They ordered in at the newspaper, Cuban food from Javier's, a new restaurant a block away. Joe was waffling, wondering whether Friday might be long enough. Just one more day. He worried about whether he could keep Lisa and Fred both out of danger for an entire weekend and how to keep them safe that night. They could go to a hotel again, but even a hotel might be too dangerous now that Earl Weinstock knew they were onto him, onto the entire sweatshop operation. By now, he had most definitely already contacted whoever was paying him. That's when Fred came up with the solution: why not camp out at the newspaper? The building was accessible only with a pass card after hours and guards watched the doors day and night. Security cameras were mounted at both entrances and along the streets. The night guards were armed. They couldn't be safer. The newspaper even had its own shower in the women's lounge in advertising, a relic from the days when men believed women needed their own lounges furnished with sofas to rest on and showers for cleaning up when they were cursed with that evil visitor, Aunt Flo. They could sleep on the sofas.

"I don't see why not," Joe said, "but I still think we need to wrap this up sooner. One more piece of evidence, even if it's not perfect, and we're done. We need to know where this place is. That's key. Police won't search every building in Iron City Heights and, even if they did, these guys would be long gone by then. They might even kill everybody, making this whole thing moot. You need to check out that bakery—get a better feel for whether that's our location. Keep your distance and watch from afar. Do not, I repeat, do not approach the building, or attempt to interview anyone who works there. It's too dangerous. Meanwhile, I'll get a reporter over to the IDA to find out what's going on, how this bakery could be functioning there with no lease on file. I don't see how anyone could pull that off for a decade or more or how the bakery could exist for that long without someone here knowing about it. Either they changed locations recently, or that's not our place. Or maybe they just change the name and nature of the business every now and then, like you suggested, Lisa. I'll have someone check on that too, on other businesses that have existed in that same location. Of course, there is always the possibility someone on the city level is involved."

Lisa munched on a few plantains but couldn't bring herself to eat more. Her appetite was long gone. What Joe said sickened her, the thought of them killing off everyone who remained. Why not? As long as they wiped out any evidence that would identify them, they could pull it off. They could leave the bodies right there in the basement. Fingerprints would be a problem though. In all this time, they must have left their fingerprints everywhere. It would be impossible to wipe the whole place clean and, given the nature of their business, it was quite likely that at least a few of the guards had records. Who else would take a job like this?

Lisa tried Toren again, hoping to relay a message to Dorothy and Bridget. Still no answer, and he hadn't returned her call. A part of her panicked, but then she reminded herself that he was both single and a hospice doctor. Maybe he'd started dating someone and had lost interest in Lisa and the whole situation with Saul. Saul was doing much better now. He didn't really need Toren's help any longer. New relationships could be so consuming. Or what if he had a patient on the edge whose family really needed him now? Toren was good like that. Most doctors would let the nurses and volunteers tend to the family and the patient in the final hours, stopping by only to offer pain medications, answer medical questions and make observations about the approximate number of hours the patient could expect to live. Toren preferred to be there when the end came. He honestly enjoyed helping people pass comfortably into the afterlife and he believed deeply in that afterlife.

Still.

Lisa and Fred stopped at a gas station with a convenience store and bought a couple of coffees and a box of crackers to keep them alert during their stakeout. They also picked up a toothbrush and deodorant for Fred. He insisted he'd be fine wearing the same clothes the next day. Lisa would have to do the same. They didn't have time to run back to her place or stop at another store. By Friday, that would be three days in the same outfit. She grabbed a can of overpriced spray deodorant with a "manly scent" from the convenience store shelf. Her clothes might need a dose of it, she figured.

"If we really start to stink, we can send an intern out for underwear," Fred teased.

Fred was in a particularly good mood. His wife had been upset when he'd called, especially since he couldn't give her details of the story he was working on. She agreed to go, but she called him back an hour later asking whether he could take a few days off when she returned, whether they could talk about a few things. He kept his cool front, but Lisa sensed an instant lightness about him that she had never felt before. She had thought this assignment might distract him—that it would be good for him—and, however cold it might seem, she had planned to take advantage of his single-minded drive. She needed a partner who was as focused as she was. It had, in fact, been good for Fred, just in an unexpected way.

Thankfully, his wall was not yet high enough or strong enough to fend off hope, and that was what his wife had given him. Fred was still Fred. He was still emotionally and intellectually smart, dependable and reliable. But something had changed with that phone call. He immediately became more complex, more animated. Lisa realized right then, in that car with a convenience-store coffee in her cup holder and a box of crackers on her console, that she missed that. She missed what she'd had with Marty when she was fifteen, eighteen years ago. How had so many years gone by? How strong was her own wall, and was she keeping more people than her parents out? Would she ever feel secure enough to tear it down?

Now she was the one who was distracted. They were in the retail district near the strip club parking lot where she had pulled over with Saul just a week before. It was a four-lane road with a forty-five-mile-per-hour speed limit and it was thick with traffic. Iron City Heights was to the west, on the other side of the city. She would have to get them there unnoticed. She needed to push other thoughts out of her mind and think.

"Okay, Fred, we need to make sure we're not being followed. No point in staking out the place when they are staking us out. So I need you to keep a close lookout behind us while I drive. Look for any suspicious vehicles, any car that might disappear and then reappear or follow just at your sight line. If you can do that, I can concentrate on making some tight moves and we can shake them fast."

"Already on it," Fred said. "It's the Jeep Cherokee in the furniture store parking lot just across the street and a bit south. It pulled into the Dunkin' Donuts across from the gas station, but no one ever got out. Then it pulled out just after we left and it's been with us ever since, staying about five car lengths behind us. It pulled over again when we did."

"Well, then. Here we go," Lisa said.

She pulled into the road, driving in the far-right lane. Then, after a few blocks and after she was sure the Jeep was trapped in the same lane behind them by traffic, she yanked the wheel to the left, cutting off another driver who was pulling into the turn lane. She made it down the narrow side street with the other driver making obscene gestures from behind her. There was no way the Jeep could make it across both lanes to the turn lane on time. It would have to go up a block. But that wouldn't take long.

Instead of taking a bunch of turns and zigzagging through side streets hoping to lose him, Lisa pulled into the parking lot of a Cracker Barrel restaurant and parked among the patrons' cars. There were plenty. Cracker Barrel was a favorite in these parts and was crowded at all hours. From where they were parked, they could see the Jeep cruise slowly by. They waited half an hour before they dared move again. It was a long half an hour, especially since they stayed on alert the entire time, watching the parking lot and street it was on. Finally, Lisa was ready to move again, to see whether they would pick up the Jeep or another vehicle. They drove around another half hour before she felt sure. Then she pulled into the lot of an Enterprise car rental business. They knew Lisa's car. It'd be too obvious in Iron City Heights, especially if they were looking for it. She rented their oldest, cheapest vehicle. It still looked too new, but it was small and the color was ordinary—dull blue. Then Fred followed her in the rental, and they ditched her car at the mall. "Much better," she said, taking Fred's place in the driver's seat. "Any sign of the Jeep?"

"None," Fred said. "I've got to say, I'm impressed. You ought to do this sneaky stuff for a living."

They drove straight to Iron City Heights. Lisa had already settled on a location, an alley on the next block over, the opposite direction of the auto restoration shop. The buildings were a little taller there, a little closer together. They could pull in from the opposite end of the alley, where no one from the bakery could see them. Once there, they would have to break into the building kitty-corner to the bakery and find a room with a view. That shouldn't be hard. That particular building, according to the property maps, was privately owned and had been abandoned at least two decades before. She had a feeling breaking in would be a simple matter of opening an already broken door. Lisa had brought two pairs of binoculars. What she hadn't told Fred was that she intended to stay until nightfall and then sneak over and get a peek. Yes, Joe had warned them to watch from afar, but what could they really see?

Fred was game. As she suspected, getting into the building was easy. The first room they entered was littered with fast-food wrappers, empty packs of cheap cigarettes, condoms and broken beer and soda bottles. Old towels and moldy blankets were scattered throughout the first room and the next. Lisa nearly stepped on a pile of used syringes. It was a big room and so was the one that adjoined it. A good-sized group could camp out here overnight, but it looked like it hadn't been used in a while. The bathroom to the left was probably the reason. Apparently, past squatters were undeterred by the fact that the building had no water. The stench of feces and urine seeped from under the closed door.

They watched for three hours, seeing nothing more than a single white van coming and going just once. Lisa didn't recognize the woman who drove the van out of the warehouse or the man in the passenger seat. On the return trip, it was the bakery owner behind the wheel with a different male passenger. Shift change, Lisa thought. That was how they did it without leaving cars in a parking lot or driving them down the street into the warehouse, though Saul had never mentioned a woman captor. They must park their cars elsewhere and use the van for transportation. They could easily deliver the illegally sewn goods with that van as well or bring a kidnapped worker to the warehouse. The van had no windows. Lisa wrote down the license plate number.

No one entered or left through the main door the entire time. Fred called Joe as soon as twilight turned to night and told him they were going to take a long dinner break and talk over some angles. He assured him he had no need to worry, but that they probably wouldn't return to the paper until eleven p.m. or so.

"We don't want to be locked in until we have to be, you know?"

With their binoculars around their necks and Lisa's voice recorder in her back pocket, they made their way across the street and up against the next building, the one next to the warehouse. There were few streetlights in Iron City Heights, or few that worked anyway. Thankfully, the two nearest the bakery were out. Lisa wondered whether that was their doing, yet another measure to keep their activities secret. But it worked both ways. The darkness hid Lisa and Fred as well as it hid the bakery.

The van had not left again, though it was long past baker's hours. Nor had any vehicles come to pick anyone up. Lisa guessed the van would make a trip again sometime soon. They must stagger someone's shift so at least one guard would be on duty at all times. They couldn't just leave the slaves unattended during shift change. Saul said there were always two guards on duty at once, but maybe he just didn't notice when there were three or one. Maybe the third had other duties at times, like taking inventory or preparing shipments.

On Lisa's signal, she and Fred darted across the lot to the back of the warehouse, staying low. They moved carefully and slowly along the perimeter, hugging the building wherever they could, until they reached the main bakery building and a large window. A thick shade covered the glass from inside, but a sliver of light revealed a gap just big enough to peer through. Lisa stood on her toes and caught sight of movement inside.

"Someone's in there and they don't want anyone to know it," Lisa whispered to Fred. "We've got to find a better window or a way to get in."

"Why not just follow me?" a voice called from the darkness.

Lisa jumped and Fred grabbed her arm. Directly behind them was a silhouette of a man, a tall, broad-shouldered man. Lisa's stomach instantly tightened, and her heart quickened as she thought of Bridget, Fred's wife, Saul, Dorothy, Chandra—all at once, all in what seemed like less than a second. They could run for it, but what if he had a gun? It might be better to comply and look for another opportunity. She thought of the gun strapped to her waist but didn't dare reach for it.

"Relax, Lisa, Fred. I have a gun, but I don't plan to use it. That would get me fired. Agent Flannigan, FBI. Now, please, be a little discreet so you don't blow our cover and follow me around the warehouse to the back door."

Chapter Twenty-Two

"How about a doughnut?" Agent Flannigan asked, sliding a half-empty carton of the chocolate-glazed variety across the table where he had invited Lisa and Fred to sit. The box had been sealed with a grocery-store barcode sticker and wherever Lisa looked, she saw nothing more than dinner rolls on the racks, and only a few at that. Through another open doorway, she could see a laptop and computer and video monitors and hear their electric hum. As she stared, a second man wearing headphones around his neck appeared in the entry to the surveillance room and waved. He was shorter and skinnier than Agent Flannigan, whom Lisa recognized as the man who had claimed to be the owner—the man who had also been at the scene of her near collision with a car. This other man couldn't be more different. His hair was wildly curly, and his black-rimmed glasses covered much of his face.

"Meet my partner, Agent Ducey. If you wait a few hours, you'll meet Agents Cory and Whitman, and maybe also Elaine and her assistant, Devon, who make the rolls that we donate to various shelters throughout the community and that make this place smell so good. I have to confess though. We buy the dough premade. All they have to do is shape it and put it in the oven for a few hours a day. They're not real bakers," he said with a smile, "but don't tell them that. We don't want to make them feel bad."

With no more chairs in sight, Agent Flannigan leaned against the stainless-steel counter and faced Fred and Lisa. The auto restoration shop, it turned out, was a chop shop, a place where high-end stolen cars were dismantled in a matter of hours and then trucked off part by part to various garages and individuals for a sizable profit. They did just enough legitimate restoration business to make their over-the-table payroll in hopes of avoiding suspicion, he said. The shop had been operating for a good fifteen years in the same location before it came to the attention of the FBI. The FBI set up the bakery, with the consent of the city, to keep it under surveillance. That was why Lisa found no records at the IDA.

"We're close," he said. "We have plenty of evidence, but we want to make sure this is a solid federal offense. We want to catch them crossing state lines. We've got an order in for Volvo parts in Vermont, and we've been promised shipment any day. We're certain this isn't the only chop shop. The boss here has another boss somewhere and runs them from his estate in Colorado. But we've gotten nothing solid on him. This operation is petty in comparison, but they might give us enough to go after him. So that's our story."

"That's why you chased me out of here," Lisa said. She was relieved to hear he wasn't one of the bad guys, more relieved than she should have been. She was suddenly conscious of her worn-off makeup, her sweat, her injuries, her three-day-old outfit and her unkempt ponytail. She tried to push those thoughts out of her head and focus.

"I have to admit, I wouldn't have chased you out of here if I didn't have to," Agent Flannigan said with a slight wink. He wasn't helping her focus. She was becoming annoyed with herself and the fact that she could be so vulnerable. So she drew her shoulders back and decided to be annoyed with him instead.

"You know I would have left you alone if you'd just done your homework. That deli I mentioned, Brody's, makes its own bread. They're famous around here for it. If I'd been one of those chop shop guys, I'd have pegged you right away."

"You're right. I'm from the Pittsburgh office and that was a stupid oversight. I honestly never thought anyone would come in here and ask me who my customers were. We've used this same cover before and the only people who have ever stopped in were looking for cakes or cupcakes. We'd tell them we were a commercial bakery, and they'd head right out the door again. You're my first repeat customer."

That smile again.

"I have an interview there tomorrow at two," Lisa said. "That must be why the owner was so reluctant and wanted to keep it short. He said fifteen minutes only and no photos. It's funny. I only wanted the interview so I could spy on you. I figured something was up here with the way you acted when I asked questions, the way the counter in back looked so clean and the fact that you didn't even have flour on your clothes. My editor was nervous that I was getting in over my head, so he asked Fred to join me."

Lisa gave Fred a look, hoping he would understand that she wanted him to keep quiet about their true suspicions. She wasn't ready to tell Agent Flannigan just yet. Now that the bakery was out of the picture, she had no idea where the sweatshop might be located. She had no good evidence. Nothing. She would have to go back to walking the streets and interviewing shop owners, this time with Fred in tow. Maybe he would notice something she had missed. It would help to talk to Saul again, but that was still too dangerous. When she saw Saul again, it would be with a police escort. She wasn't telling anyone where he was until she was certain he would be kept safe.

"Go ahead and do your interview," Agent Flannigan said. "We'll be watching from here. You'll be fine. But do us a favor. Not a word about any of this to anyone. We've been working on this for a year, and we don't want to blow it. You'll be the first in the media to know when this goes down, and I'll give you an exclusive interview. Do you think you can handle that, both of you? Can you do this interview without giving anything away?"

"Of course we can," Fred said. Lisa noted the offense in his tone. "Our jobs aren't that different, you know."

"Yeah, well, we're a little better at the sneaking around part. We don't get caught," Agent Flannigan said. "Did you guys really think no one would see you crossing that road? It's dark, but it's not that dark. You didn't even wear dark clothes."

"And just who are your customers?" Lisa said.

"Touché. Now let's see if we can get you back to that rental car you hid in the alley without raising any suspicions, shall we?" Agent Flannigan stood and Fred and Lisa did the same. "I'm going to send you out the back door and I'd like you to go in the opposite direction, down the block and turn right, making a circle back to this street and the alley so you stay out of the line of vision from the shop. Okay?"

"Fine." So they'd known about the rental car, too. Lisa and Fred had been so careful to shake anyone who might be tailing them, yet the FBI had managed to spot them in the alley. All those hours they'd spent watching the building, and the entire time Agents Flannigan and Ducey had been watching them. Lisa was feeling foolish. Why did she think she could pull this off, find the sweatshop without getting herself and Fred killed first?

"Did you follow us here? Is that how you knew where the car was?"

"Why would we follow you?" Agent Flannigan asked. "We're looking for a delivery, remember? A Volvo. Our monitors picked up the engine noise nearby and then it stopped. So we used our neat little tools to peek down the alley. I got the plate, checked with Enterprise and your name came up. Not that you're not worth following. I mean, well, under other circumstances. Okay. I'd better shut up before I come across as a stalker."

Lisa thought she saw him blush.

"But you were there when I dodged that car. I saw you."

"Very good eye," he said. "How is that shoulder, by the way? You really kissed that concrete. Our Seneca Springs office is just around the corner from the newspaper, as I'm sure you know. I wanted to help, but I couldn't risk it and plenty of other people pitched right in. I wish I'd been paying more attention when it happened though. I didn't catch the plate. I could have caught that idiot."

"It's getting better. Thanks." He said nothing about the driver, Lisa noted with relief. If he'd noticed, if he'd thought for a moment someone had tried to run her down, he'd ask why. Then she'd lose her last opportunity to find that sweatshop.

"Here's my card," Agent Flannigan said, handing one each to Lisa and Fred. "If anything comes up, if anything is said during that interview you think is important or relevant, give me a call. We don't have bugs inside. These guys are around 24/7 and they rarely let any strangers in the shop. They even do their own background checks on their legitimate customers. That's why I was surprised to see you go in the other day. I guess what we really needed was a pretty female agent with a flat tire, though I doubt that would have worked for anyone else."

Lisa felt herself blush again and was suddenly anxious to get out of there.

"One more thing," Agent Flannigan said as he ushered them out. "You really should wear a looser blouse with that gun. You know, untucked and falling just below the hips to cover it up. I'm not trying to be smart with you. You're too skinny to hide it that way. Maybe think about an ankle holster."

By the time they left the bakery, Lisa and Fred were famished. It was ten p.m. and the nearest restaurant that was still serving was a Chinese takeout place with four booths for eat-in customers. Fred swallowed an entire serving of garlic chicken in a matter of minutes, but Lisa found she could only pick at her rice and take a few sips of her wonton soup. She pushed her sweet and sour pork over to Fred, who ate that, too. Lisa's stomach was expressing all of her frustrations, and there were plenty of them.

It was too late to return the rental car, so they drove to the mall lot, got Lisa's car and she followed him back to the newspaper. Sleeping in the lounge had seemed like a great idea early in the day but, in reality, it was awkward. Joe had found a couple blankets and pillows and left them on the sofas along with a note that said he would meet with them at seven thirty a.m. That would give them plenty of time to be up and showered before the advertising staff came in. The room had an emergency light that gave a soft glow to the darkness. Lisa set her cell phone alarm for six and crawled under her blanket, but her eyes wouldn't stay closed, and it didn't help that she was sharing a room with Fred, a coworker she barely knew outside the newsroom. After half an hour of silence, she spoke up.

"You asleep yet?"

"No way."

"I'm too wired," Lisa said.

"That because you're thinking about Agent Flannigan. He's got a crush on you, and I think the feeling is mutual."

"Oh yeah? Well, you've got a crush on your wife."

Fred was quiet for a minute and Lisa thought maybe she had crossed a line. They'd become friends but not that close of friends. They'd only been working together closely for a day, and in all their years together at the newspaper, they had never even shared lunch. Fred was someone Lisa had always shared a quiet kinship with, the kind of person who seemed to think like she did. She had always avoided real friendships with coworkers. It was hard enough to balance her passion for journalism with her passion for Bridget. If she started socializing with people from work, she feared the two lives would bleed into each other and she would lose sight of her priorities. But Fred was growing on her and his relationship with his wife intrigued her, the fact that someone who seemed to share her cynicism—who seemed equally protective of himself—was still unafraid of being vulnerable at times.

"I think you're right," Fred said finally. "When she called, she sounded so scared, so worried, and it occurred to me that we'd never been much for showing our emotions, or rather, that I'd never been much for showing my emotions. Maybe that's the problem. Maybe I'm the problem. Anyway, I'm thinking counseling might be worth a shot."

"I'm glad to hear that, Fred."

"Now shut up and go to sleep. Just keep those X-rated dreams to yourself."

Lisa grabbed Joe's note from the end table, balled it up and threw it at him, hitting him in the face. Then she curled up, pulled the blanket tightly around herself and tried to dream of anything but Saul and Chandra and the others. But not even visions of Agent Flannigan could help with that. Every time she closed her eyes, she saw Saul with his welts and scars and protruding bones. Her heart raced and her eyes flew open again. She would get no sleep tonight.

Chapter Twenty-Three

Dorothy had felt uneasy all day, an uneasiness that seeped into her bones. Part of it was Toren, the fact that he had still not called back. His voicemail was full. She hadn't known him long, but she knew this was not like him. Something was wrong.

The other part was the crickets. Their chirping had always been persistent. Sections of crickets would pause sometimes when a guest walked down a certain path, or perhaps some creature came running through a field, but never did they stop completely. Not until this evening. She had been sitting on the porch with a few of the guests just after the sun had set when it happened. Even they noticed. The silence lasted for only a few seconds, but it gnawed on Dorothy the rest of the night. What would make all the crickets stop chirping at once like that? The deer were not in the field either.

Perhaps she was just paranoid. Saul had been with her for almost a week now and it could be tiring sometimes, keeping such a secret. Still, when Bridget told Dorothy how much she wanted to go to the movies with Ben, Dorothy told her to go ahead and to stay the night with her best friend, Claire. She argued that Bridget would awaken the guests, who often liked to rise early, by coming in so late, and that she deserved a night off. Bridget didn't put up a fuss, and neither of them brought up Lisa's orders that Bridget stay put. Bridget would be leaving for college soon and she would miss her boyfriend and friends. So Bridget called them both and filled her backpack with toiletries and a change of clothes. Dorothy gave her an extra-long, extra-tight hug before she left and warned her, once again, to stay away from her mother's house. When Bridget gave her a suspicious look, Dorothy forced a smile and attributed her own high emotions to the fact that Bridget had grown up so much recently, and that she would miss her when she was gone.

But now, at four in the morning when Saul and all the guests were fast asleep, Dorothy still couldn't shake the feeling. Once again, she made the rounds, checking all the doors to ensure they were locked, checking all the windows, feeling vulnerable for the first time since she had built this place. Not even in the old days when she had lived with her husband and son in the small house at the foot of the same hill had she been nervous to be so far away from the rest of civilization. She had always taken comfort in the distance, in the isolation. But not tonight. For the third time that night, she settled into the recliner in her living room and pulled a blanket over her body, concealing the handgun in her lap. She slept fitfully for two hours until the sun rose again, bringing the comfort that comes with daylight.

It wasn't enough.

Something still felt wrong.

"Good morning."

Dorothy's fingers instantly clenched the handgun's grip when Saul walked into the living room. She was not yet accustomed to the strength of his voice. He was less raspy these days. His words were deeper, smoother. More like that of a stronger man. She relaxed her hold when she saw it was him and sat up straight, letting the blanket drop from her shoulders to her lap.

"Guess I fell asleep here," she said, rubbing her face with her hands.

"I'll start the coffee. If there is any cooking I can do in here for your guests, let me know. I'm feeling pretty useless these days and I do like to cook. With Bridget gone, maybe I can help. I really would like to be of help."

Saul moved into the kitchen and Dorothy knew she had to pull it together. Her guests had paid a lot of money to stay here, and they didn't deserve to see her red-eyed and dragging her feet around like a teenager with a hangover. She went into the bathroom, turned on the shower and dropped some Visine into her eyes before she let the water course over her body. By the time she was dressed, it was a little easier to push her dread into a small corner of her mind. Saul handed her a cup of coffee and motioned to the table, where a

134

plate of bacon and eggs with a side of whole-wheat toast awaited her.

"The least I can do," he said as he pulled out her chair.

He wasn't fooling Dorothy. She had heard him moaning several times through the night. He needed this to end as much as she did, even more than she did. Saul needed counseling, more medication and a slow reentry into the world he had left more than ten years before. A lot had happened in the past decade. The changes were likely to shock him, to leave him mourning. Those years were gone. He could never get them back. If anyone could do it, though, it was Saul. There was something about him, a resiliency that left Dorothy with no doubt he would eventually succeed. He had talents, too—talents that had gone unnurtured for all those years, but had somehow managed to develop regardless. He could cook and, she thought, might even have developed a more sensitive pallet from all that sensory deprivation. In everything he made, there was a perfect balance, a perfect blend of flavors.

He was not a visual artist. His sketches weren't much better than those of the average sixth grader. But he could write, and lately, he was spending more time on the verses that accompanied his sketches than he spent on the sketches themselves. His words were painful, intriguing, poetic and lovely all at once. They painted portraits of despair and hope, of ugliness and beauty. Dorothy found herself drawn to his writing, picking up his notebook whenever he happened to put it down, to read and reread. She hoped Saul didn't mind. Her forays into his notebook had become something she looked forward to each day.

It was Friday, early breakfast day. Most of the guests would be leaving, and checkout time was eleven. Some—those who had traveled long distances—would want to get an early start. The few who stayed often used this time to go into town and shop. Dorothy encouraged it, handing them brochures she had made up with a map and the names and descriptions of several art galleries, co-ops and antique stores. No lunch was served on Fridays. She needed time to clean rooms and change sheets. New guests would arrive at four. Dorothy was glad Saul was here. She really could use his help with breakfast.

"If you could just do all the bacon in here, that would be a huge help, and maybe cut up the fruit when you're not busy with that. I'm serving omelets made to order, pancakes and home fries. The home fries are boiled, seasoned and ready to fry. So I can handle that on my own. I'll just need to do omelets and pancakes, which shouldn't be a problem if I set it up right. I'm so glad I decided to do drink stations instead of serving drinks when I opened this place. Can you imagine what it would be like without you or Bridget if I had to pour coffee and orange juice for each of my guests while flipping pancakes? I'd go out of my mind."

When she was a child, the smell of bacon cooking had always soothed Dorothy. Bacon was something special, a treat they could rarely afford, so it was always an indicator of a good day ahead. She tried to recapture that feeling as she stood in the kitchen, chopping green peppers, red onions, mushrooms and ham and sliding them each into their own bowls. But even that irresistible aroma seeping through the doors from her tiny kitchen into the large commercial kitchen couldn't suppress the feeling that rose inside her, the urgency to get her guests out.

Chapter Twenty-Four

Lisa was up before her alarm went off and so was Fred. He didn't look like he'd slept much either. He offered to wait out in the advertising area while she showered, and then they traded places, with Lisa guarding the lounge door in case some woman with her period decided she needed an early morning nap. By the time they were through, coffee was brewing in the cafeteria and fresh doughnuts and bagels had arrived. They each grabbed a cup and Fred bought a doughnut, but Lisa still couldn't stomach the thought of food. They were worse off now than they had been before. Someone was still trying to hurt Lisa, someone who desperately wanted Saul back, and now she had no idea where to start looking.

"I have the interview with the florist this morning and the interview at the auto restoration shop this afternoon," Lisa told Fred and Joe. "Either of those could lead to something. You never know. At least they give us legitimate reasons to be in the neighborhood. I think we ought to spend the time in between looking for anything Saul had described. Pretty much every dumpster out there is green and most of them are in alleys, so that doesn't help much. But we should find a freshly boarded-up basement window near one of them. I know it's a long shot, but it's the only one we've got."

Fred and Lisa had told Joe about Agent Flannigan, but they'd left out the part about getting caught outside the building. He would have been furious. Instead, they let him assume they'd been caught in the building across the street, just before leaving for that dinner they'd told Joe they were about to have. Joe was too excited about the story that would come out of it to worry anyway.

"At least we know you'll be safe in the auto shop with the FBI watching. I always knew Iron City Heights was a high-crime area, but I never imagined it was a haven for sweatshops and chop shops," he said. "This is unreal. Today is the day though. No more messing around. You two get what you can and stick together and at five p.m., we're going to the police. Got it? I really don't like the idea of you going down there at all. They know you're onto them. They must by now. Weinstock would have told them."

"But, Joe—"

"No 'buts,' Lisa. There is only so much I'm willing to risk. We can keep it low key, maybe find a way to get you two to the police station without being noticed or arrange a meeting somewhere discreet. If the bad guys don't know you've contacted police, nothing has changed. Has it? A lot of cops work out at the YMCA, don't they? And you both have memberships through work. Whoever is following you couldn't get in without a card, and somehow I doubt they're members. I'll make a few calls and arrange a meeting with a detective. Bring a duffle bag to make it look good."

Lisa sighed and Fred threw up his arms. Joe was right. They'd taken on too much and they'd need a whole force combing the streets to find that window. They needed help. Saul was still safe, and Lisa would not reveal his whereabouts until they could vow to protect him 24/7. They'd done the best they could, and they still had the entire day ahead of them. They didn't have to give up just yet.

"You win, Joe," Lisa said. Her chest felt suddenly heavy. "Thanks for letting us take it this far. I know I've put you in a terrible position and at least we were able to get the Weinstock interview. They should have enough to maybe get something out of him. Fred, we've got to return that rental before the florist interview and find you a duffle bag. And I could really use a change of clothes. How about we get going?"

"Yeah." Fred was deflated, too. Lisa could hear it in his voice.

"Let's go."

Lisa didn't bother to look for tails as they drove to the Enterprise office. Let them follow her. What were they going to do here in broad daylight? She was surrounded by witnesses and Fred, and she still had that gun. Agent

Flannigan hadn't taken that. Somehow, his oversight made her feel better about getting caught so easily.

Fred lived half an hour out of the city in the suburbs and Lisa's house was only ten minutes away, so they decided to pick up a duffle bag for him there. Lisa hadn't been home in two nights now anyway, and she was anxious to check on things. Besides, she was certain her clothes were starting to reek. Nothing looked out of place from the outside, but the front door was unlocked, and the security system was off. How could it be off? Only Lisa, Bridget and Dorothy knew the code. Bridget wasn't supposed to return, but maybe she came by anyway. She was a teenager. A forgotten tube of lipstick of a certain hue could be considered an emergency.

Still, Lisa and Fred walked in carefully, scanning the foyer and the living room before they went farther. Lisa's skin felt hot where the gun rested, a constant physical reminder that it was there if she needed it. At least now she knew how to shoot one, and she was pretty good at it. Dorothy had made sure of that.

The answering machine was not flashing, but it showed four messages that had been played and not deleted. Lisa was certain she had cleared her answering machine when she'd left. It should be either empty or flashing. She hit play and listened to a reminder from her dentist that had recorded two hours after Lisa's last visit home. It was followed by a message from Toren, a call from Uncle Lee asking her to dinner next weekend and a request for her participation in a survey. Toren had called at ten Wednesday night.

"Hi. This is Toren. Just wanted to let you know, I checked on our mutual friend and he's fine. I'm amazed really. I'll catch up with you again in a few days."

Lisa cringed. His reference to their "mutual friend" would have been obvious to anyone who knew about Saul. But even if someone had managed to bypass Lisa's security system and listen to her messages, how would they know who Toren was? It was an uncommon name, but there were a lot of people in Seneca Springs, and he gave no indication in the message that he was a doctor. They hadn't dated long enough for anyone outside Lisa's tightest circle to know they'd been dating at all. As a doctor, he maintained a private cell phone number, so it wouldn't show up on her caller ID.

All at once, Lisa's body started to quiver. Bile rose in her throat, and she was dizzy. She couldn't see straight. She grabbed the phone table for support.

"Lisa," Fred said. "Lisa, what's wrong?"

Lisa pushed past Fred and ran outside to her car. She pulled open the door and touched the panel that opened a storage compartment in her dashboard. All her business cards were gone, including Toren's. The day someone broke into her car—the day she found the photo—that must be when they took them. They had Toren's name and his occupation. It wouldn't have been hard to find his address. Between the phone message and the business card, they had a perfect match.

Lisa's body was overcome with dry heaves. She could feel Fred's hand on her back, and she could hear him somewhere in the distance asking again whether she was okay. No, she was not okay. She had pulled Toren into this. She had let this happen. She had to pull herself together. It might not be too late. He left the message Wednesday, the same day her car was broken into, but there were other messages on her machine. Some were from Thursday. Whoever broke into her house—if someone broke into her house—had done so Thursday afternoon or this morning. She had to remember that she could be wrong. It was always possible only Bridget had listened to the messages.

"Give me your cell phone," Lisa said, straightening her body out and thrusting her hand toward Fred. "I can't risk using mine."

Lisa took several deep breaths and tried to convince herself she was overreacting. When she had calmed down, she called Joe and told him what she'd found and what she suspected. She gave him Toren's address and phone number and asked him to have the police check it out. He could say she got a phone message from him indicating some kind of emergency. She could be wrong. He might be fine, so she didn't want to give police any more information than they needed at this point, but that would get them there.

"Lisa, forget the five o'clock deadline. Come back here now and let's tell them what we know."

"Let's just see what the police find, Joe. Maybe Toren's on vacation. Maybe I'm just paranoid. Bridget might have turned off the security system and forgotten to switch it back on," Lisa said, trying to convince herself as much as Joe. "Nothing else appeared to be missing or disturbed."

"Okay, but if they find anything at all, if there's any indication that Toren has been hurt or taken against his will, I want you and Fred back here immediately."

When Lisa ended the call, she found Fred leaning against the car with his hands in his pockets, staring at her. It was not a friendly, caring stare. He was angry. He held out his hand to take the phone.

"Next time, do me a favor and fill me in a bit before you freak out," he said. "Okay? We're in this together, or have you forgotten that? I deserve to know what's going on. You scared the hell out of me. Do you really think they have Toren?"

"I'm so sorry, Fred. I don't know. God, I hope not. What have I done? Why did I get involved to begin with?" Lisa didn't even try to stop the tears. She just let them roll down her face and neck silently. She had no energy for shaking sobs, moans or anything else. She just stood there in her driveway pushing wisps of hair from her face, letting the tears flow freely. He had to be okay. She could not possibly live with the guilt if they killed Toren.

"See, this is the stuff I have to work on," Fred said. "I know I should hug you right now, but I find that kind of thing awkward. If I can't even hug a crying coworker who's being followed by killers who might have come after her ex-boyfriend and who have been holding a bunch of people in captivity as slaves for at least a decade, then what kind of husband have I been to my wife?"

He grinned, reached into the car and grabbed a napkin from the console.

"Here, they didn't take this," he said, holding it out to her.

Despite it all, Lisa smiled. He was wrong. He knew how to comfort others, just in his own way. She accepted the napkin and dabbed her eyes until they were dry. Then she turned back toward the house and motioned for Fred to follow.

"Come on," she said. "We'll still need a duffle bag for you, and we have an appointment to keep. Plus, I apparently need to wear a longer, looser shirt. Until we hear from Joe, we keep on working. Let's take both cars, though. I want to be ready to fly if something has happened to Toren. If something has happened—if it's bad—you go to his place and talk to the cops, and I'll go to Dorothy's and ask the sheriff's department to meet me there. Unless..."

She stopped abruptly on the stairs to the porch and turned to face Fred. "Unless you have other ideas. I'm being a jerk again and telling you what to do rather than getting your input, only a few minutes after I left you in the dark, ignored you and called Joe. You're right. We're in this together and we have to work together."

"In all honestly, Lisa, this cops and robbers stuff is your thing. I wouldn't know what to do. That's why I like the courtroom. All the drama without the stress. Just be sure and tell me first if, say, we're being shot at, or bad guys are heading for us or you find Chandra Bower. You know. Anything like that. Don't make me listen to you explain it over my phone. And it would have been nice to know you were carrying a gun. I like to know that kind of stuff."

"Deal," Lisa said. "We'd better get moving. I still have to change, and we're supposed to be at the florist in half an hour."

Chapter Twenty-Five

L isa was parked in her driveway with the engine running waiting for Fred to move his car out of the way when she heard the squealing of tires and a crash on the street far too close for comfort. She looked to her far right and saw that a Jeep Cherokee parked along the curb toward the end of the block had apparently tried to pull away, but another car, a dark blue Chevy, had blocked it, crashing into its front side. While she watched, a white Honda Accord pulled in behind the Jeep, preventing it from backing up.

The Jeep's driver-side door opened and a tall thin man in dress slacks and a golf shirt jumped out like he was about to flee, but he was greeted by two armed men and a woman wearing U.S. Marshal t-shirts and vests who had already gotten out of cars with their guns drawn. The Jeep driver threw his arms up and the marshals shouted instructions. Fred was already trotting down the street with his camera bag over his shoulder by the time Lisa shut down her engine and got out.

"There she is! There's the bitch," the man yelled, indicating Lisa with his chin. "Do you know what I get paid? Do you have any idea what kind of hell it is to work for Trammel? All you had to do was run the story. That was all. It wouldn't have hurt you one bit."

"Shut up unless you want to waive your rights," the female marshal said as she approached the man. The marshal grabbed him by the shoulders, turned him around and told him to put his hands on the Jeep. Then she frisked and handcuffed him while the other two kept their guns trained on him. As Lisa drew closer and the marshal turned the man back around, she recognized his narrow face and dark eyes. It was Robert, the junior partner who had given her the IDA contract. Then another familiar man emerged from one of the marshals' cars—Uncle Lee.

"Hey, baby girl," Uncle Lee said, approaching her with open arms. He pulled her close and held her tight for what seemed like a long time before he released her. "Sorry about all this. It looks like you've made yourself an enemy. He set up the account and forged the documents, and from what he's hollering at you right now, it appears that someone paid him some good money to do it."

"What was he doing here?" Lisa asked. She shivered despite the summer heat. What had she missed? She could understand his anger and even his desire for revenge against Trammel. Trammel was hated among many of the junior ranks, especially those who finally admitted defeat, quitting after failing time and time again. They wasted years in his firm, earning next to nothing and getting nowhere. But this scheme involved a lot of money. Someone had financed it. It didn't make sense.

"You didn't run the story and he probably knew something was wrong. We followed him here from his office after my guy matched his signature from the IDA contract with the forged signatures on the bank papers. We're not sure what he was planning, but the Jeep's a rental. He's had it for a week. He probably used it when he dropped off the papers so no one would connect him with the plate if he was spotted. Of course, all the FBI had to do was call the rental company. He stopped along the way and picked up a can of gasoline, a pair of rubber gloves and a box of wooden matches from his garage. Then he headed here. I'm hoping he was at least going to wait until you were gone before he torched the place. These guys let me come for the ride. I am so glad to see you," he said, hugging Lisa one more time.

Lisa sensed movement beside her and realized she'd forgotten about Fred. He was looking through his camera lens, clicking one photo after another, but Uncle Lee put a hand in his sight line and politely asked him to stop.

"Go ahead and shoot if you can keep the marshals and their cars out of the photos. They agreed to help us out with the arrest, but marshals usually prefer to lie low. A lot of people out there would like to get their hands on them," Uncle Lee said. Fred lowered the camera and seemed unsure how to react.

"Fred, this is my uncle, Lee Vickery. He's a lawyer, but he's also former FBI. I gave him some documents last week someone had left at my door that would have proved the head of the IDA was taking kickbacks from Trammel. If they'd been real. Uncle Lee, this is Fred, a coworker of mine. We're working on a story together and we're running late for an interview. I really don't want to leave now, though. This is crazy. Was he really going to burn down my house?"

Robert was in the back of the undamaged marshal's car now, leaning his head back against the seat—defeated and deflated. Already, two other vehicles had arrived—a hook-and-chain tow truck and a flat bed. A city police car had arrived as well with its lights flashing. A marshal was taking photos of the damage to both vehicles and of the inside of the Jeep. A man in a shirt and tie, probably an FBI agent, emerged from yet another vehicle and headed in Lisa's direction.

"Nothing more is going to happen here. They'll tow the Jeep and bag the evidence, and they'll take their time booking him and calling his lawyer. I have a feeling it won't be long before he tells them who paid him to do this. He's not that smart and he's a little on the wimpy side. No point in you hanging around. They'll need a statement from you eventually, but that can wait. This is Agent Juarez," he said, as the FBI agent came within hearing distance. "He'll need your contact information and maybe some basics, but I'm sure he can get whatever else he needs later tonight."

"No problem," Agent Juarez said. "I think we're going to be tied up with this guy for a while anyway."

"Uncle Lee, I don't even know what to say. You probably saved my life. I think he's been following me for a few days now. Somebody has, and that person was driving a Jeep. I slept in a hotel the other night. We both slept at the newspaper last night, thinking it has something to do with a story I was working on. But I didn't see this coming."

Before this, Lisa had felt lost. Now she was confused. What else was she missing? Robert had probably followed her—Fred confirmed the Jeep was the same make and color as the one he'd seen tailing them the previous day—and he was definitely the person who called her a bitch on her cell phone. He had used that same tone, that same mix of anger and whining. The inflection was unmistakable. But he didn't leave the note. It wouldn't make sense. Robert wanted her to do something, but it had nothing to do with giving someone up. The note asked her whether "he" was worth it. And the incident with the car—that required two people. Someone had tried to run her down, and someone else had taken the photo. Suddenly Lisa felt even more vulnerable than before. She scanned the street wondering whether anyone else might be watching.

"I have a feeling there are plenty of people who would like to stop this project from going through," Lisa said. "Between you and me, the FBI is investigating a chop shop down there and I've got some evidence that a sweatshop exists somewhere in Iron City Heights, too."

"We'll know soon enough. Go ahead to your interview. We'll take care of this mess. Call me when you get home tonight, though. You make me nervous with all this poking around. You were like that when you were little, you know. Always asking questions," he said. Someone shouted Uncle Lee's name and Lisa saw a marshal motioning for him to get in the car.

"That's my ride," Uncle Lee said, turning to go. "You stay safe and make sure you call."

Lisa promised, and then watched as her uncle got in the front of the car Robert sat in and the car peeled away. It had happened so fast that it was only just beginning to occur to her how much danger she had been in. At the very least, he would have burned her house down. All the photos of Bridget, her swatch of baby hair, her first baby shoes—all that would have been gone. But what if Lisa had not been working on the sweatshop story? What if Saul had not come into her life? She'd have had no reason to send Bridget away, no reason to believe she might be in danger. Bridget could have been home. Lisa couldn't bring herself to follow that thought further. She closed her eyes and drew her arms tightly around herself.

"Are you okay?" Fred asked. He looked up at Lisa from the sidewalk where he was crouched over his camera case, removing the lens and putting his equipment away. When Joe had first suggested assigning another reporter to work with her, Lisa had accepted it as a necessary burden, a way to placate Joe. But now Lisa was thankful Fred was there. She couldn't do this. She couldn't waste time wallowing in the possibilities, and Fred's presence was a good distraction. So she simply nodded and blew out a long breath.

"I'm glad I had this with me, but what do we do with this?" he said as he stood and threw his camera bag over his shoulder again. "Do we go back and write this story or go ahead with the interview? This is big news—front page. Bert Trammel's own employee set him up along with the head of the IDA and was planning to burn your house down. We can't sit on it too long."

"The marshals are pretty quiet about this stuff, and I doubt many television reporters have FBI connections," Lisa said. "I don't think we have to worry about getting beat until they at least interview me. They'll want to do that before they arraign him. Let's go ahead with the florist interview and then meet with Joe tonight to discuss it. We'll give the FBI some time to get him talking. Personally, I'd like to see them nab whoever is behind this, or at least formally book Robert, before we run a story. I'd like to go to bed at night knowing I won't wake up in a house full of flames."

Lisa had other reasons for holding off. As big as this story was, Robert was in custody. He was no longer a threat. But Chandra and the others grew closer to death every minute she and Fred wasted. They were suffering at this very moment, and their suffering would not end unless they were found. The sweatshop story was more important, and time was limited. If someone beat her to the IDA story…well, let them. She could live with that.

Fred shrugged his shoulders, but he didn't argue.

"It's your call, but I'm going to get these photos on the computer as soon as we get back. We have some time between interviews. Let's do takeout for lunch and eat at the newspaper before we start searching the alleys. We need a better plan for this sweatshop story now that the bakery is out of the picture, and I want to know more about this Robert guy and the papers he sent you. Maybe it's time to bring Saul in. Maybe if you and Joe and I all talk with him, we can help him remember something more."

"No. I'm not taking Saul anywhere until the police or the FBI can guarantee his safety. We'll meet over lunch and go over the maps, but then I want to go back to Iron City Heights. The sweatshop is somewhere near that bakery. I saw that sedan drive in that direction, and I can feel it. We're just going to have to walk every sidewalk and every alley near there until we find that bathroom window. I was able to rule out about half the alleys with Google Maps, so it won't be as overwhelming as it seems. We can get in a little time before the interview with the chop shop guys and an hour or two after."

Lisa wished she could cancel the florist interview, but it was too late. Already they were a few minutes behind schedule. Cancelling now would be even ruder than arriving late. Regardless of what happened with the sweatshop story, Iron City Heights and the development were still her responsibility. She couldn't afford to make enemies and blowing off feature interviews was a sure way to do that.

With their shadow in custody, Lisa and Fred decided to take separate cars and meet there. They would both keep an eye out for other suspicious vehicles, but Lisa had had a few minutes to think, to become more rational. Robert was obviously the driver of the Jeep that had been following them. His Jeep was the same color and model, and he had a motive. So they didn't have to worry about that anymore. Whoever took the photo of Lisa diving for the sidewalk had probably been waiting there a while. Most likely, they had followed Lisa long enough to know she was in the diner and would be returning to the newspaper to at least fetch her car. They had probably set up the supposed accident with the driver dropping off the photographer and then parking around the corner with his engine running. Maybe the driver had not intended to kill her but had wanted to scare her into submission with an injury and a photo. Regardless. it was unlikely that person was watching her now. Lisa was beyond caring at this point anyway. Tonight, it would all be out of her hands. All she wanted was to gather as much information as possible in the hours she had left.

Chapter Twenty-Six

Only three guests remained registered at the retreat Friday—two women who had traveled together from Florida and Cesar Medina, a well-known artist from Detroit who had come to Dorothy's retreat for a little productive privacy. The women had tried all week to befriend Cesar, but he had rebuffed them, making it clear that socializing was not part of his plan. Dorothy had supported him, shooing other guests away when they tried to peer at his work in progress or engage him in conversation and serving his meals in his bedroom or workspace. But Cesar had lightened up Thursday night and joined the others for wine and cheese near the fire. Dorothy was surprised when he declined breakfast in his room this morning and joined the others at the shared table, announcing plans to tour antique shops with the two women, who were so excited they barely touched their food.

They left at eight thirty, an hour after the other guests had packed up and checked out. With no one left in the retreat, Dorothy was finally free to give Saul a tour, and she would still have plenty of time to clean the three rooms that would accommodate new guests. Bridget would be back by two o'clock, and maybe Saul could help set up for the upcoming week as well. Dorothy was still worn out from her lack of sleep, but she was feeling better, less paranoid. She had called the newspaper a few minutes earlier just to make sure Lisa was still okay and was told she was out of the office on an interview. Dorothy had been careful to dial the city desk, not Lisa's direct line, and she had not given her name. Toren had finally returned her call at about seven a.m. Dorothy had been taking out the trash and had missed it, but Toren left a short message saying he would be out of town for a few days. He sounded upset and sick, like he had a bad cold or maybe he'd been crying. Dorothy guessed he'd had a death in the family or some other crisis that had pulled him away. She made a mental note to have him for dinner when this was all over.

Still, as she walked up the stairs with fresh sheets draped over her arm, uneasiness overwhelmed her. Something felt wrong, different. She could hear Saul in the main kitchen, where he was working on three pans of an old favorite of his—baked French toast made with thick bread, cinnamon, nutmeg and praline topping—for the next morning's breakfast. A soft breeze flowed through the windows she had opened earlier, warming even the coolest corners of the house. Four gallons of iced tea in large glass containers brewed in the sun on the concrete patio by the side door. But the crickets still bothered her with their oddly sporadic song, and the birds were not singing their share of the melody. Dorothy hung the sheets over the railing at the top of the stairs and started back down, surrendering to the urge to survey the land surrounding the house. She had her hand on the front doorknob when the door flew open, hitting her in her face and knocking her to the ground. Blood immediately coursed from her nose, and she looked up to see a gun pointed at her, held by a bulky man with broad shoulders, pasty skin and hair shaved close to his head.

"Don't move," he ordered, keeping his gun trained on her as he peered toward the kitchen. Dorothy could no longer hear Saul banging cupboard doors or tossing utensils into the sink. Instead, she heard something being dragged. She thought she heard the door to her quarters swing open and then nothing. Silence.

"Devon," the gunman hollered, his eyes continually shifting from Dorothy to the kitchen and back. "What's going on?"

He waited for a reply. Nothing.

"Devon, you bastard. Answer me."

The man motioned with his gun for Dorothy to get up. She tried to remain calm and keep her face toward the man as she rose, trembling, from the hardwood floor. She was unsteady, dizzy, and she nearly slipped in her own blood. Dorothy had read somewhere once that it was psychologically easier to shoot people from behind, less traumatic. She did not believe this man would be reluctant to shoot her from any position, but it was worth a try. He wanted her to walk into the kitchen, so she moved sideways, keeping her hands up and letting the blood flow freely down her face and her chest. She alternately looked ahead while making eye contact with the gunman. Where was Saul? What had she heard? She was terrified by what she might see in the kitchen, but she knew she couldn't let terror win. If Saul was dead, nothing she did now would help him. If he was alive, she had to keep her cool and think. This man would not expect her to think.

From the foyer, only a sliver of the kitchen was visible, but as they moved through the great room, she could see the gas stove and a good chunk of the counter space through the four-foot opening. Saul had left a mixing bowl and a glass rectangular pan on the counter. A rubber spatula lay on the tile floor in a pool of batter, and a cast-iron frying pan rested unevenly on the edge of a burner. A few dots and streaks of blood were scattered on the tile, forming a path that led to Dorothy's door. Saul's blood. It had to be Saul's blood. But when Dorothy's mind tried to envision what she might find behind that door, it was not Saul she saw. It was her son, lying motionless on a gurney in the ER with a gaping hole in his head. His expression was peaceful, she remembered, but entirely without life. What remained of him was a shell, and the sight of it had made her ache more than she had ever thought possible.

When the gunman started to push her into the kitchen and toward the door and that ache began to rise again, she realized why she had trusted Saul so much, why she had been willing to risk her own life for him. Everything about him—his slight build, his quiet determination, his artistic nature, his sense of righteousness—everything reminded her of her son. She held her body stiff against the next shove. She could not and would not lose him again.

Chapter Twenty-Seven

Stems and Petals was bustling with activity when Lisa and Fred arrived. Tall, narrow buckets full of roses, baby's breath, lilies, carnations and other flowers that looked familiar to Lisa but that she could not identify filled the room, their scents mingling in the moist air, but not quite blending. Lisa spent the first few moments standing in the doorway breathing deeply through her nose and taking it all in. The crew was preparing for three different weekend events, shearing stems, plucking leaves, arranging vases, corsages, altar bouquets with just the right mixes of colors and textures. They moved about with grace, often grazing each other's arms or legs or shoulders but never disrupting the flow.

Lisa was so entranced by the fluidity of it all that it felt like an intrusion when her cell phone rang. She wanted to ignore it, to remain fully within this Eden where Saul, Chandra and the evil they had experienced did not exist, but she knew she could not. The call was from Joe and, as she suspected, he had news about Toren.

"The landlord let the police in," Joe said. "It looks like he took off on a trip. Nothing was disturbed. There were no perishables in his fridge, his garbage was empty and he left a list on the table of things he needed to do—reserve a room, pick up toiletries, call you. Apparently, he forgot that last item. His car was gone from the parking lot, too. The space was left empty overnight, according to the landlord."

Lisa was relieved, but she also felt foolish for getting so worked up. It didn't seem like Toren to just take off like that, especially with Saul in his care, but how long had she really known him anyway? He seemed eager to have a woman in his life. Maybe he went someplace where he could meet people. Maybe he met some new woman, and they went on a spontaneous trip. Maybe someone died or was hurt, someone important to him. Lisa was not the center of his world and Saul, last she'd known, was doing well. Saul didn't really need him anymore. Why shouldn't he just up and go, and why would he have to tell Lisa?

"Thanks, Joe. I'm sorry to be so paranoid. It looks like the marshals caught the guy who was following me, too. A whole other story that's unrelated, but very interesting. An employee of Trammel's was trying to frame his boss and the head of the IDA. He sent me some papers that were too good to be true. I turned them over to my uncle, who gave them to the FBI. I guess he was mad that I didn't write a story. Fred's got photos. I'll fill you in more tonight, but I've got to wait until the arraignment to write it. I know I have a scoop though, because they won't charge him formally until they interview me, and that's not going to happen today."

"Whoa. When did all this happen? Why didn't you tell me about these papers? Lisa—" Joe sighed. "Never mind. We'll talk later. Remember that you're supposed to write the news, not make it, Lisa. I'm glad they caught this guy, but be careful anyway and keep Fred by your side. We know these people are dangerous regardless. If we don't have to do this cloak-and-dagger thing anymore though, I'll call someone I know with the FBI and arrange a meeting for six tonight in my office instead. I'll call the police chief, too, and ask him to send a detective. You've done a great job on this, Lisa, but I have to say I'll be happy to turn this story over to the authorities. It's too big for us and too many lives are at risk."

"I know, Joe. I know. I'll be back at five to prepare, but Fred and I are going to do one more search of the area before we give up. I've asked around here at the florist. No one knows anything about a garment factory or anything unusual. Maybe we'll stop by some of the other shops, too, especially the ones that have been around a while. Someone must know something, even if they don't realize it's important."

"I still want you and Fred to work together," Joe said. "It's not safe out there. Saul is still missing in their minds and that guy you saw that morning is still out there, probably looking for him. If he sees you snooping around the neighborhood, walking up and down alleys, especially after the Weinstock interview…I don't even want to think about it."

"Will do," Lisa said, watching Fred as he snapped frame after frame of hands dancing with stems, leaves and petals. It was nice to see this softer side of him. She wondered sometimes how she came across to her coworkers, to her sources, to men. Did she ever show her own softer side? Did she even have one? She assured Joe she and Fred both had their cell phones and each other's backs, and then breathed deeply again.

Lisa decided Stems and Petals deserved her undivided attention, so she tried to push thoughts of the sweatshop out of her mind and concentrate. She gave in to the aromas, to the beauty around her, and let it all envelope her. Lisa immersed herself and, within thirty minutes, she knew more about flowers than she ever knew she could. She felt calm, relaxed, for the first time in more than a week. And she was hungry, ravenous.

"I know it isn't the healthiest choice, but I could really go for a burger at Molly's," Lisa told Fred. "A half-pounder with cheese and bacon and a side of steak fries. No lettuce. No tomato. Just pure meat and carbs right there in a booth. No takeout. You know that if we try to eat at the paper, we'll never get out of there. Somebody will need something. Plus, Molly's is quick at this hour. We eat and go."

Molly's was just around the corner from the newspaper and a favorite among journalists, especially the night shift. They served beer until two a.m. and food until four. Molly's burgers were probably at least partially responsible for the higher-than-average heart attack rate among editors and reporters. But Lisa was so hungry, she didn't care.

"Sounds good to me," Fred said as he pushed open the door to the florist's and gestured for Lisa to walk ahead. "But I really want to upload these photos. How about I stop at the photo department first and then meet you there? I'll keep my head down and I won't talk to anyone outside of photo. I promise. I'll take the same burger as you with a large Coke. A real Coke, not the sugar-free kind."

The contrast was overwhelming as Lisa stepped into the bright noon sun.

It had been so cool and fragrant inside, so beautiful. An oasis. Lisa only now realized how accustomed she'd become to the stench of the river and grimy dust of the neighborhood streets in the past few weeks. She doubted that river could ever be truly cleaned, but she was grateful someone was willing to try. As long as everything was on the up and up, this development could only be good for the city. Without it, Iron City Heights would eventually lose businesses like Stems and Petals and become an even more appealing haven for mold, mildew and crime.

"Okay," Lisa said. "I'll be right along. I'm just going to make a quick call to my uncle and find out what's going on with Robert, that guy they arrested, and then I'll go. I didn't see anybody following us and I'll go straight to Molly's, so no worries."

Fred was reluctant, but he left after Lisa promised not to linger. Lisa leaned against her car and dialed her uncle's cell phone number. No answer. Uncle Lee was probably listening in on the interrogation. There was no way he'd be able to resist this one. His partner wouldn't be able to defend the guy because of Uncle Lee's involvement in the arrest, but he wouldn't want to take the case anyway. She called his office phone and left a message, asking him to update her when he got a chance. Just as she ended the call, her phone rang. It was Dewey, the man she'd hired to keep an eye on the Canadian, Rousseau.

"I'm following a white box truck with New York plates DFY three five six. I'm already through Malone and we're on Route Eleven, probably headed to Interstate Eighty-One. I had to wait for a cell signal before I could call you. There is a guy driving and I think someone in the passenger seat. It was hard to tell when they passed me."

"Dewey, you're wonderful." Lisa didn't even try to hide the excitement in her voice. "Keep following them. I'm getting in my car now. I'll get on Eighty-One, turn around and wait in the rest area just north of Oneida Lake. Do you think you could follow them that far and call me when you pass exit thirty-three? That would give me just enough lead time to pull on the highway and drive slowly until they pass. What kind of car are you driving and what color?

"It's a gray Ford pickup. Pretty beat-up. I'll call you in another half hour or so and give you an update."

Lisa climbed into her car, peeled away from the curb and told her phone to call Fred's number, but then changed her mind. Before he could answer, she grabbed her phone off the passenger seat and disconnected, swerving for a moment into the opposite lane in her effort to see the screen. Lisa took a deep breath after she regained control, and then looked around for the flashing lights of a police car. She didn't have time to get pulled over and she didn't have time to deal with Fred. If she told Fred exactly what was going on, he would insist on joining her. Then she might be late and miss the truck as it passed by. She couldn't take that chance. Not now. Instead, she pulled over and sent Fred a text: *Going to be a bit late. Something came up. Phone battery dying. I'll call when I get my phone plugged in. Eat without me. I'll grab something along the way.*

For nearly about forty-five minutes, Lisa sat in her car at the rest area, waiting for Dewey's call and ignoring calls from Fred. Dewey called once when they passed the Watertown exit, which meant they were near. Very near. She could have called Fred then, but she didn't dare. What if they pulled off? What if they took a different route into the city? She couldn't take the risk that Dewey would be unable to reach her for those few seconds she was on the phone. She didn't want any distractions. Not when she was so close, so close to finding Chandra and the others. Then came the call she'd been waiting for. They'd just passed exit thirty-three. It was time.

"You can drop off as soon as you see me," Lisa told Dewey. "I'm in a black Toyota Camry. I'll catch up with you after I find out where they're headed. You're the best, Dewey."

Lisa pulled onto the highway slowly, going just fifty miles an hour in the far-right lane. Dewey said they were going about sixty-eight. That should give the driver a chance to catch up and pass her. She was on the road only about three minutes when she spotted them. She picked up speed, staying in the right-hand lane, and read the plate on the truck—an older model Ford with a box about twelve feet long. This was it. This was the one. Lisa allowed her car to fall behind so she wouldn't be so obvious and started to call Fred. Her hands shook and she had trouble punching in the numbers while keeping an eye on the truck. His phone instantly flipped to voicemail.

"Dewey found the supply truck. I'm following it now on Interstate Eighty-One. We're almost to the city limits. I'll call you when we stop."

The driver turned off the highway at the exit for Iron City Heights. He wasn't even bothering to cover his tracks, but why would he? Delivery trucks matching the same description passed through Iron City Heights all the time. This was easy. Way too easy. The truck slowed down, easing its way through traffic, which was thick with daytime activity. She had expected the driver to take Fairview. Instead, he turned toward Reading, winding through a part of Iron City Heights that was less familiar to her, the warehouse area on the western fringe. Here, no tall buildings hugged the streets, providing her with cover when the truck turned corners. The traffic was thin, making her car obvious. She dropped back as far as she could without losing the truck and finally pulled to the side of the road when the truck turned into the wide-open parking lot of an abandoned factory.

With her eyes focused so intently on the truck, she didn't notice the sedan that had pulled up behind her. She didn't notice the gun either until its owner pulled the driver's side door open and pointed it at her head.

"Move over."

Behind the gun was a thickly built man in his thirties with fingers stained black with grease or oil, a slate-blue uniform shirt and navy-blue work pants that looked like they'd been through a few oil changes. She'd seen him before—at the auto restoration shop. He was there when she met with Greene and arranged the interview.

"I said, move over, and don't do anything stupid. My buddy there will be following us, and he has a gun of his own."

Lisa lifted her body over the gearshift and awkwardly slid into the passenger seat of her own car, barely daring to breathe. This couldn't be happening. She was tempted to fling open the passenger-side door and run. But where would she run? There was no one around. There were no businesses, no cars, no people in this part of Iron City Heights. He'd shoot her on the spot and probably leave her there or toss her back into her own car and drive it into a river or something. If she cooperated, at least she had a chance. She might find another way out. Besides, she still had her gun. She tugged on her shirt, ensuring it draped over the metal bulge inside her waistband.

The car was still running. The man with the gun eased it back onto the road and into the parking lot, stopping beside the truck. Another man came around the side of the white truck and opened its back doors, indicating that Lisa should get out of her own car and step inside. The truck was stacked full of boxes, probably full of materials, but they weren't the only cargo. On the floor with their hands tied behind their backs and gray duct tape over their mouths were two women. Both had dark hair and pale white skin. They looked terrified.

"Thanks to you, we were unable to drop off part of our cargo," the man with the gun said, motioning toward the women with his pistol. "These women were headed to New Jersey, where they were supposed to work for one of our colleagues, but we had to cancel our rendezvous when you started following us a few miles back. Do you think we're that stupid? We knew you were onto us. We recognized your car. What we need to know, though, is how you knew about this delivery. But Mr. Eckhart can talk with you about that in some place more suitable. Hop in."

Lisa expected to be bound like the two women, but the other man simply pulled a stowaway ramp from under the truck and shoved her aboard. The truck was padded inside, probably for soundproofing. No one would have heard these girls yell even without the duct tape. No one would hear Lisa scream either. Lisa could feel her own heart beating hard against her ribs as the doors slammed shut, the lock bar dropped and darkness closed in around her. She scrambled across the floor to the women and immediately started peeling off the duct tape. The first one burst into tears as the truck's motion jostled them from side to side. The second woman simply took deep, deep breaths. They tried to talk to Lisa in a flurry of sounds and Lisa tried to communicate with them, but neither spoke English. Russian. Lisa could make out that much from their accents. They were most likely Russian or maybe Ukrainian. With no light, she could not even communicate with them nonverbally. So she worked the ropes off one woman's wrists, feeling the knots with her fingers in the dark, and let her start working on the other's. Then she fell back onto the floor and focused on her pistol.

They wouldn't expect a journalist to be carrying a gun, and this was a small one compared to most. She needed a better hiding spot. She removed the waistband holster and flung it back into the truck, where she hoped they wouldn't find it immediately. Then she unzipped her right boot, grateful that these particular boots were high and loose in the calf area, and shoved it inside her sock, stretching her sock as much as she could to cover it. She had no idea whether she could walk with a pistol in her boot, but she would have to try. Maybe she could feign an injury that would allow her to limp. Lisa stood up in the truck, using the truck wall for support. She took one step before the truck jerked, sending her crashing back down onto the floor. But one step was enough. It would be awkward, and she prayed it wouldn't work its way out of her boot or accidentally fire, but she could walk.

It wasn't long before the truck stopped, backed up and came to a stop again, a stop too long for a traffic light. The engine was still running, and Lisa heard a strange noise. A rumble, like a garage door opening. The truck jerked again, moved backwards, and stopped once more. This time, they cut the engine. They had arrived at what Lisa assumed was the auto restoration shop. It must be a cover for the sweatshop, she thought. It made sense—a chop shop and a sweatshop working together with one functioning, in part, as a legitimate business. At least the FBI was watching. They would see the truck enter, though they would have no way of knowing Lisa was inside and they would have no reason to suspect the chop shop was a front for slavery.

Lisa immediately recognized her surroundings when the truck doors opened, along with the men who greeted her. James Greene waited with his feet spread wide and his arms crossed over his chest, watching Lisa as she stood. Harley was slightly behind him. Harley caught Lisa's eye once, and then turned away.

"You're about fifteen minutes early for our interview," Greene said with a smirk. "Stupid, stupid, stupid. I was just talking to a business associate who was trying to figure out how he could kill you without anyone ever knowing when we got the call. Come on down. I'd like to show you your car. You'll get a better idea of how our business works."

Lisa turned to look at the two women who were huddled in a back corner of the truck, probably hoping to avoid attention. Had she helped them by untying them or made things worse? What would happen to them? Where would they go from here? She couldn't think about that now. She needed to focus, focus on the gun in her boot and on trying to walk naturally—focus on looking for opportunities. She took a deep breath, hoping Greene would not notice how badly she was trembling inside, and started down the ramp. Greene offered a hand, but Lisa refused. The thought of touching him, any part of him, made her sick. As soon as her feet reached the concrete floor of the bay, she felt the barrel of a pistol in her back.

Greene pushed on a door that was designed to look like part of the shelving, revealing a dimly lit passageway that arched around a downward staircase. He instructed Harley and the gunman, whose name was Rodney, to follow behind her. She allowed herself to limp a bit in the darkness of the passage, relieving some of the pressure from the gun, which was rubbing hard against her ankle bone. Greene led them past the stairs and through another door that opened into a second double-bay garage. In one bay sat her car.

Lisa had been to the back of this building. She had walked all the streets in this neighborhood and had examined them from above on Google Maps. From the outside, she'd seen two old garage doors that were boarded up and looked like they hadn't been opened in years. The building had appeared abandoned and did not seem to be part of the auto restoration shop's operation. But from inside, she could see that the old doors were attached to newer functioning doors and that the windows were not windows at all. They were fake. The room was long, and her car occupied less than half the space. In a corner near the garage doors, far from her Toyota, were a charred metal barrel and a steel table with a thick mat that looked like a large potholder. There were several containers in the room of various sizes along with a few long carts, like those used to collect lumber at Home Depot.

Lisa once more felt the prod of the gun in her back. Greene told her to sit and learn, and then ordered Rodney to handcuff her to a pipe near a folding chair. The cuff was too tight and the metal cut into her wrist. She had to lean against the pipe to ease the tension. As she watched, Rodney and Harley each opened a door of her Toyota and began pulling out her insurance cards, her registration, her purse, her notebooks—anything and everything. Even gum wrappers. They tossed it all into the barrel and set it on fire. The flames were well-contained within the walls of metal and the smoke was too far away to cause problems. Next, they each unbolted a license plate. Rodney easily snipped the plates into small pieces with metal cutters, while Harley filled a large steel bowl with sand and then set it on the table with another smaller steel bowl inside it. As Rodney added pieces of the license plate to the bowl, Harley set a blowtorch to them. They worked quickly and smoothly together.

"Clever, isn't it?" Greene said. "That's a little recycling trick I learned. The aluminum will cool in the steel cup, and then we can throw it away. It will no longer be recognizable as a license plate. Keep watching. Normally, we would save your airbags, maybe your fender, seats, doors, any parts we could sell, but we're interested only in getting rid of your car and making sure it cannot be traced back to us. If only this were a different situation. Camry parts are in high demand."

When they were was done, Harley and Rodney pulled off the wipers and a panel from under the hood, and then popped the windshield free. Harley drilled out the rivets that held the VIN plate to the dashboard and replaced it with a new one. Then they dropped the windshield back into place. While Harley swapped out the VIN plates inside of the door jamb and underneath the passenger side seat, Rodney smoothed pre-taped masking film over the windows, lights and wheels, and sprayed foam in the locks and door jambs. Harley was ready with a spray gun when he finished. Soon, the car's body was covered in a fresh coat of deep red paint. Rodney attached new license plates and stepped back.

"Not a great paint job, but it will do. Cops won't recognize your car on a tow truck and the paint matches the color of the new VIN," Greene said. "We have someone coming to take it away shortly. They're getting a good deal on this car and will probably use it for parts. If they choose to sell it,

Chapter Twenty-Eight

L isa tried not to think beyond the moment. If she did, she would have to admit she was probably going to die. Then she would be mentally dead before they actually killed her. She would have no chance of doing anything but waiting, waiting for death. She did not want to think about dying. She did not want to wait. She did not want her mind to ponder when and how they would do it. She had to hang onto hope, every last shred of it, and to do that, she had to calm down and focus. She had to be ready to fight.

But her body ached for Bridget. The pain was almost unbearable. Bridget was eighteen. She was legally an adult, and she had her father's family and Dorothy, but if Lisa died, she would have lost both of her parents to murder. She would never recover from that. How could anyone? Lisa had gone through her late teens and her adult life without her parents. She had survived. But her father was physically well and deep down, a part of Lisa knew there was a chance her mother was still out there somewhere. Maybe strung out, maybe in jail or shacking up with some grizzly, greasy guy, but maybe not dead. She had no desire to see her, but there was a certain level of comfort in knowing she might still be alive. Bridget wouldn't have that.

And Dewey. Did they know he'd followed them, too? They hadn't mentioned him, so she could only hope they hadn't noticed and that he was safe. It was her car they were familiar with. Her car they'd been looking for. What about those women? Where would they take them now? They looked so scared. So helpless. They couldn't even understand their captors. They likely had no idea where they were headed or what they had gotten into. Lisa was their only hope. Lisa and her gun. The pistol was rubbing her raw now, probably tearing the skin off her ankle. She wasn't sure how much longer she could take it. She gritted her teeth against the pain just as Greene raised his own gun to her chest and told Rodney to unlock the handcuffs.

"My part in this is done," he said as another man came down the passageway and stepped into the garage—a tall, broad-shouldered man with a shaved head, bright blue eyes, a strong jawline and small rounded glasses. He wore a black t-shirt and leather pants. He looked like a skinhead trying to get modeling work. Behind him came another man, the man from the sedan. This time when he looked her up and down, it was not flirtatious. It was with obvious contempt. He motioned for her to stand.

"Such a pleasure to see you again, Ms. Jamison," he said through tight lips. "And so kind of you to join us. Have you told her, Mr. Greene, about her friends, that she needn't worry about them anymore?"

"That's your thing, not mine. And I don't want to hear anything more about it. Our joint operating agreement did not include murder. I fetched her and I took care of the car. Now please get her out of my shop," he said, dropping his gun-bearing arm to his side. "The rest of us have work to do."

"Very well," the man said. He was not dressed in business clothes like he had been the day he searched for Saul. This time, he wore casual slacks and a black t-shirt like the man who stood with him. He seemed smaller, too. His brown hair was dull and somewhat greasy. His teeth were stained with tobacco. He had a shadow of a beard. He clearly had not slept well since Saul had escaped, and that gave Lisa a slight bit of pleasure. Greene seemed to make him nervous, too. He shifted on his feet, and then motioned to the tall man who had already drawn his gun.

"Allow me to introduce myself. I am Peter Eckhart, small business owner, entrepreneur and revolutionary. Your friends—Saul and that woman, Dorothy—should be wrapping up a meeting with a few of my employees right about now. Did you really think you could hide him from me?" he asked, bringing his face and his foul breath close to Lisa's. "Do you have any idea who I am? I will not have all my work destroyed by some wisp of a girl who likes to write stories."

What had he done? How did he find them? The room started to close in around her. He didn't mention Bridget. Please let Bridget be alive, Lisa thought. Dizziness was overwhelming her, and she felt bile rising in her throat once again. Her stomach muscles began to cramp, and her body lurched. She couldn't let this happen. This was what he wanted. She tried to remember what Ricky had taught her about mental control, about focusing. This guy wanted her to react. He wanted to weaken her. She could not give him that. She would not. For all she knew, he was lying. She straightened herself out and forced herself to face him.

"That's enough," Greene bellowed. "I told you to get out. I've had it with your philosophy. I'm here for one reason—to make money, and I can't tell you how happy I am that we will be going our separate ways. If I'd known what a lunatic you were all those years ago, I never would have agreed to this.

"And this mess—you should have just had your men run her down when they had the chance. I gave you an untraceable car. You obviously didn't succeed in scaring her into giving him up. You just gave her more time to do more damage. If you'd have killed her then, your missing guy would have eventually gone to the police, and you'd have him by now. Your incompetence baffles me."

A deep red hue started at Eckhart's neckline and crept into his face. He pulled back from Lisa and spat on the floor near Greene's feet. Greene did not even flinch. He simply rolled his eyes and walked away, leaving Lisa with the man he'd just called a lunatic. Lisa wanted to know more about Dorothy and Saul. She wanted assurances they were still alive, assurances she knew he would not give her. She had to believe they were alive, or she would crumble. She had to block his words from her mind.

Lisa concentrated instead on the present and on her surroundings. The tall man got behind her and gave her a push toward his boss, who led the way through the false door and down the hidden stairs. So this was how they came and went without the FBI's knowledge when they needed to be especially careful, how the sweatshop guards came and went. The chop shop could maintain a legitimate appearance on the one block, sending shipments for both businesses out the front door. They could even take sweatshop guards in and out in their vehicles. But the chop shop could receive stolen vehicles through the building in the back, a building that did not even appear to be connected. Did Agent Flannigan know about this? Was he watching? Did he know she was here? She doubted it. She had stolen glances at their monitors when she was inside the bakery. She had not seen the driveway or the garage doors to the second auto shop. Just the exterior of the main building.

As they walked slowly down the stairs, a wretched odor rose to greet them. How could they stand it? It was a mix of sweat, urine and mold. The air felt ancient and dense. When they reached the bottom, Lisa stopped, terrified of going any farther. The tall man shoved her again and she stumbled forward, almost crashing into Eckhart. Now she could fake it. She favored her left foot and limped slightly as if she had just twisted the right. It still hurt, but the pain was more bearable. They walked about twenty more feet through a hall lit by uncovered light bulbs that dangled from wires above until they reached a door. Lisa could hear people moving about beyond the wood barriers. Someone was shouting orders. She heard scraping along the floor, like furniture being moved about.

When Eckhart finally unlocked the door, Lisa threw her hands over her mouth and nose. It smelled like death, and the people she saw looked like they were headed there. At least twenty people, as many men as women, were loading a variety of materials into boxes along with thread, needles, zippers, scissors—all kinds of sewing necessities. More than a dozen aging sewing machines filled the center of the room with narrow paths around and between them. None of the workers were white or even light skinned. They were mostly Black, but also Hispanic and Asian, as far as Lisa could tell with such a quick look. Like Saul, they were walking ghosts, their bodies void of any fat and their eyes sunken into their faces. A few looked up when Lisa came in, but they showed no reaction. They simply went back to work. Lisa scanned the faces—some with purple swollen lumps and scars—knowing it would be nearly impossible to pick out Chandra. It'd been seven years and she was still practically a child when she was kidnapped.

Under normal circumstances, her looks would have changed some. But under these circumstances, she was probably unrecognizable.

She was about to give up, unable to take in their suffering any longer, when a woman looked up whose eyes seemed to plead with Lisa. It was her, definitely her. Before they could communicate even nonverbally, another black-shirted man knocked Chandra's head with his palm and ordered her back to work. She obeyed.

Lisa didn't believe in telepathy, but she was willing to try anything. She closed her own eyes and concentrated on the woman's eyes. They're coming, she thought, as loudly and as strongly as she dared. They are coming and they will save you. Don't give up hope. Fight with me, she thought, forcing herself to believe it was true. She opened her eyes when she felt another push from behind, afraid she'd accidentally spoken aloud. But nothing had changed. Lisa stared at Chandra as long as she could until finally, Chandra lifted her face again, and Lisa saw what she swore was a slight smile.

Chapter Twenty-Nine

They moved more deeply into the sewing room. The tall man held the gun against Lisa's spine as they watched Eckhart survey the progress. A spool of white thread fell to the floor a few feet away, and it seemed everyone suddenly grew even more silent than before. The prisoners continued working, but the fear they carried had clearly become heavier. They worked more cautiously with sideways glances and arms raised just slightly toward their faces when possible. Eckhart walked over to the man who had lost the spool from his box and ordered him to pick it up. As the man started to retrieve it, Eckhart punched him hard in the stomach. The man dropped his load and tried to silence a moan. He clenched his abdomen with one hand while he grabbed the thread with the other and tossed it into the overloaded box. He immediately picked up the cardboard carton and continued working.

"That ought to help him bend over faster," Eckhart said with a laugh as he walked back toward Lisa. Lisa felt sick. She wanted to help the man, who was still obviously trying to conceal his pain, and it took everything out of her not to run to him. She had to keep reminding herself of the gun at her back.

"You don't approve?" Eckhart asked. "Too bad, because you could be such a help as a journalist. You could make people understand. Spread the word, you know? You see, Ms. Jamison, that's how you have to treat these creatures. They don't understand simple directions and they're lazy by nature. You have to break them, just like you break a horse or a dog. You have to bring them under control and make them obedient. That's why our economy is going downhill, because some idiots decided Blacks should be free. Then they let the Hispanics and the Asians and all those other breeds run lose around the country, mating with whites and diluting our genes. They weren't meant to live untamed. They need us to guide them."

He smiled.

She needed to keep him talking, to buy time.

"Those other women—the two women in the truck—are white, not Black, Hispanic or Asian. How do you explain them? How do they fit into this sick world of yours? I want to understand." There were worse fates for women than sweatshops. Lisa didn't want to think about where they might be headed or what might happen to them.

"Oh, but they're not mine. The other sweatshop owners, they're just after the money. Shallow people, really. They bring people in from all over the world, luring them with lies about nanny jobs or waitress work or factory jobs that pay more in a week than they could earn in a lifetime in their countries. Those poor people fly into Canada with fake passports, happy as tourists and all expenses paid, until they get cuffed and shoved in a van. Rude awakening, but that's what ignorance gets you. They're trouble, though. Too feisty. Not worth it. They were not born to be slaves, not like these workers," he said, gesturing toward Chandra and the others with a sweep of his arm.

"Someone has to rebel. Someone has to undo the world's mistakes. If I can do this, if I can make enough money to be an influence, I can change things. The government just makes it so hard. They call it kidnapping. They call it imprisonment, and torture, and abuse, and whatever. But then again, parents are arrested for whipping their own children these days. Dog owners face jail if they leave their animals out in the cold. And you can't even look at a woman without inspiring a lawsuit. The world, our country especially, has gone crazy. But the climate is changing, the political climate. Our day will come."

His face looked honestly pained, like he really believed in his mission. It took everything out of Lisa to hold herself back, to prevent herself from using a few of those moves Ricky had taught her. Instead, she willed herself to calm down, to treat this like an interview. She needed to disassociate. She didn't have to like her subject or agree with him to appear interested.

"Why are there no female guards? Are men the only people who will work with you? How do you even find people who think like you do? If your employees are ever caught, they'll be charged with kidnapping, assault, unlawful imprisonment. And not just one charge each. One each for every person in here and for Saul and for Frank Tomey. Add murder charges for Tomey, the man you lynched, and for the pregnant woman, the one you left to die from infection. These men will never get out of prison. How much are you paying them to humor you in this sick game of yours? What do you do when they want to quit? Kill them?"

The hand struck her face so hard and fast, Lisa didn't even feel the pain until seconds after. The entire right side of her face throbbed, but she refused to touch it. Instead, she lifted her eyes and focused on Eckhart, daring him to answer. The workers didn't miss a beat. The rhythm and flow of their sewing continued despite the scene she was creating. Beside her, the man who had been punched was already back in his chair behind his machine, pushing fabric through it like nothing had happened.

"These men work for me because they believe in the cause. Some of them might enjoy the violence more than others, and I do pay them well, but what does it matter? Every nation has people with different motivations. What matters is that we all work toward the same goal. And women? They are like you. Weak. Untrustworthy. My boss doesn't get it. He's making me move out, clean the place up and go elsewhere, all because I lost one piece of property. He said I make Mr. Greene nervous and that the chop shop brings in steady money with less risk. This is no Aryan Nation, he says. Well, I'm not stupid. He's going to move me out of here, get me to clean it all up and then kill me. Let someone else take over. So we're not going there. I found my own place in New York City. The guys and I are going into business for ourselves. We're going to expand our model and, someday, show the world how it's done."

Eckhart moved nearer to Lisa, once again bringing his face too close to hers. He traced her injured cheekbone with his finger as he spoke. "Too bad you're not one of them. If you were, you could be broken, and I could let you live. It's a shame to kill you, really. You're strong, you're healthy and—"

Lisa slapped his hand away from her face. This was too much. "Saul is not broken. You never broke him. He's no animal and neither are the rest of these people. Did you hear me? I said 'people.' You are evil. Sick and evil. You are insane. Not even criminals want you working with them."

She'd blown it and she knew it.

The tall man pushed the gun's barrel even harder into her back, making her wince with pain, but Eckhart just laughed again. Harder this time.

"Not broken? He's dead. I would have preferred to bring him back here, to make an example of him, but you made that difficult. He wouldn't have gotten away without you. These creatures are not intelligent enough to do that kind of thing on their own. But he was very good. We'll miss him. I'll have to find a replacement and that will cost me a lot. I'm not happy. But I've got you now and this little mess is nearly cleaned up. You'll forgive me, I hope, for what we're going to do to you, but I have to know whether you've told anyone else. So I'm afraid it won't be an easy death. You might have to beg for it."

She would not show him fear. She could not. Just minutes ago, when they were upstairs, he told her his employees were "taking care of" Saul and Dorothy at that moment. That meant he hadn't heard back yet, that there was still hope. Fred was still free and so was Toren. Those were the things she needed to focus on. She needed to concentrate on staying alive, just for a while, for just long enough. Long enough to use her gun and get help. He was wrong about Saul. Saul could have done this without her. He escaped. He found Lisa. He convinced her not to call the police. He stayed to help the others when he could have run and saved himself. If Lisa had not helped him, he would have found another way. Lisa slowed her breathing—four seconds in, eight seconds out; four seconds in, eight seconds out—and tried to think. She would have to stall somehow, buy even more time.

"Now come with me," Eckhart said, leading the way to a partially opened door toward the back of the room. The tall man prodded her forward and Eckhart moved aside, allowing Lisa to enter first. Despite her efforts, Lisa's heart quickened, and her legs nearly gave out. She felt the room suffocating her as the tall man shoved her in. Slumped in a corner with one hand chained to the wall was Toren, his face so swollen and bloody he was barely recognizable. One eye was swollen shut and the other stared off in another direction. He was naked except for his boxer shorts and his body was covered with welts and bruises.

"Your friend here was kind enough to tell us where to find Saul." Eckhart had followed her into the room. "He wasn't so sure about you, though. Apparently, you are on the go quite a lot. You've saved him more suffering by showing up. Now we can just kill him. We're not quite ready yet though, because they make a real mess when you kill them, you know, even when you do it neatly. Void themselves and all. We don't have time for that at the moment, so he gets to watch you suffer for a while first."

He turned to the tall man. "Nate, chain her up there right next to her ex-boyfriend. Don't they look cute together? Too bad they broke up, huh? Oh, you should have seen him, Lisa. He was so good about writing notes to leave behind and giving us his keys. We didn't even have to hotwire his car. I think he really believed we would let him go eventually."

Nate said nothing and his face showed no emotion. He scared Lisa more than Eckhart, the way he looked at him. The way he obeyed him without question. It was clear that Nate was a believer and a follower. How did Eckhart find people like this, people who bought into his philosophy, did his dirty work and were willing to keep his secrets for all these years, people who were willing to spend their lives in prison if it all went wrong? He said he paid them well. Lisa couldn't help hoping most were after the money. The alternative was too sickening.

Lisa had no more time to think. Nate gave his boss his gun, yanked her by both arms and dragged her to the corner. The back of Lisa's head smacked the wall when he shoved her down onto the concrete floor. Before she could recover, he grabbed her left arm and snapped a metal cuff around her wrist. Lisa pulled. The metal cut into her skin and bruised her wrist bones. She was stuck. There was no way out, she thought, looking around the windowless room. This must be the room where they punished the workers. On the wall opposite her whips of different lengths hung below shelves of weapons that seemed to come from the Middle Ages. She was losing hope again. She looked down. Thank god she'd gotten rid of her holster. Her jeans had ridden up slightly, revealing the skin just above her boot line. But the gun was still there, tucked in tightly and covered by her sock. She moved her leg carefully, trying to change the angle so they couldn't see down into the boot. Her right hand was free. She could grab the pistol and shoot them both. But what good would it do? The others would just come running. Still, if her life was going to end, better to end Eckhart's life, too. But guys like Eckhart liked to brag. If she could just get him talking more, maybe he'd keep going. Maybe she could buy another ten or fifteen minutes, and that might just be enough. Maybe the FBI was watching the back entrance after all.

"Tell me one thing. How does Oakwood fit into all this, and Earl Weinstock? Why do you need him?" she asked, struggling to keep the fear and adrenaline out of her voice. "I don't get it. He doesn't seem very bright and he's a hothead. Why would you involve him in a sophisticated operation like this?"

Eckhart had been standing a few feet away from her, leaning against that awful wall, talking to Nate. He raised his eyebrows when Lisa spoke and crossed his arms over his chest. He was getting comfortable, Lisa thought. That was good.

"Very perceptive," he said. "No, he wasn't very bright, but he was useful. I'm surprised you haven't figured it out since, according to Earl, you linked him to our operation through the police report on our runaway. It's simple really. Earl Weinstock liked money. It didn't take long to figure that out about him. So we came up with an arrangement. We dropped the word 'Oakwood' now and then to our slaves, just often enough to make them believe Oakwood is the name of the building or the location where they are being held. Then, if they escape and go to the police, how do you think that sounds? It worked perfectly in the case of Frank Tomey. There he was at the police station—a disoriented Black man babbling about being enslaved, whipped and tortured. When they asked where this took place, where he had escaped from, he told them he'd been held at Oakwood. Who gets the call when police find an escapee from the psychiatric hospital? Earl Weinstock, head of security. Per our arrangement, Earl ensured that the police called him and only him when escapees were located. He had a special cell phone for such circumstances and that's the number he gave police. It was almost too easy. They handed Frank Tomey right over to him, no questions asked. All we had to do was send two of our guys down in white coats, carrying restraints."

"You keep referring to Earl Weinstock in the past tense," Lisa said. She didn't really want an explanation, but he was fully engaged with her now. He was feeling clever, enjoying the opportunity to boast.

"You didn't know?" Eckhart laughed. "Poor Earl. After your chat with him, he gave me a call. He said he needed to leave the country and he wanted enough to live on for a decade or so. If he didn't get it, he'd leave the country anyway, but he'd send computer files to the police with evidence, too. Like you said, he wasn't very bright. Nate here stopped by his house with the money and a big bottle of whiskey last night. Sort of a goodbye celebration. He brought him some sleeping pills, too, out of the kindness of his heart, of course. Who can sleep when you are about to flee the country?

"Unfortunately, he forgot to tell Earl that he had mixed the sleeping pills with the whiskey. Nate's a beer man himself, so he didn't have any. After a few drinks, Nate suggested they try the hot tub. He told him he had called a few hookers who were on their way. It's a shame. Nate says Earl slipped slowly down under the water just a few minutes after he'd turned on the jets. He didn't even struggle. A peaceful ending, though, don't you think? It could have been much more painful. We're pretty good at that here."

As he said those last words, Eckhart uncrossed his arms and began fingering some of the items behind him, admiring a bone-handled whip as he let the leather slide between his fingers. Then he turned to Lisa and smiled again. "Wait a minute. Of course you don't know about Earl. I don't believe anyone's found him yet. That's not a story you'll be writing, so you needn't concern yourself any further."

Then he nodded in Nate's direction.

"You had your fun last night, Nate. I think I'll start this one."

Eckhart selected a leather glove that was embedded with metal on the knuckles and started toward Lisa. If she tried to stall again, it would be too obvious. He might wonder what she was waiting for, what she was hiding. Maybe they'd search her for a wire and find the gun. She would have to move quickly, leave fear behind and concentrate just as Ricky had taught her. This was just another round, just a little sparring. She could do this. Just as he bent down and Lisa leaned forward, sliding her free hand toward her boot, a voice from the sewing room called to him.

"Boss, Mr. Greene needs you a minute. He says it's urgent."

Eckhart crouched in front of Lisa, slipped off the glove and dangled it before her. Her hand had not yet reached the gun. She pulled herself back and glanced at her boot. It was still hidden under the sock. "I'll be back shortly. I'd ask you first who you've told and give you a chance to avoid the pain, but I know you'd just lie. I don't have time to waste, so we'll be starting with a good beating and moving on from there."

The calm Lisa had achieved seconds ago was gone. Her heart made up for it, racing so hard she felt her chest was going to break. Eckhart followed Nate out of the room, and she heard him holler at the other guards to start moving boxes up the stairs and into the truck with the supplies. Saul had said they worked in shifts of two, but it seemed like all of them were here now, overseeing the move to the new location and preparing to dispose of two bodies.

"Tonight," Eckhart said. "I want to be out of here tonight. No excuses."

She didn't speak until she heard him stomping on the stairs and his voice fading away. When she could finally breathe again, she turned to Toren, whose shoulder almost touched hers. "Toren. Can you hear me? My god. Toren, please say something. Move something. Show me you know I'm here. I am so, so sorry. So very, very sorry."

Lisa lifted her right hand and gently touched his lips, which were split in several spots and bleeding. She fought back her tears, fearing Eckhart or one of his men would see them and take advantage of her show of weakness. Toren's chest rose and fell rapidly and ever so slightly. Each breath seemed to take all his strength and he was clearly in pain. Broken ribs, she guessed, hoping no bone had pierced a lung or a vital organ. How long had he been

175

here? How much had he suffered?

"This is my fault, all my fault. Why did I get you involved? I am so sorry."

Toren slowly turned his face toward her and focused with his one good eye. She had to lean in and still, she could barely understand him as he spoke. His voice was weak and broken. "I betrayed you. I am the sorry one. I just want to die."

"No, Toren. No. You don't want to die. It isn't over. The FBI—they've been watching this place. As long as we're alive, there's always a chance. You can't give up on me, Toren. You can't do that," she said, caressing his bruised cheek. "Please stay with me. Please try. This isn't your fault."

She'd barely gotten the words out when she heard heavy footsteps and voices on the stairs. He was coming. Lisa focused on her breathing again, forcing her heart to slow down, and closed her eyes. She envisioned the gun and her hand pulling it out in just the right way at just the right moment. She would kill Eckhart and maybe Nate. They would all come running, and they would shoot her, but they wouldn't think to kill Toren right away. He was defenseless. She could buy him time, maybe enough for the police to come. Maybe she could at least save his life.

Chapter Thirty

Dorothy planted her feet more stubbornly as the gunman shoved a second time. She tumbled to the floor, catching herself with her hands. Without a word, the man yanked her by the arm, and she experienced his strength as that single movement lifted her from the tile. But the tumble had given her a moment to think, just a few extra seconds to observe. Along with the blood on the floor, Dorothy noticed black marks—the kind shoes would leave—leading in the same direction. Saul had been wearing flip-flops. They hadn't been able to buy him shoes yet. He wasn't the one who was dragged. Just then, Dorothy heard a loud pop from the great room, and then a closer and louder pop that brought with it a burning sensation in her left side. She turned to see the gunman's body twist as he crashed to the floor, revealing Saul, who stood in the great room with a gun—Dorothy's gun—at his side.

Months or even years later, Dorothy still could not explain or understand what prompted her to reach down, despite her pain, and wrench the gunman's pistol from his hand. But she did. Before she and Saul could even speak, the door to her quarters snapped open and bullets flew past Dorothy's ear. She fired instinctively, remembering her technique and her form. In her mind, she was in the field far behind the retreat, firing at a target tacked to a bale of hay. She focused on the yellow circle in the center and pulled the trigger. Instantly, the other gun grew quiet, and the second attacker collapsed, his blood filling the grout in the tile and slowly making its way toward Dorothy across the kitchen floor.

Saul started toward Dorothy, but she motioned for him to stop. They didn't know for certain whether there were more. They needed somewhere safe to hide. Dorothy tucked the gun into her waistband, walked carefully across the tile and grabbed two dishcloths from a drawer near the sink. She pressed one against her nose and the other against the wound in her side. There was no point in hiding if she left a blood trail leading the way. Then she stood by the portable phone, whispering to Saul that he should take it. When Saul had the phone in hand, Dorothy headed toward one of the guest bathrooms, indicating that Saul should follow. This particular bathroom had no window and was large enough to have been a small bedroom. Once inside, Dorothy locked the door and she and Saul moved around the corner from it in case anyone decided to shoot through the wood. Only then did Dorothy drop the soaked cloths, dial 911 and examine the wound in her side. It was not terribly deep, but it was bleeding badly. She had the gun in her hand again now and she didn't dare let go of the trigger long enough to press another towel against it.

Dorothy and Saul said nothing while they waited. They simply pressed their bodies against the wall and focused on breathing and listening while keeping their guns trained at the door. Dorothy concentrated on lowering her heartrate and decreasing the flow of her blood. If someone did attack, she had to be strong enough to react. She wasn't generally a religious person, but she found herself praying Bridget would not come home early and that no guests would arrive before their time. She also thanked God for sparing her right side, which included the hand she favored when she painted. But when the sirens came and they heard the sliding of tires on gravel and the screeching of brakes, Dorothy finally lowered her gun and asked Saul what had happened.

Saul had clearly been elsewhere in his mind, and it took him a moment to awaken. His body began to shake slightly as he became more aware of his surroundings, and Dorothy wished she could offer a blanket to warm him. She couldn't even begin to imagine the fear he had lived with every day and every night for an entire decade. With his own gun still aimed at the door, Saul reached for a hand towel from the rack near the sink with his free hand and gave it to Dorothy, who applied it to her side.

"When you live like I did," Saul said, "your senses develop differently. You always knew when they were coming. You could tell who it was, even in the dark, by the weight of their steps and by their individual smells. He came through your quarters, but I smelled him, I felt him as soon as he entered the house. I could see him in my memory, and I almost forgot. I almost put my hands up to protect my face because that was all I could ever do. But then I saw the batter and I remembered. I remembered that I was free and that I had options. I had the advantage because he didn't know that I was aware of him."

Saul paused and took a long deep breath. He pulled his shoulders back and smiled.

"I felt strong, Dorothy. For the first time in more than ten years, I felt strong. I grabbed the frying pan, that heavy cast-iron one, and stood to the side. Then I whacked him in the back of his head when he came through the door. I dragged him into your living room and ran outside to see whether there were others. I thought he was unconscious or dead. I never would have left him if I'd thought he would move."

Dorothy heard shouts from outside—a sheriff's deputy, most likely—yelling through a bullhorn. Then she heard footsteps on the porch and the crack of wood slamming against wood, like someone had swung the front door open hard. People started to move about the house in heavy boots, slowly at first, and then faster.

"I came from the porch in case others were out front. I ripped a window screen, opened the window and climbed through it into the great room. I saw his gun aimed at you, but I figured I didn't have a choice. If I didn't shoot, he would kill you anyway. If I shot right away, I thought maybe we'd both have a chance. He must have had his finger on the trigger and gotten a shot out before he went down. I am so sorry, Dorothy. After all you've done for me. Your nose, your side...you don't deserve this."

Dorothy reached for Saul's hand and squeezed it tightly. The footsteps were getting louder and there were more of them. The deputies were all over the house now, scattering throughout the main rooms and the upstairs. Dorothy heard one deputy shout to another that they'd found two shooting victims and that both were still breathing. Then another deputy yelled that the caller said she was hiding in a bathroom.

"My injuries will heal. We're both safe and alive. That's all that matters. But it's time now to tell the sheriff's deputies your story. You can't hide anymore," she said. "And you don't have to."

She squeezed his hand again, and then yelled through the door.

"We're in here. We're coming out. We have guns. We'll leave them on the floor."

Dorothy slid the gun she'd taken from her attacker across the floor and encouraged Saul to do the same. It was hard for him to let go, she could see that, but he did. Still holding his hand, she opened the bathroom door, stepped out into the hallway and let go of consciousness, collapsing into the arms of a waiting deputy.

Chapter Thirty-One

Eckhart did not come back to Lisa immediately. Something was going on. She could see his profile from where she was chained. His face was the color of a fresh bruise—purple and crimson—and veins bulged from his neck. His fists were clenched. He had stopped in the sewing room and was shouting orders. Louder than before. All boxes that were already packed should be loaded into the truck now, he told the guards.

"Get the second truck ready for the slaves and forget the sewing machines. That bastard upstairs knows we're not going where we're supposed to. He's giving us one hour to get out before he calls the boss. I ought to shoot him dead, but that would only make the boss look harder for us. We have to get out now."

He was gone for what seemed like at least half an hour, giving more orders and running up and down the stairs. Once, she heard shouting from above so loud it traveled through the open door, down the stairs and along the corridor. She prepared herself for gunfire, but it didn't happen. Both men probably knew that was a bad idea. This was not what she had expected. She slipped her fingers into the boot and felt past the sock. The gun was jammed in there hard, and her ankle stung each time she touched it. She would have to take a chance. Slowly, carefully, she pulled the gun out of her boot and slipped it under her thigh, keeping her finger on the trigger. And barely a second later, there he was, standing just outside the doorway.

"No time for you," Eckhart said, turning toward Lisa while he pulled a gun from his waist. "You make no difference anymore. If I'm leaving all this behind, I might as well leave the two of you. Let Greene clean you up. No one will have time to figure out where we're going, no matter what you told them."

Lisa had envisioned the spot on his upper chest to the right where she would have a good chance at an artery and had already mentally practiced the shot several times. As he stepped over the threshold and into the room, she lifted the gun and fired. Then she fired a second time and a third, allowing herself to feel nothing as he stumbled backward and fell. She fired a fourth time when she sensed more movement in the doorway, watching, stunned, as Nate gripped his stomach and buckled over. He still had his gun in his right hand. At the same moment, Lisa heard commotion from the direction of the corridor, lots of commotion. Shouts. Too many voices, far more than the handful of men she had seen. Then she heard heavy boots, a couple pairs, crashing down the stairs, along the loose floorboards, headed her way. She aimed for Nate's head and fired again, but this time, nothing happened. She squeezed the trigger once more. Nothing. Only four shots, and she was out of ammo. She was dead. There was nothing more she could do.

Lisa let her hand drop to the floor and closed her eyes when Nate lifted his face to look at her. She didn't want to see his expression, his pleasure, when he did it. She didn't want to see the others, their faces full of anger and spite. She just wanted it over with. She focused on sending a message to Bridget. She had never believed in such things, but she seemed to have connected with Chandra and now was not a time to be cynical. She needed Bridget to know that she would always be with her, that she had what she needed to thrive and succeed even without her, that she was sorry.

"I love you, Bridget. I love you so much," she said. This time she was certain she said the words aloud. She didn't care.

But instead of a gunshot, Lisa heard a growl—a low, fierce growl—and a scream. She opened her eyes to see a long, muscular German Shepherd with its teeth deep in Nate's arm. Nate screamed again as he dropped the gun and tried to beat off the dog, who only clamped harder, pulling him down to the floor. Within seconds, another man came from behind, grabbed the gun and ordered the dog to release its target. Lisa was overcome with relief. The second man held a rifle high, pointing it at Nate's head. Emblazed across his bulletproof vest was the word "Police." The police had come and, other than a bump on her head and a sore wrist, Lisa was fine. Unscathed. Another S.W.A.T. member came into the room and lowered his gun when he saw Lisa and Toren.

"He has the keys," she said, pointing to Nate. "I think I saw him put them in his t-shirt pocket. Toren needs help first. He's barely hanging on. Please, please, get him out of here. Get him to a hospital."

Lisa watched, still chained and holding her breath, while the officer freed Toren and checked his pulse. Toren seemed so lifeless, so helpless. He had not made a sound since Lisa spoke with him earlier and his chest movements were almost undetectable now. The officer radioed for help and two EMTs came immediately, and that was when Lisa saw it. Toren lifted his left hand just an inch or so and moved his thumb into an upright position. A thumbs-up. He gave Lisa a thumbs-up. Lisa allowed herself to breathe again, but she couldn't smile. Not yet. She had to know about Bridget, Dorothy and Saul.

As soon as he finished helping the EMTs lift Toren, the officer unchained Lisa and helped her to her feet. He tried to examine her, but she broke free from his hold and ran. Lisa heard the sobs but did not bother to take in the scene in the sewing room, where S.W.A.T. team members were comforting men and women who'd probably given up hope years before. She pushed past an investigator and an FBI agent who were coming down the stairs. The FBI agent tried to stop her, but she wrestled her arm free. She flew through the chop shop to the parking lot outside, ignoring the throbbing in her head that worsened with each stride. And there she saw him, talking to Agent Flannigan and Fred, very much alive and well. It was Saul. She scanned the lot, where emergency crews were setting up tents, gurneys and IVs, preparing for the victims to emerge from inside. She counted five ambulances and three rescue vehicles with more on the way, she assumed, from the sounds of the approaching sirens. No Dorothy. No Bridget. She couldn't move, but Saul spotted her and rushed to her.

"Where are Dorothy and Bridget? Tell me they are okay. Please, Saul." Lisa grabbed Saul's arm and looked into his eyes, unwilling to free him from her grip or her stare until she had answers. She expected him to turn away, unable to maintain eye contact while he told her the terrible news. Instead, he smiled.

"Bridget's at the retreat, trying to find temporary rooms for the guests elsewhere and looking for a cleaning company that specializes in blood removal while the sheriff's deputies and the FBI do their investigation. Two guys attacked us—Dorothy and me. Bridget wasn't there and she didn't see anything. Dorothy, that brave and wonderful friend of yours, is in the hospital with a broken nose and a minor gunshot wound. She's going to be fine, but I think she'd appreciate a little help for a few weeks. You should have seen her in action. She was amazing."

Lisa pulled Saul into a hug so tight she feared she might hurt him. When she finally released him, she felt a hand on her shoulder. "Thought you might like to see who is coming out now," Agent Flannigan said.

Fred lifted his camera and start clicking frame after frame. Saul ran toward the fragile figure being helped from the garage and across the driveway by a police officer and a firefighter. He stopped in front of Chandra Bower, took her perfectly oval face into his hands, caressed her cheeks and kissed her—filthy cracked lips, bruises and all. He didn't seem to care, and her entire demeanor visibly lightened. Saul took over for the police officer and Chandra leaned into him, her eyes moist with tears. This was a story Lisa had not anticipated. They were in love, clearly in love. Before she could say or do anything more, Agent Flannigan took Lisa by the elbow and began to lead her to the medical tents.

"We've got more than a few questions for you, but first, you need to be checked out. That's blood I see in your hair and I'm guessing you've got a good-sized lump there. We want to make sure your head's straight before you give a statement."

Lisa started to protest, but then he moved his other hand to the small of her back and she felt her knees give way. Thankfully, she could blame her head injury. He was an FBI agent, she was a journalist, and they were at the scene of a major organized crime bust with several victims. She had just shot and probably killed one man and had definitely injured another, and she didn't have a gun permit. She had to pull herself together, so she tried concentrating on that pain in her head. She absolutely could not get involved with Agent Flannigan, and this was not the time or place to even think about it.

Agent Flannigan left Lisa sitting on the edge of a gurney with an EMT at her side and instructions to stay put unless she needed a trip to the hospital. "And if you end up at the hospital, stay there until we find you."

Then he disappeared into what was becoming a swarm of FBI agents, S.W.A.T. team members and other city police officers. The gurneys were quickly filling up. Police had stretched crime scene tape from one light pole to another, keeping all reporters except Lisa and Fred back. Television news reporters arrived with their satellite trucks and Lisa recognized another photographer and reporter from her own newspaper. Then Lisa saw two more familiar faces that made her smile: Mr. and Mrs. Bower.

The couple ducked under the tape escorted by a city police officer and ran to their daughter, almost falling on her. Mrs. Bower moaned loudly and long, covering her daughter's face with kisses and nearly lifting her off the gurney. Mr. Bower sobbed uncontrollably and nestled his head into their daughter's stomach. And then Lisa's own eyes welled up. Seven years. For seven long years, they had held onto the belief that their daughter was alive, when so many others were urging them to accept closure, to hold a memorial service, to bury her in spirit. They never gave up hope. Never. Somehow, they knew she was alive.

Lisa obeyed the EMT who encouraged her to lie down and looked up at the tent ceiling. All these people, seeing sunshine, daylight and open skies for the first time in so many years. Who knew how long it had been for some of them? Many came out with hands covering their eyes. It must have been too painful. How would they adjust? Would their families welcome them back? Lisa had always considered herself enlightened in terms of racial relations. She had thought the world was becoming a better place with fewer and fewer instances of discrimination with each year that passed, despite the recent uptick in racial incidents. But who was she fooling? She understood nothing.

"Animals," he had called them. Animals who needed to be broken and trained. It would be easy to say this was the work of a singular sick man, but the "masters" had concurred with him, and several others had simply let it happen. Maybe they did it for money. Maybe they would have been equally ruthless if they had worked for an owner with white slaves, but maybe not. It was possible they bought into Eckhart's philosophy and were attracted by it. Regardless, they were complicit, just like so many others had been over the centuries, during Black slavery, during the Nazi regime, during recent protests over the treatment of Black people by police. Lisa doubted there would ever come a day in the United States, in the world, when we could just relax and say, "we're done." The power that comes with oppression is too tempting. The weight of history is too heavy.

But then she saw Saul again. This time, he was embracing Chandra's parents and they held him just as tightly. She remembered the day she'd first seen him. A dead man, she'd thought at first glance. No muscle, no energy, no life. But she was mistaken. There was life in him, and plenty of it. Eckhart, Nate and the rest thought they had snuffed that out of him. They thought they had taken from him all that had made him human. They couldn't. The will to live—the will to think and breathe freely, the humanity in him—was too strong. Saul and the rest of these people had not become what Peter Eckhart had tried to make them, nor had Lisa saved Saul, as Eckhart had proclaimed. Saul saved himself and the others. Even in the state he was in, he knew how to hide, when to come out and whom to trust. He came to Lisa. She didn't find him.

Part of her wanted to go see Mr. and Mrs. Bower, to celebrate with them. But there would be plenty of time for that later and they deserved to be alone with their daughter. Right now, they seemed unable to take their eyes off Chandra, and Lisa had the overwhelming urge to hold Bridget. She asked for a cell phone and called the retreat. When Bridget answered, Lisa could not speak. Her voice was weakened by tears and Bridget, too, could not get past "Hello." They laughed and they cried, and they laughed some more until the EMT said it was time to go. Two hits to the head in a week required a scan and maybe some observation, he said. She managed to tell Bridget she would be there as soon as she could, and then she returned the phone to the medic.

As the EMT walked Lisa to a waiting ambulance, she saw a line of parked squad cars and investigators' sedans, all with men in their backseats. They put only one man in each car, a smart move, Lisa thought. Greene was in the vehicle closest to her. Though the windows were closed, she could see he was shouting, demanding to be heard by the investigator at the wheel. She couldn't help hoping that the prosecutors, the judges and the guards in the prisons that held these men, that none of them would be white.

Lisa climbed onto a bench in the ambulance, which she shared with one of the victims, who was lying on a gurney with an IV in the top of his hand and his eyes closed. As dehydrated as they were, the paramedic probably couldn't find a good vein elsewhere, she thought. She couldn't even imagine how good those fresh, clean sheets and the softness of the gurney padding must have felt to him. This man looked much like Saul had when she first encountered him: relieved and relaxed and on edge all at the same time. Lisa reached over and placed a comforting hand on his arm. Then she closed her eyes, grateful this was over and anxious to go home.

Chapter Thirty-Two

Lisa was appreciative of the doctor's concerns, but she had a story to write. So they struck a deal. She could conduct interviews, make phone calls, do whatever she needed to do, as long as she stayed within the confines of the emergency department for four hours. She had to check in with the nurse every half hour to be examined for signs of concussion. If all was well, she would be released. That was eight hours ago. She'd been too busy to leave.

Fred had brought her a newspaper cell phone since hers was destroyed in the chop shop. He also gave her cash, a voice recorder, a couple notebooks and some pens. Everyone she needed to see was here—Dorothy, Toren, the investigators, the victims, Chandra's parents. Only those who were arrested and the two women who had been in the truck were not present. The women were examined at the hospital and then taken to FBI headquarters, where an interpreter would help them give statements. Some of those arrested were taken directly to FBI headquarters. Others—the two men who had attacked Dorothy and Saul, and Nate, the man Lisa had shot—were in another emergency room far away from their victims. Eckhart was at the morgue. Lisa had killed him. It still hadn't sunk in.

No one asked for a pistol permit during her interview with the FBI agents, so Lisa was anxious to finish tomorrow's story before they remembered. So many things had come together at once to save Lisa, Toren, Chandra and the others, she learned. Robert Burke, the lawyer who had tried to set her up, broke a short-lived silence after his arrest and told the FBI everything. Lisa had been wrong. The two stories were related. Robert was known in criminal circles for both his legal and accounting expertise. He had been contacted a few months ago by Greene, who had set up a meeting at the restoration shop with himself, Eckhart and a woman who represented their boss.

The trio offered Robert a hundred thousand to frame the head of the IDA and Bert Trammel in hopes of derailing the project, more than he'd make in a year as a junior partner in the law firm. They figured if this project went south, no one would consider developing the area again for a long time. Robert hadn't asked what types of business he was protecting, but Eckhart couldn't keep his mouth shut. He walked Robert out after the meeting and espoused his business plan and philosophy.

"The meeting took place before we started surveillance. Otherwise, we might have put two and two together sooner," Agent Flannigan told Lisa. "Apparently, Mr. Burke had been assigned a large mall project in the Adirondacks that failed, and he was bumped back down the ladder. He wasn't too happy about it, and he was more than thrilled to potentially send Bert Trammel to prison. Then you blew it for him. Without your cooperation, there was no hope of money or revenge."

The series of the day's events, the way they came together so perfectly, was too unbelievable for Lisa to comprehend and horribly confusing. Lisa found herself drawing diagrams in her notebook as she spoke with Agent Flannigan over coffee in the hospital cafeteria, trying to figure out exactly what happened when and who was involved. For the story that appeared in the newspaper the next day, she developed a timeline with the help of the graphics department.

"Here's what happened," Agent Flannigan said. One of the agents who had been interviewing Robert Burke called Agent Flannigan to let him know a sweatshop was operating in conjunction with the chop shop that was already under surveillance. About the same time, Fred came bursting into the bakery asking for help. He said Lisa had been following a supply truck trying to locate a sweatshop in the neighborhood and hadn't been heard from since. He also told them she had been threatened previously.

"Fred said he went looking for your car in Iron City Heights after he got your message, figuring you would pull over somewhere when you reached the truck's final destination. Then he saw your car go by with a man behind the wheel and no passenger. He followed it until it turned the corner onto the street behind the chop shop, but he had to hang back a bit so he wouldn't be noticed. When he finally turned the corner, it was gone, but he could see a slight bit of movement as the garage doors closed. Then he saw the dumpsters in the alley and the broken storm drain in the street that Saul had described to you. When he checked out the alley, he found a freshly boarded-up basement window. We checked with the florist, and you hadn't returned there. You're lucky he acted so quickly. He could have waited for you to call back, looked for you further and gotten caught himself—anything could have happened. I feel terrible, Lisa. We heard them bring your car in through the back, but we thought it was the Volvo. Our shop in Vermont was told to expect shipment this weekend. We have cameras back there, but our feeds weren't clear enough. We could see it wasn't a Volvo, but we couldn't read the plate. We knew there was a problem with the feed yesterday, but we couldn't get anyone back there fast enough. We thought we were dealing with criminals, not killers."

While Fred was filling in Agent Flannigan and his partner, the county sheriff was on the phone with the local head of the FBI and the city police chief to tell them about the shootings at Dorothy's retreat and about Saul's claims that he'd been forced to do slave labor for a sweatshop in Iron City Heights. Saul had insisted on talking to the sheriff immediately and on going with the police to Iron City Heights. Agent Flannigan interrupted that phone meeting with an urgent phone call, telling his boss about the information from Fred and requesting permission to act. For the FBI, the fact that these people had tried to kill Dorothy and Saul confirmed Fred's fear that Lisa was in immediate danger, and so they decided to move.

The FBI quickly came together with the city's S.W.A.T. team. They grilled Saul about the layout of the basement. The man Dorothy shot had regained consciousness and told them about the false door, the hidden garage and the passageway in hopes that his cooperation would lead to a lighter sentence. Agent Flannigan indicated the man might have been further motivated by the fact that one of the agents had taken control of his morphine pump.

"We had to get the information quickly," he said. "You do what you have to do. While that was going on, we picked up an argument between Greene and Eckhart. We were never able to bug that place, but we have long-range microphones, and they were shouting loud enough. Greene gave him one hour to get out, so we knew we had to act fast. Less than an hour had passed from the moment Saul spoke with the sheriff's deputies until we moved in on the sweatshop. It was pretty amazing."

Agent Flannigan said everyone was excited about the leads they'd gained from the Russian women and the truck. The men who had transported them still had their cell phones, which held phone numbers for their contacts at the New Jersey sweatshop and the offices of the organization's bosses, a couple in Colorado. They also still had the women's fake passports, which they were supposed to dispose of once they delivered the women to their owners. From what little they'd gathered so far with the help of the interpreter, both women were from a part of Russia with few jobs, high rates of alcoholism and intense poverty. They were promised cleaning jobs at a Florida resort, where they would have free rooms and be allowed to enjoy the amenities during their spare time. They thought they were doing the right thing for their families.

The FBI also arrested Rousseau when he walked across the border onto his American property. Canadian police found all kinds of contraband stored in his Canadian house—a dresser full of marijuana, a kitchen cupboard loaded with prescription drugs, cocaine stuffed in the sink drains. Investigators were still searching the homes on both sides of the border. He had a complex operation going that involved picking up goods with groceries, from bakeries in cake boxes, from hardware stores crammed into shells of lawnmowers, power washers and generators. Some clients pretended to be friends visiting and brought goods over multiple visits by car. He feared trucks would raise suspicions, so he generally didn't allow them. Then they had to pick up the goods from the U.S. side using vehicles with New York plates, preferably cars or SUVS. Eckhart had to pay extra when his organization needed a truck because of the risk to Rousseau. A great deal more. Rousseau had bought the American land under the name of a man who died in the fifties.

"There's more, Lisa, but this part is off the record," Agent Flannigan said, leaning in more closely as he lowered his voice. "Are we clear? If the information I'm about to give you gets out, it could put the investigation and a whole lot of lives at risk."

Lisa agreed.

"We already have warrants for taps on all the phones and one of the guys from the truck is talking. He's giving us locations of sweatshops in hopes that he'll get a better deal. He might, but first we need to know more about his involvement and his criminal history. This goes far beyond the FBI, Lisa. These guys have slave suppliers all over the world. They make a fortune selling human beings to sweatshops and brothels, to wealthy families as servants, and the victims are not all adults. A lot of them are children. Kids as young as nine or ten. People believe slavery is dead, but it's not true. There are more slaves now than at any other point in recorded history, but it's concealed better than it used to be. It's all in the shadows and as long as it is, the politicians can pretend it doesn't exist."

Agent Flannigan fell back into his chair. He looked tired, worn.

"It makes me sick, Lisa. It really does."

Lisa made a mental note to investigate his claims. The information was off the record, but she could always try to put the sweatshop and the plight of the two women from the truck into perspective by looking at the information already out there. Statistics, previous busts. That kind of thing. She made him promise to let her know if there were any more arrests related to the Iron City Heights sweatshop, chop shop or the two women.

"You know I will, Lisa," he said. "We owe you that much."

Less than four hours had passed from the time Lisa was kidnapped until she was freed during the raid, and in that time, all those dominos fell perfectly, cleanly. Lisa was still having trouble taking it all in. There were too many "what ifs." If even one person involved had not acted how and when they did, she would have been dead. Bridget would have been an orphan. The captives might have died, especially if the guards or Greene had been given time to panic after she had started shooting. More than anything, Lisa wanted to see

Bridget right then, but they both had jobs to do. Bridget wanted everything to be in order at the retreat before Dorothy returned, and she understood that Lisa had to finish what she'd started.

"I love you, Mom, but I want to do this," Bridget said over the phone. "I can finally do something for Dorothy, and I want to do it right. She needs me. Ben is helping me out and so is Claire. And you worked hard for this. My god, you risked your life. You at least deserve to write the story. I'll see you tomorrow. I promise."

Dorothy's nose was badly broken, but the hospital called in a specialist to reset it. She was still in surgery. The bullet that tore through her side had not hit any major organs. She needed plenty of stiches, but she was strong enough for the OR, the doctor said. Toren suffered broken ribs, a cracked cheekbone, a broken leg, a concussion and internal bruising. He would be in the hospital for several days while doctors watched over the bruising to ensure nothing turned into a bleed and for observation of the head injury. Some of his wounds had also become infected, but the infections had not spread into his bloodstream.

Fred was at FBI headquarters trying to get names and backgrounds for all the suspects. The FBI had given Lisa a list of all the victims and the communities they were abducted from. With the help of city police, they were trying to contact family members, but they saw value in the newspaper publishing the list, which would hopefully be picked up by the Associated Press and published online and in some of the victims' hometowns. All the victims would recover physically, but Agent Flannigan said he doubted any of them would ever be what we would call "normal" again. They would likely all suffer from some form of post-traumatic stress syndrome.

"None of them saw it coming," he said. "One day, they were living normal lives, going through their daily routines, and the next day, they were living in a squalid basement, forced to work eighteen hours a day, fed next to nothing and beaten almost daily with no hope of seeing their families or sunlight ever again. I don't know how you recover from that."

Still, Agent Flannigan said, he was amazed by their resilience.

"There's fire in every single one of them. They all insisted on walking out even if they needed support on both sides. They've all been asking about each other, concerned more for the health of their fellow victims than for themselves. They bonded in there when they could have just given up. They all said there were opportunities to end it, but they couldn't do it. They couldn't let go of that hope that one day they'd be free."

Lisa had gotten the same impression from the victims she'd interviewed. One woman had been kidnapped twelve years ago when her children were just four and seven years old. City police had reached her family in Florida. Her husband had remarried, believing she was dead or gone for good, and the children were teenagers now. She expressed no anger at her husband, only relief that nothing had happened to him and that her children had been raised in a good home with two parents who loved them. Her oldest, her son, was going to the University of Maryland in the fall.

"So many times, they told me they were going to kill my husband and leave the kids on the street. Sometimes, they'd describe the kids, telling me they'd sold them drugs or offered them small illegal jobs, and that if I didn't behave, they'd frame them and get them sent to juvie. They were just babies when I was taken, but I knew them, you know? I knew my kids down to their souls. They weren't like that, and I couldn't make myself believe it. And now I find out my oldest is going to college, studying computers. My boy is okay. My daughter, too. Can you imagine how it feels to know that? To know they are okay?"

Another man was about to lose a foot. It was still attached to his leg when he was freed, but it was fractured in several places and had gangrene caused by lack of blood flow to the tissues. His toes were black, almost mummified. There was no possibility that his foot could be saved. They took him immediately into surgery, but Lisa had the chance to speak with him beforehand. He had asked for her, just in case he didn't make it through, he said. He was seventeen when he was abducted.

"I just want my parents and my little sister to know they got me through this. I thought of them every single day, and they kept me alive. I'm sure they thought I ran off, got into drugs or something. I wasn't the best kid. I was failing out of high school and hanging out with a bad crowd, and I don't want them to feel bad for thinking that. That's probably what would have happened to me if these guys hadn't gotten me first. I have a chance now, and if I get through this, if I pull through…well, I can't imagine what I can do. I've been given another chance at life and I'm sure there is a reason."

He paused to rein in the tears.

"He dropped a sewing machine on my foot, you know. The owner. The machine stopped working and one of the guards said it didn't look like it could be fixed. I took something away from him, he said, so he was going to take something away from me, and then he just dropped the whole thing on my foot. I had to go right back to work, sewing jeans by hand. The others helped me out. They sewed faster than ever and sneaked pairs into my pile. We all got in trouble for it. They were producing too little and, even with their help, so was I. But it's a lot harder to punish a group. Somebody had to work, or the guards and the owner didn't get paid. We knew they couldn't get too brutal. They didn't feed us dinner or breakfast and then, finally, they gave me another machine. These other people, they all took a huge risk for me. They all suffered, just for me. I owe them my life."

Chandra's parents had taken her home. The hospital wanted to keep her overnight, but they arranged for a private nurse and promised to bring her to their own doctor for follow-ups. They were afraid to leave her, and everyone seemed to understand that. Saul got her contact information and let his lips linger on her forehead for what seemed like a long time before he let her go. When he turned to face Lisa again, she saw a strange mix of sadness and elation in his expression. He would be with the FBI and sheriff's investigators off and on for several more hours. The sheriff offered to return him to Dorothy's retreat when they were done. He looked at Lisa, who smiled and nodded.

"You take care of Bridget until I get there, will you?" Lisa said.

And then she hugged him long and hard, unafraid this time that he would break. Saul had proven to everyone that he was strong. He was unbreakable inside and out.

Chapter Thirty-Three

Dorothy adjusted her body in the kitchen chair to avoid stretching the side with the stitches. In just a few short days, the stitches would come out, and not too soon after, she would be allowed to remove the metal splint from her nose. Bridget and Ben had done a wonderful job of keeping things running smoothly while she recovered and so had Saul, despite his distractions. Saul had helped cook, served drinks, chatted with curious guests and bowed out of conversations when it was appropriate. He complimented their work but provided constructive criticism that was impressively on point for someone with no art background. He was a natural host, good with people. They all loved him.

So she was surprised by Saul's reaction when she asked him to stay. She had assumed he would remain at the retreat—that he knew he would always be welcome, that Dorothy considered this place his home. But Dorothy had forgotten that despite his outward demeanor, Saul was still insecure and unsure of his place in this new world. He was young when he was kidnapped, and he had next to nothing. He'd lost his family, his girlfriend and his job. He had even less when he escaped. He was having some trouble accepting this thing we call unconditional love.

"I am not offering you a job out of pity or obligation or anything like that, Saul. I need you here," Dorothy said. "We're already booked four months in advance thanks to all the interviews, especially the one where they airbrushed the picture of me shooting at a target and made it look like a bloody canvas on an easel. Now everybody wants to get creative with the gun-slinging artist who runs the retreat and her mysterious chef, who's a pretty good shot himself."

Saul looked up at her across the table where they were having a late dinner, and then he did something Dorothy had never seen him do. He cried. In all this time, throughout the entire ordeal, he'd held back those tears. Now, when all was finally good, he cried, letting his sobs shake his entire body. Dorothy was honored to be the person he let go in front of. He was a good man, and Chandra was a lucky woman. Dorothy could only hope that someday they would both be free enough of the past to live as a couple and start a family, if that was what they wanted. She stood up and took the fleece blanket from the recliner. Then she wrapped it around his shoulders.

"I'll take that as a yes," she said.

This would not be his only job, and he would not likely remain long term. She knew that. A literary agent had contacted Saul with an offer. One of the big publishing houses wanted a memoir, a recounting of his experience in captivity. He was uncertain at first. But he was growing more comfortable telling his story and he had already seen how much it had helped some people, especially those who had missing family members or friends. They found hope in him and the other victims. They found strength.

Saul was still debating whether to accept the book contract when the agent called him back and told him how much the publisher was offering, and that there was already interest in the movie rights. Saul had hoped to get his master's degree when he was younger. That hope remained despite all his lost years, and this money could make that dream a reality. Dorothy knew thoughts of a future with Chandra colored his decision as well.

So he accepted.

"We obviously can't keep sharing my quarters, so I thought I'd convert the guest room on the end of the main hallway into its own little suite with a separate entrance. I'll add a bathroom and a combination kitchen and living room. Will that be enough space for you?"

Saul laughed, the tears finally under control.

"Enough? I shared a single room and an overflowing toilet with twenty smelly bodies for ten years. I think that'll do. I don't know how to thank you, Dorothy, for everything."

"Thank me? You undersell yourself, Saul. Soon this will be the home of the famous author, just when this whole gun-slinging thing has started to fade. Then we'll be booked a year in advance. Plus, with you on board, I'll have more time to paint again. Have I told you the prices people have been offering me? I thought artists only made that kind of money when they were dead."

Saul laughed again and pulled the blanket around his shoulders. Dorothy got up and poured them each a cup of tea. What she didn't tell Saul was that he was growing on her, that she greatly enjoyed his company and that she needed to create separate quarters for him because she might become too dependent on him. It was nice having someone to tend to, to care for, and she'd found that her own dreams about her son had become less severe. When she dreamed of him now, they were pleasant dreams, memories of the good times rather than flashes of those few moments of horror. Saul had done that for her. He had changed her dreams.

In just a few more minutes, they would begin serving drinks in the great room. It was a good crew this week with a good balance of productivity and socializing. The guests would leave here feeling good about the place and that was Dorothy's ultimate goal. If they felt good, they would return. Dorothy usually tried to stay out of sight and out of the conversations. But when they asked her to join them for a drink toward the end of the evening, as they most always did, maybe tonight she would accept.

Chapter Thirty-Four

L isa had been critical when Bridget settled on the small red Toyota pickup truck as a graduation gift from her paternal grandmother. A car seemed like a more practical choice. But now she was grateful, especially for the cap that came with it. Bridget insisted on taking everything with her to Arizona, including all her winter camping gear in case she had the chance to spend time in Flagstaff or the White Mountains. It was a tight squeeze, but everything fit, and there was still plenty of wiggle room in the cab for Lisa and Bridget.

She and Bridget planned to spend a week driving across the country, taking detours along the way to see some of the sights. Lisa would help Bridget settle in at Arizona State University in Tempe, just outside Phoenix, and then she would fly back alone. She dreaded the return trip already. Between the flights and layovers, she would have far too much time to think about the piece of herself she'd left behind. It was harder than ever to believe that she was three years younger than Bridget when she first held Bridget in her arms. Bridget was still a child to Lisa. She guessed she always would be.

"Ben and I are going to run up and say goodbye to Dorothy and Saul," Bridget said, slipping her arm around her boyfriend's waist. "Do you want to come?"

Ben was leaving the next week for Ithaca College. They would be a country's width apart. Bridget had said little when Lisa asked whether she thought it would last. "It is what it is," Bridget said. "We both know we have a lot of changes ahead. We're not putting pressure on ourselves. I mean, I love him, but I really need to do this. I need to figure out what I want to do for the rest of my life before I decide who to spend it with."

Regardless, Ben had been good for her, Lisa thought as she watched Bridget lift her eyes to catch a smile from him. They'd been together more than two years and he'd become as much of a son to her as she'd ever have. She would miss them both. She would miss them together.

"I'm supposed to meet Uncle Lee for lunch," Lisa said. "He's got some new partner or employee he wants me to meet. A total set-up, but he sounded so disappointed when I tried to get out of it. Bring me back some of Saul's banana bread though if he's got any left, and take him the package, will you? It's in the foyer. I wanted to do it myself, but it's not fair to make him wait any longer."

The package had arrived two days before. It was from Saul's former landlord in Cincinnati. He had read about Saul in the *Cincinnati Enquirer*, and he immediately contacted Lisa at the *Sun Times*. Inside the box were all of Saul's legal documents—his birth certificate, Social Security card, high school diploma, college diploma—along with photos of his mother and other personal items. He also threw in a check for Saul's security deposit along with the interest it would have earned. He couldn't bear to take Saul's money after reading about what had happened, he wrote in the accompanying note.

"Will do," Bridget said.

Bridget turned her attention back to Ben, who wrapped his arms around her. Lisa left the couple in the driveway while she went inside to redo her ponytail and maybe apply a little lipstick. Who knew? Maybe this new guy would turn out to be kind of cute. Saul and Chandra were proof that love found us in the strangest of circumstances. It had been only a few weeks since they gained their freedom and Chandra and Saul were just beginning to tackle their psychological traumas, but there was strength in their relationship that seemed to be pulling them through.

Then there was Dorothy and Saul—a different kind of love, but it was definitely love that had grown between them. The tables were turned now. This time, Saul was nursing Dorothy back to health, doing most of the chores around the retreat and all the cooking. It made Lisa feel good to know someone would be up there at the retreat with her throughout her recovery. Lisa worried about Dorothy sometimes, though she supposed she'd proven she was capable of taking care of herself.

Ben and Bridget were pulling out of the driveway in Ben's car when Lisa came back outside. Bridget waved through the open window as they disappeared around the block. Though it was still August, the air was starting to hint at early fall with lower humidity and the earthy aromas of decaying leaves and late summer flowers. The mail carrier had just come through the neighborhood, so Lisa reached into the box and pulled out a few catalogs and envelopes. Among the envelopes was a business-sized one with no return address.

Lisa had just opened it when a car pulled up alongside the curb. It was Toren, his face nearly absent of the bruises and swelling that had covered it just weeks before. Aside from a few traces of yellow and green where the skin was still healing underneath, his face looked just as it had before all this happened. He still had to be careful of his kidney—it had a good-size bruise that would make him vulnerable for a while—but his leg was another matter. His right foot rested on the passenger-side of the car, the length of his leg encased in plaster, while he drove with his left. He'd been through two surgeries, but the doctors told him it would never quite be the same again.

"Hey, lady," Toren said with a smile. "I'm on my way to see a patient on your side of town and I thought I'd swing by and wish you well on your trip. I'd get out, but then I'd have to get back in, and that's not fun with this thing on my leg."

It still pained Lisa to see him, to think of what he went through. He had rejected her sympathy several times over, insisting he was getting more attention from women than ever thanks to his role in all this. The television stations and newspapers had described him as a single doctor, plastering his image all over the news. People couldn't get enough of him. Not only was he considered a hero for risking his life to treat Saul, but with his chiseled looks, he'd become a national heartthrob. His refrigerator quickly filled up with donations of food and bottles of wine. He received letters and cards daily from women asking him out. He'd had to change his phone number because of all the calls he'd received. "And I finally have a story that won't bore my grandchildren." He laughed.

In more serious moods, Toren talked about the captives—the pain and suffering they endured. He couldn't possibly feel sorry for himself when he knew they had not only suffered, but had lost years of their lives, years they could never get back. A local group had formed to raise money for the victims and to provide temporary food and shelter until the police and the FBI were ready to let them go home. Toren was part of that leadership, but he'd taken its mission a few steps further.

When the captives reunited with their families, most were initially welcomed with tears, hugs and joy. But those were extreme overwhelming emotions, born of shock. They overwhelmed reality. Already, many of the former sweatshop workers were finding their return had become a burden to their family and friends. People didn't know how to react to them, how to make room for them in their lives. Toren pulled together psychologists and therapists from all over the country who were willing to meet locally with the families or to provide counseling as best they could over the phone or by Zoom. He created a private online forum for family members and a separate one for the victims themselves. He researched instances of people who had endured similar circumstances and found articles on their recoveries. He put those together in booklets and distributed them to the victims and their families.

He helped find homes for the few who no longer had family here in Seneca Springs, where they could count on the support of Saul, Chandra and dozens upon dozens of other people who wanted to help. Those victims—there were two of them—needed the most help adjusting. They had counted on family or friends still being there when they were freed. That hope had helped them survive captivity. But when they were released, everyone was gone. In one case, a woman's husband and infant daughter had died in a drunk-driving accident. The driver hit them head on when he swerved into their lane on a highway. She had no siblings, her parents were dead and she had not been married to her husband long enough to connect emotionally with his family. They had settled nine hours away from his parents.

In the other case, the man's family simply couldn't offer what he needed. His father had died when he was young, and his mother was in a nursing home. His siblings were struggling financially, and as much as they wanted him home, they couldn't take him in. The advocate group had paid for a trip home to see his family, but then he returned to Seneca Springs, knowing he would find more support here.

"In some ways, people like Saul have it easier," Toren said. "He has no ties to the past. Everything is new. Everything is a discovery. He's not trying to return to anything or recapture anything. Saul is only trying to move forward."

Saul's half-brother wrote him after he read about Saul in the newspapers, but they'd never had much of a relationship before. There were no expectations, except of the possibility they would meet when Saul was feeling stronger physically and mentally. Toren was right. Saul was captured at a time in his life when he had next to nothing, nothing except the most valuable thing: his freedom.

Toren didn't stop with the local victims though. He reached out to victims in the other communities as well—in New York City, New Jersey, Philadelphia, Washington, D.C.—where other sweatshops had been busted, and offered his newfound expertise. In all, the FBI, together with local law enforcement, had freed three hundred and thirty-nine slaves who all worked under the thumb of Billy and Serena Henderson. The Hendersons had two slaves on their Colorado ranch—one who cared for the horses and another who cleaned and cooked. Both slaves had been told their visas were no good and that they would land in prison if they went to the police. They spoke little English. Their situations were different. They would likely be deported, sent home, but at Toren's urging, the FBI arranged for counseling while they remained on U.S. soil as witnesses in case any of the defendants opted for trials.

Six chop shops were shut down along with the sweatshops, and a total of eighty-three people were arrested as part of the stings, including Greene and the woman who represented his boss. The man who ran it all was still on the run and had presumedly left the country. The FBI would not release his name. Lisa finally learned of the St. Lawrence Seaway connection as well. The Iron City Heights chop shop often stole cars from the wholesale lots on the banks of the Seaway, where newly imported foreign vehicles awaited distribution to car dealerships throughout the country. The lot was so huge that security was not as tight as it should have been. One missing vehicle every now and then wasn't enough to raise an eyebrow, but the chop shop could make at least three times the car's worth by selling the parts on the black market. That explained the choice of Seneca Springs as a location, something that had baffled Lisa. Most chop shops were in bigger, busier cities, but the proximity to the car lot made Seneca Springs desirable.

She learned more about Eckhart in the aftermath of the arrests as well. He had apparently become a skinhead in the late eighties when the movement carried itself like a college fraternity, empowering its members with tight-to-the-head haircuts, combat boots, swastika tattoos, white power t-shirts and a sense of belonging. At the time, he was broke and ready to drop out of college. He needed someone to blame. White supremacists were crawling all over campus, looking for people like him. They convinced him that all the scholarships were going to Blacks and Asians and that soon they would have all the jobs as well. They gave Eckhart copies of *National Socialist Skinhead* magazine and told him whites were under siege and that a war was being waged. Most important, they told him they needed him. Eckhart was a narcissist, so it didn't take much to recruit him. They gave him a place to stay so he could save money on food and housing, and he graduated. He became an active member and a loud voice for the movement. By the late nineties, he was a chapter leader for the Hammerskin Nation, the most powerful skinhead organization in the country. But then it all fell apart.

His chapter members complained that he was too heavy handed and controlling. They ousted him and the chapter folded. That was when Eckhart met a sweatshop owner and agreed to work for him. He immediately saw the potential to apply his philosophy, and he worked his way up until the organization gave him his own place to oversee. He made good money for the crime ring, so they forgave his eccentricities, allowing him to recruit his own guards and find slaves domestically. But then Greene overheard him telling an employee about his plans to eventually take over all the sweatshops and Greene told his boss. Eckhart was right to flee. They were planning to kill him.

Toren played an essential role in those arrests and in the freeing of all those people. If not for him, Lisa would have been forced to take Saul to the emergency room. Weinstock would have sent a few guys to fetch him, and he would have been dead within hours.

"It's great to see you, Toren, but aren't you still on disability?" Lisa said. "I thought you had another three weeks to go. And why are you driving? Are you supposed to be driving? Toren, you drive me crazy."

"It's just this one patient," Toren said. "I started working with the family six months ago when she was diagnosed with ovarian cancer, and she's declined further chemo. Her kids are having a rough time with the decision, so I thought I'd stop by and try to help them see where she's coming from. It's a good decision in my opinion. She'll feel better and she'll have some clear-headed time with her family."

"It's just like you to come up with some incredibly unselfish reason to break the rules. Promise me you'll go right home after. I know you're bored being all cooped up, but you're a doctor. You know better. You'd be awfully upset if a patient behaved like you."

Toren gave Lisa an exaggerated eyeroll.

"I promise, but you'd better be careful, too," he said, pointing to the bundle of mail in her hands. "You just dropped something out of that envelope and you're about to lose one of those catalogs."

Lisa tucked the rest of the mail under her arm and reached down to pick up the white sheet of paper. "Thanks for coming by, Toren," she said as her eyes scanned the document. "I'll tell Bridget you were here. I've got to run myself. I'm late for an…"

Lisa couldn't finish the sentence, couldn't say anything at all. She stared at the paper in her hands, not quite sure she was reading it right. She read it again and then a third time.

"What is it?" Toren asked. "What's wrong?"

"Nothing. Nothing at all," Lisa said, breaking into a laugh. She held the document up to Toren's open window so he could read its message.

"It's a pistol permit, backdated one year, issued by city police. And look," she said, pointing to a line of letters and numbers. "My gun is registered, listed on the license. These things take forever to get in New York State. You have to go through all kinds of background checks and fingerprinting."

"That's good news, I take it," Toren said. He took the license from Lisa, looked it over and handed it back, looking up at her with raised eyebrows. "From what I remember, you're a good shot."

"Good news? It's great news. When this goes to trial, I'll have to testify about shooting those two men and any good defense attorney would ask whether I had a permit to carry. I'd have to admit it right there in court, on the record, that I didn't have a license and that the gun wasn't registered to me. They'd have no choice but to charge me."

Lisa stared at the license for a moment, thinking about the events that occurred after the shootings, after city police and the FBI converged on the sweatshop. During all the interviews that followed, she'd waited for that one question, the accusation, the charge that would have to follow. She had hoped for a legal slap on the wrist given the situation. She'd hoped the courts would forgive her. But she had never even dreamed of this.

"That's why no one asked me about the gun. Someone was already working on this. If they'd asked me earlier, it would have been in my official statement. They couldn't have backdated the permit without getting caught. But I never said anything, because no one asked."

Lisa hadn't realized how much it had weighed on her, waiting to be confronted, to be arrested. She suddenly felt light, eager to face the days ahead and even excited about the road trip to Arizona. She leaned in through the car window and gave Toren a kiss on the cheek, promising to call as soon as she returned. Toren was not the one, she knew that, but he was a good friend, and she was learning she could never have too many good people in her life.

It would have taken the cooperation of several people to get this pistol permit for Lisa. They'd put their jobs on the line for her, these people who would probably remain forever anonymous. As Toren drove away, Lisa hugged the document to her chest, closed her eyes and, for the first time in more than a month, released all her anxiety. She breathed out long and slow and just let it go.

Chapter Thirty-Five

It was already growing dark when Lisa's plane landed at the Seneca Springs airport. The clouds she'd passed through were thick and heavy, threatening the season's first snowfall. It was such a contrast to Arizona, where she and Bridget had spent Thanksgiving climbing the steepness of Camelback Mountain and hiking the trails of Cave Creek and Sedona in shorts and t-shirts. Arizona suited Bridget, but Lisa found herself aching for clouds after only four days, while her skin craved the humidity of the east coast.

Leaving Bridget there was hard, but Lisa was growing more accustomed to her own independence. She was getting to know more of her colleagues outside work, accepting invitations to barbeques and group dinners. She had been out for drinks with Fred and his wife when they announced his wife would be their designated driver for the next nine months thanks to the baby in her belly. She was even teaching a cardio kickboxing class once a week at Ricky's gym.

Of course, she wasn't really alone in all this, she thought as she passed through the doors leading to the security-free zone of the airport, and that helped. Standing a few feet away, with her leather jacket draped over his arm and her winter gloves in his hand was Agent Flannigan, better known to her now as Patrick.

"You're late," he said, wrapping her in his arms and holding her tight. "You must be starving. I thought we'd stop for some dinner on the way home."

He pulled back, took her face in his hands and kissed her long and deep. Lisa could feel the stares of the other disembarking passengers and those who had come to fetch them, but she didn't care. Patrick had been her distraction all the way home from Arizona. He was the reason she could leave Bridget behind with only a few tears.

"God, I've missed you," he said.

Lisa would always remember her shock and the rush of warmth that instantly overtook her when she arrived at lunch to find Patrick sitting at a table with her Uncle Lee that day three months ago. She couldn't speak at first, especially when he looked up at her with that smile, a smile that left her no doubt he felt the same way. He no longer carried a badge. He'd been taking law courses and was anxious to pursue a degree, but he couldn't attend law school full time as an FBI agent. Uncle Lee had offered him a job as a staff investigator. He readily accepted, moved to Seneca Springs and applied to law school. He learned just before Lisa left for Arizona that he had been accepted for the January semester. He'd also been awarded a fellowship especially for former federal agents that would cover most of his tuition.

Lisa thought she knew love when she was with Marty, Bridget's father, as a teenager. She realized now that was something different—more like affection, lust and attachment born of shared rebellion, of the shared fear and excitement that came with growing up. Their relationship might have evolved into a more mature kind of love had they stayed together. It probably would have, Lisa thought. But it never had the chance, and, thanks to Patrick, she didn't regret that.

"I am starving, but let's get takeout. I just want to be home with you," she said.

Lisa reluctantly pulled her body away from Patrick's and slipped her hand into his. As they walked toward baggage claim, she wondered how Patrick and Bridget would get along. Bridget was flying home for Christmas. She had always been the center of Lisa's world, the focus of all her attention. But she was growing up. Lisa saw so much change when she visited her in Arizona. Patrick didn't have any children, but he always listened so patiently, so attentively, to every detail about her daughter. He seemed to realize that without a doubt, Bridget was part of the package—that Lisa was a mother first and foremost—and he seemed to appreciate, almost admire that.

Lisa felt Patrick's hand let go of hers and slide around her waist. She leaned her head against his shoulder as they walked, thinking about how quickly life could change for her, for the captives, for Dorothy, for Bridget, for Saul, for Patrick, for anyone really. How quickly and how beautifully.

A Note from the Author

I hope you enjoyed *Never Broken*. Feel free to contact me at lori@loriduffy-foster.com with any questions. Reviews are greatly appreciated if you have a few minutes to spare.

Acknowledgements

The seeds for *Never Broken* came from a "what if" scenario: What if Lisa Jamison found a near-dead man in the back of her car? But the plot and the characters were nourished and enriched by a book I read while the story was gestating, *A Crime So Monstrous: Face to Face with Modern-Day Slavery* by E. Benjamin Skinner. Skinner's book opened my eyes to the suffering of human trafficking victims in ways that nothing else had. When I told my good friend and fellow writer Bill MacFarland about my deepened interest in the issue, he introduced me to his cousin, Laura Cusack, who has been a crusader for victims of human trafficking for at least a decade. Her stories and her work touched me deeply as well.

At about the same time, the political climate in the United States was changing and white supremacists were becoming louder and bolder. It was frightening to see how quickly we could slip backward as a society and just how fragile human rights remain. I reread Philip Roth's *Plot to Kill America*, thinking about apathy and racism and the danger of group thought. All those forces and influences came together to inspire *Never Broken*.

I would like to thank E. Benjamin Skinner, Laura Cusack and Phillip Roth for their influences along with Christopher Carr, who read the finished book to ensure that I wrote with sensitivity. He provided prospective that I never could have. High school classmate Don Fadden and his father, John Fadden, of the Six Nations Iroquois Cultural Center in Onchiota, NY, also contributed to issues of sensitivity. I cannot thank you both enough.

Fellow author and Pennwriter David Freas saved me from embarrassment with his mechanical knowledge. I owe you big time, Dave. My niece, Trish Druetto, was a valuable resource as well. Editor Rachel Jackson made some great catches in her review of *Never Broken* for my publisher, Level Best

Books. Thank you, Rachel. I look forward to working with you again. I owe a huge debt of gratitude to The Dames of Detection–Shawn Reilly Simmons, Verena Rose, and Harriette Sackler—owners and co-publishers of Level Best Books. You had faith and me and gave this book life.

Thank you to my sister, Angela Bader; my college friend, Tina Sabrin; and my husband, Tom, for reading *Never Broken* in its early drafts and providing input that made it better and stronger. Thanks also to my former agent, Elizabeth Trupin-Pulli, who encouraged me to turn the first book, *A Dead Man's Eyes*, into a series, featuring journalist Lisa Jamison, and who provided valuable feedback on *Never Broken*.

My sister-in-law Linda Duffy was a huge supporter of my writing and of the arts in general. She was a creative and generous soul who left this earth too soon. As *Never Broken* nears publication, my thoughts turn to Linda. She is with me in spirit.

So many people and organizations have buoyed me on this publishing journey. I would like to acknowledge the unwavering support of my stepdaughter, Kelly Foster, and my siblings and their spouses: Angela and Andy Bader: Patricia Bardua; David and Jean Duffy; Ed (Linda) Duffy; James Duffy; and Andrew Duffy. Thank you to my cousin, Kelly O'Leary; my aunts Kathleen Lahue and Dolores Martin; and my friend Georganna Doran.

My children–Riley, Kiersten, Matthew and Jonathan—have been nothing but proud and patient throughout my publishing journey. They are my heart and my motivation. My husband, Tom, is my greatest supporter and my best critic. He has encouraged me through multiple bouts of financial and parenting guilt and has never let me quit. He has always believed in me. I would not be where or who I am without him.

Last, but not least, I would like to acknowledge the writing organizations I have leaned on all these years. We all need our tribes and they have been mine. Thanks to the people of Pennwriters, Mystery Writers of America, Sisters in Crime, International Thriller Writers and The Historical Novel Society for the comradery, advice and support. It is invaluable.

I am sure I have failed to mention some people. It's inevitable. You might not be listed here, but please know I am grateful and that you are in my heart.

About the Author

Lori Duffy Foster is a former crime reporter who writes and lives in the hills of Northern Pennsylvania. She is author of *A Dead Man's Eyes,* the first in the Lisa Jamison Mysteries Series and an Agatha Award nominee. *Never Broken* is book 2 in the series. Look for her debut thriller, *Never Let Go,* in December of 2022. Her short fiction has appeared in the journal *Aethlon,* and in the anthologies *Short Story America* and *Childhood Regained.* Her nonfiction has appeared in *Healthy Living, Running Times, Literary Mama, Crimespree,* and *Mountain Home* magazines. Lori is a member of Mystery Writers of America, Sisters in Crime, The Historical Novel Society, International Thriller Writers, and Pennwriters. She also sits on the board of the Knoxville (PA) Public Library.

SOCIAL MEDIA HANDLES:
　　Facebook @loriduffyfosterauthor
　　Instagram @lori.duffy.foster
　　Twitter @loriduffyfoster.

AUTHOR WEBSITE:
　　www.loriduffyfoster.com

Also by Lori Duffy Foster

A Dead Man's Eyes: A Lisa Jamison Mystery